Two for the Show

A **C**OMPANION **P**UBLICATIONS BOOK

To my Little Phyllis Valentine, with all my love. Thank you for believing in me.

ALSO WRITTEN BY CHRIS PAYNTER AND AVAILABLE NOW FROM COMPANION PUBLICATIONS:

Playing for First (Book 1 in the *Playing for First* series)

Come Back to Me

Survived by her Longtime Companion

And a Time to Dance

To Love Free

COMING SPRING 2015:

From Third to Home (Book 3 in the *Playing for First* series)

Two for the Show

by

Chris Paynter

This is a work of fiction. All characters, locales and events are either products of the author's imagination or are used fictitiously.

TWO FOR THE SHOW

Cover design by Ann Phillips

Published by Companion Publications

www.ckpaynter.com

ISBN: 978-1-942204-05-3

First edition: April, 2011
Second edition: January, 2015

Printed in the United States of America and in the United Kingdom.

Acknowledgements

Thank you to my publisher, Emily Reed. By taking a chance on me in 2009 with *Playing for First*, you allowed me to bring Lisa, Amy, and Frankie to life. I couldn't ask for a better publisher. It's been a treat watching Blue Feather grow over the past two years, and I'm proud to be a member of the family.

A huge thank-you to my editor, mentor, and friend, Jane Vollbrecht. Please continue helping me to hone my craft, even when I grumble about making the changes. If I could, I'd embroider you a pillow that says, "Jane knows best." But you'll just have to take my word for it because, trust me, you wouldn't want to see my needlework.

Em and Jane, the years ahead look bright for Blue Feather. I look forward to sharing them with you and seeing what the future holds in store.

Thanks to my baseball buddy and the best line editor in the business, Nann Dunne—I even forgive you for being a Philadelphia Phillies fan. A big thank-you to Cathy, K.C., and Patty for their readings of *Two for the Show* in its infancy and for their invaluable suggestions. And to cover artist extraordinaire Ann Phillips, thank you for the freaking awesome cover!

Thank you for the support of my wonderful parents, Nancy and Morris, my brother, David, my niece, Cassie, and my sister-in-law, Grace. A very special thank-you to my dad for instilling in me the love of The Game.

Again, I save the last acknowledgement for the one who's first in my heart—my wife, Phyllis. Without your love and constant encouragement, I never would have achieved my dream. You overwhelm me with your patience and understanding when I retreat into the world of my characters. I thank God for the day that He brought you into my life.

Chapter 1

Amy Perry dove in the hole between first and second base. She snagged the ball on a line, jumped to her feet, and stepped on first base to complete an unassisted double play and end the top of the sixth.

"Damn." Lisa Collins watched from her vantage point in the Victory Field press box. She pounded on her laptop keyboard for a few seconds as she recounted the play in her article for Minor League.com.

"Yeah, I agree. The woman can flat out play the game," Sarah Swift said. Sarah, Lisa's friend and fellow sportswriter, was covering Amy's story for *Baseball Weekly*. "I don't know if I'll ever get used to seeing her out there with those guys, looking like she should have been there years ago."

"Nice to see, isn't it?"

"Yes, it is. Should've happened before now, but at least one major league baseball organization got their heads out of their collective asses long enough to notice her talent and give her a chance."

"Amen to that. She was something to watch last summer for the Chattanooga Lookouts. And the September call-up when the Reds gave her a look-see was impressive. She's been outstanding this whole month of April for the Indianapolis Indians."

The Indians went out in order in the bottom of the inning.

"Wonder when the Reds will call her up again?" Sarah asked.

"Don't know, but I'm sure it'll be soon."

The game ended with the Indians on top, 4-2, in the Saturday night contest against the Toledo Mudhens. Lisa and Sarah entered the clubhouse, and Sarah went to talk to the Indians starting pitcher who'd pitched a complete game. Lisa walked up to Amy as she finished answering the last question from a *USA Today* reporter.

"Hey, Aim." Lisa smiled at the woman who had become a good

friend and got a crinkle-eyed smile in return. "Helluva play in the sixth." Lisa gestured at Amy's uniform, which was dirt-covered from the top of her jersey all the way down her six-foot frame.

"Thanks. Sometimes I love making those defensive plays more than hitting a home run."

"What about that pitch in the third that you hit out of the park?"

Amy grinned. "Okay. I still love hitting the long ball. He threw me an inside fastball. He had tried to sneak it past me in the first. Thought he might try it again."

Lisa scribbled down the quote. "Tell Stacy I said hi."

"Will do."

Lisa was about to leave the clubhouse when Sarah called her over to a corner.

"Hey, Collins, just heard it from Kipper of *Sports Illustrated*. He's leaving the job to become an analyst for the MLB Network. Talk is that Ted Hillary, the Major League.com beat writer for the Reds has been offered the *SI* job."

"No shit?"

"So, when are you going to apply?"

Lisa's head was spinning. "I don't know…"

Sarah stared at her. "You're going for it, aren't you?"

"I guess."

"What do you mean you guess?"

"Jesus, Swift. Don't yell at me."

"Well, somebody's got to talk some sense into you."

"I'll think about it, all right?"

Lisa walked away before Sarah could assault her eardrums any further and left for the press box to file her article.

*   *   *

Lisa stood in front of the bedroom mirror and fiddled with her shirt collar. She grabbed her jacket draped across the nearby chair, shrugged it on, and readjusted the collar as she studied her reflection.

"Hey, isn't it about time to get you to the airport?" Frankie called from the kitchen.

"Yeah, but I'm still not sure if this whole outfit works."

Frankie entered the bedroom. "Let me." She stepped behind Lisa and smoothed out the collar as Lisa shifted in place. "I don't know what you're so nervous about, Leese. It's not like they don't know what a damn good writer you are." Frankie turned Lisa to face her.

"Besides, you're hot and charming and—"

"Stop, will you?" Lisa said with a laugh. "You're a tad prejudiced, don't you think? I mean, I've known you six years. Wait. Let me rephrase. We've been best friends for over five years, but I've known you in the biblical sense for a year."

"True." Frankie pressed her lips to Lisa's. "And it's a blessing."

Lisa returned the kiss.

"If we keep doing this, you won't get to the airport in time for your flight."

Lisa ruffled Frankie's salt-and-pepper hair. "You started it."

"But we could finish it together." Frankie gave Lisa a peck on the cheek.

She glanced over Frankie's shoulder at the bedside clock. "We should've been on the road thirty minutes ago."

"I'll crank it up a little on I-465."

Lisa checked out her reflection again and ran her fingers through her short-cropped blonde hair. "This is as good as it gets. One butch, ready for the interview of a lifetime."

"You have the job. Major League.com would be crazy not to hire you. And remember, *they* called *you*."

"I guess you're right. They called me, but I'm still frigging nervous."

Frankie grabbed her by the shoulders and pushed her toward the hallway.

Lisa stopped abruptly and turned to face Frankie. "You and I haven't finished our talk about me moving down to Cincinnati if I get this job. What about the Watering Hole? You've worked so hard on your bar."

"I told you, this is an opportunity of a lifetime and I'll support your decision."

"Which is still not getting into what all—"

"Listen to me. I love you, honey. I love you enough to see you reach your dream. We'll work out the other stuff later." Frankie's dark eyes held hers.

Lisa was about to continue her protest, but Frankie again pushed her toward the front door.

"All right. I'm going. I'm going."

"Don't forget your overnight bag and briefcase. It's always impressive to carry a briefcase."

On the drive to the airport in Frankie's Dodge Ram, they chatted about work. They pulled into the roundabout for departing passengers. Lisa hopped out and grabbed her briefcase and bag before a security officer on one of those funky upright wheelie things ran her down for loitering.

Frankie gave her a fierce hug. "You'll do fine. Just be yourself."

Lisa hurried toward the automatic door and waved at Frankie.

"Call me after they tell you they gave you the job," Frankie shouted.

* * *

"Jesus Christ, Perry! What the fuck happened to your footwork?"

Amy sighed. *Curt Reed is such a hard-ass.*

"We're doing this until you get it right," her manager shouted. "If it means we stay out here until two, then that's what we'll do."

Reed smacked another ball to the shortstop, who fired it to Amy. The throw was to the right, almost out of reach. Amy stretched and still kept her foot on the bag.

"Better. Try it again."

Reed hit one to the second baseman. Amy adjusted her footing for the throw.

"Whaddya know? You are capable of listening to the old man."

Amy almost smiled, but she didn't want to endure another tirade from Reed. Twenty minutes later, he halted infield practice.

Amy did a little skip over the first baseline like she always did. She didn't have many superstitions, but she'd held onto this one since her fast pitch softball days. She entered the clubhouse with the rest of the Indians players and headed for her locker.

"Perry, come to my office after you shower," Reed said as he passed by.

Amy sat down and took off her cleats.

"What'd you do this time?" Jody Harrelson, the third baseman, asked from his chair beside hers. "You haven't been making more front page news, have you?"

Amy held her cleats and gave Jody a look. "You mean like coming out publicly right before opening day? You know I had to do that, right? I couldn't pretend Stacy was just my roommate."

"Not a problem with me. Anybody bother you about that?"

"Not our teammates. I got some comments from the other teams—a slur here, a jab there. No big deal."

"So what's buggin' Reed?"

She shoved her cleats into her locker before answering Harrelson. "I don't know. I can't think of anything I've done lately that might have pissed him off."

"Doesn't he ride you more than the rest of us?" By now, Harrelson was half-dressed and about to take off his pants.

From the onset, back to the Arizona Fall Instructional League where the Reds first assigned her, Amy shared the clubhouse with the rest of the team. She took it in stride, ignoring the sweaty and sometimes nude bodies around her. She'd adjusted to waiting until they finished showering before taking her own.

"I guess it depends on how you look at it. I try to think of it as he's working me to be my best." Amy pulled off her practice jersey and undershirt and waited to shed her pants. She sat back in her chair, still in her sports bra, enjoying the air conditioning against her exposed skin.

Harrelson turned his back on her as he continued peeling off his uniform. He tugged off his jock strap and quickly wrapped a towel around his waist. She suppressed a smile. Yes, they stripped in front of her, but it didn't mean they wanted to parade it around.

"Hang in there," Harrelson said, while grabbing his soap and shampoo. "You're a hell of a player, Perry. They'll call you up soon enough."

She got lost in her thoughts, remembering everything she'd gone through to get to where she was—fighting to play on her high school baseball team, starring on the Kansas City Bandits professional women's baseball team, and getting sent to Arizona and Double-A Chattanooga.

The last player trickled out of the shower, dressed, and left the clubhouse. Amy finished undressing, showered, and dressed in her jeans and Indians polo shirt before making her way to Reed's office. His door was open, but he had his head down. She tapped on the doorframe.

"You wanted to see me, Curt?"

"Take a seat." He leaned back in his chair and put his hands behind his head.

She'd seen this body language many times before. Reed was from Mississippi, and like his slow drawl, he took his time in passing on any news.

"You're adjusting well to Triple-A pitching. It doesn't surprise me. You've met every challenge along the way. You did good with the Reds last September during your call-up. Maybe not as good as you wanted, but enough to impress them. What'd you bat—.270?"

"About that."

"I don't remember your other offensive stats exactly, but here with us…" He picked up a sheet of paper from his desk. "You're batting .297 with six home runs, eight doubles, and twenty-two RBIs. You've made only one error. I remember the game. It was a lousy scoring decision. That winter ball you played helped you, plus, starting spring camp this season with the Reds." He set the stat sheet aside. "You've probably guessed where I'm going with this. I spoke with Max Murphy. Seems the Reds are thinking of calling you up again by the middle of next month."

Amy tried to remain impassive, like this news wasn't anything she didn't expect. Inside, her heart rate picked up and her stomach fluttered.

"Of course, you need to keep on doing what you're doing. Question is, are you ready for the next step? Not only the physical stuff but also the mental stuff."

"I think I am. I never thought all this would come easy."

"I know that." He waved off her comment. "Perry, if the rest of the guys on this team had your attitude, my job would be a lot easier. Some of them think it's a given they'll move on from here. What they don't realize is some guys are destined to be career minor league players. I know because I was one of them. Every time the Rangers called me up, I choked. Major league pitching ain't Triple-A. You found that out last September, not that you didn't already know it. But you're a woman, and despite how these players have treated you, there'll still be some jackasses. You've also added pressure by announcing your sexual preference." He gave her a hard stare. "Are you ready to face more shit in the bigs?"

She wanted to tell him she'd been through enough crap to understand the implications of what she was doing, but she calmed herself before answering.

"I know I'll need to have a thick skin, but I think I can handle it. Baseball's in my blood, Curt, and I can't give it up."

He rocked in his chair and nodded. "I figured that's what you'd say. Keep it going out there. It won't be long."

Amy headed back to her locker and grabbed her gym bag, anxious to see Stacy. She hoisted the strap over her shoulder and stood a little straighter on her walk to the parking lot.

* * *

Lisa gave Frankie a quick call after she landed in New York. She hailed a taxi and told the driver the address for Major League.com on Ninth Avenue. As they drove through traffic, an old Beatles tune poured through the speakers. She tapped her thumbs on her thigh in time with the beat. Frankie was right. She shouldn't be nervous since they contacted her, but doubt still crept in, and not just about the job possibility. Regardless of Frankie's reassurances, she worried about their fledgling relationship. What would Frankie do about the Watering Hole? She was the owner, and it was her baby. Lisa didn't expect her to give it up. At the same time, how would being apart affect them? She'd had a difficult enough time living in Chattanooga last year when she was covering the Amy Perry story.

You don't have the job yet, Collins.

The cabbie dropped her off in front of the building. She would meet with Lonnie Craftman, the head editor, and Ross Barnes, his assistant whom she'd spoken with on the phone.

She took the elevator up to the twentieth floor and approached the receptionist seated out front.

"Hi. Lisa Collins to see Lonnie Craftman and Ross Barnes."

The woman clicked her mouse a few times and studied her computer screen.

"Yes, Ms. Collins. They're finishing with a meeting and should be ready for you in a few minutes. If you'd take a seat over there, I'll let you know when they're done." She gestured to a waiting area.

"Thanks." Lisa carried her bags to one of the leather chairs in the corner of the office and sat down. A few wrinkles in her slacks caught her attention. She smoothed out the material and raised her hand to her collar to check it once again. But she caught herself before she started tapping her dress shoe on the carpet. Instead, she picked up a Website media guide from the table.

She wasn't sure how much more time had passed, but it felt like hours instead of minutes. She resisted the urge to push back her cuff to see the time.

The receptionist answered her ringing phone. "They're ready for you now, Ms. Collins."

Lisa picked up her bag and briefcase and followed her down a hallway with even plusher carpet.

Before the receptionist opened the door, she reached for Lisa's overnight bag.

"Why don't you let me take this and store it up front? I'm sure you want to keep your briefcase with you."

"Yes. Thank you." Lisa handed over her bag as the receptionist opened the door.

A short, portly man, with thin wisps of gray hair sprinkling his balding head, stood and held out his hand to Lisa.

"Hello, Ms. Collins. Lonnie Craftman, but please call me Lonnie."

"It's Lisa."

"All right. I think we can be on a first-name basis. This is Assistant Editor Ross Barnes. You spoke with him on the phone."

A tall African American stood up from one of the three chairs in front of Lonnie's desk.

Lisa clasped his hand.

"Nice to meet you, Ross."

His smile was genuine, and she returned it.

Lonnie motioned to the chairs. "Would you like some water?" he asked, holding up a pitcher of water and a glass with ice.

"Yes, please." She took the offered glass and gulped down a couple of swallows to try to calm her nerves.

"Ross called you at my request." Lonnie settled into his high-back leather chair. "As you're aware, Ted Hillary, our beat reporter for the Reds Website is leaving for *Sports Illustrated* in about two weeks. We'd like to have someone else in place before he leaves. In fact, we'd like to have the person we hire ready by the end of next week so Ted can get his successor acclimated. Next Friday night, the Reds will be playing Houston in Cincinnati, in the middle of an eight-game home stand that ends Monday afternoon. They then fly to Milwaukee for the start of a six-game road trip ending the following Sunday in Chicago. The new hire will go along to watch Ted cover those games—especially to get a feel for how things work on road trips."

"We've kept up with your reporting on Minor League.com, Lisa. Your writing has impressed us," Ross said.

"Thank you." She hoped her penchant for blushing at compliments was in check, but when the rush of heat hit her cheeks, she knew it was hopeless.

"We were also impressed with how you shot down the false steroid accusations against Amy Perry," Lonnie added. "I'm sure you're aware there's a good chance the Reds will call her up next month. It's another reason we'd like to get the new hire in place as quickly as possible." Lonnie leaned back in his chair and smiled. "We'd like to offer you the job."

Lisa's heart thudded in her chest.

"You're an Indianapolis native, correct?" Lonnie asked.

"Yes."

"Then the question is, do you want to be uprooted from your home city?"

She'd thought she would blurt out "yes" if he asked her pointblank if she wanted the position. She instead took a moment before replying.

"I'd like to discuss this with my partner before I give you my decision. I hope you understand." Lisa watched for his reaction.

To her relief, Lonnie's expression didn't change.

"Of course." He reached for a sheet of paper on his desk and passed it over to her. "Here are the conditions of the job."

Lisa stared at the print and the salary line and managed to keep her expression impassive despite the fact it doubled the salary she pulled in from Minor League.com.

"I trust the salary is to your satisfaction," Lonnie said.

"Yes, sir."

"Good. In addition to covering the Reds while they're in town, you'll travel to all road games. This job can get to be a real grind, Lisa. The season lasts at least six months, maybe longer if they make the playoffs. The Reds may not make it this year, but I anticipate it happening soon. They have a lot of good young talent, as do their farm teams. You're aware of that since you've covered the Lookouts and Indians. The season can take a toll on you. I'm glad you plan to talk to your partner. You don't want to make a snap decision about something like this."

"Thank you for understanding."

"We hope you'll sign on as a member of the Major League.com team," Ross said. "We'd love to have you on board."

"Thank you." Lisa put the sheet of paper in her briefcase and shook his hand before following Lonnie to the door.

"I know you need a little time to think this over, but I'd appreciate having an answer by the end of the week. It'd help us settle things down there, knowing we have someone lined up to make the transition."

"Yes, sir. I'll let you know by Friday morning."

"Good. We'll look forward to hearing from you."

Lisa retrieved her bag from the receptionist. Dazed, she took the elevator back down to the main floor. As she stood at the curb and flagged down a taxi, her mind spun. A car pulled to a stop, and she gave the driver the name of her hotel.

One question played over and over in her mind. Is this really what we want, Frankie? The query hung with her as she sank into the backseat.

As she got comfortable in her hotel room, Lisa doubted the wisdom of her decision to stay overnight rather than catch a late flight back home. She unclipped her phone from her waistband, flopped into the chair beside the bed, and propped her feet up on the mattress as she hit the first number in her speed dial list. Frankie picked up on the second ring.

"So?" Frankie asked.

"They offered me the job."

"That's fantastic, Leese!"

"But I didn't accept it yet."

"What do you mean you didn't accept it?"

Lisa leaned her head back on the cushion. "I told them I needed to talk it over with you. I have until Friday to give them an answer."

"Which will be yes."

Lisa sighed. "Frankie, can we at least talk about this a little more when I get home? It'll be a big change for us, and I think this is important enough to discuss it face-to-face."

A long moment passed. "All right. Let me know when your plane lands, and we'll have the talk when you get here about how perfect this job is for you."

The tension eased in Lisa's shoulders. "I love you."

"Love you, too. Have a safe trip home."

Chapter 2

Amy pushed through the front door of the Watering Hole. She searched for Stacy but didn't see her. The basement door swung open, and Stacy appeared, struggling with a crate of liquor. She attempted to push the door shut with her hip.

Amy hurried over. "Need some help?"

Stacy's face lit up with a smile.

Amy almost stumbled. *God, she does it to me every time.*

"Hey, you," Stacy said as Amy took the crate from her. "Curt give you a break and set you loose for the afternoon?"

"Yeah." Amy carried the crate behind the bar and set it down.

Stacy sidled up behind her. "Aren't you forgetting something?"

Amy leaned down and kissed her. "That?"

"Yes, that." Stacy opened the crate and put the liquor bottles on the shelf.

"Where's Frankie?" Amy asked as she helped shelve the bottles.

"She said something about taking Lisa to the airport. She said Lisa's been a nervous wreck since last week. Maybe a new job? I didn't catch all the details."

"Lisa has a job interview?" Amy tried to sound calm. She and Lisa had been lovers, briefly, but now she considered her one of her best friends.

Stacy glanced back at Amy. "I think Frankie said Lisa had to fly out to New York."

Amy frowned. What could be in New York?

"What's that look for?" Stacy asked as she finished unloading the last of the bottles.

"Nothing."

"Come on, Perry." Stacy rubbed against her. "You should know by now you can't hide anything from me."

"How do you know I have anything to hide?"

"Oh, I don't know. Maybe that I love you and that I've learned to read a lot of your expressions?" Stacy pushed up on her tiptoes to kiss her.

Amy tugged her closer for a long, passionate kiss.

"Hey, hey, break it up there." Frankie's husky voice ended their embrace.

"Sorry, Frankie," Amy said.

"No you're not. You've got it bad. Take it from someone who has the same malady." Frankie joined them behind the bar. "Lisa and I've been caught in the same compromising position back here."

"Speaking of Lisa, boss, how'd the sending off go?" Stacy asked.

"I had to shove her out the door to make it to the airport in time, but her nervous ass finally got on the plane to New York."

"I know it's none of my business…" Amy started to say.

"One of the head editors of Major League.com called her last week and asked her to fly in today to interview for the Cincinnati Reds reporter's job. Just got off the phone with her. They offered her the position."

"That's awesome!" Amy said.

"It is. When she gets back tomorrow, I'll need to convince her to take it."

"Why would she hesitate?" Stacy asked.

"Oh, we need to talk through her concerns about her working in Cincinnati while I stay here." Frankie picked up a dishcloth and wiped down the bar. "Stacy, take the rest of the afternoon off. You only have another hour anyway."

"I'll get my jacket in the back room, Amy."

Amy watched Stacy walk away and then turned to Frankie. She caught her worried expression. "Something wrong?"

"Everything's fine. I just need to talk some sense into Lisa. We'll work it out."

Stacy came toward them, pulling on her jacket. "Ready?"

They walked outside.

"I know we just dropped it off this morning, but I already miss our SUV," Stacy said as she opened the door to Amy's Mazda. "When will they finish with the tune-up?"

"By tomorrow afternoon, I think. You have a problem with my car?"

"Not at all."

"It's over ten years old, but still gets good gas mileage and—"

"It's okay. You don't need to defend the car. You've told me how much it means to you." Stacy covered her mouth. "Repeatedly," she said under her breath.

Amy keyed the ignition and backed out of the parking spot onto Massachusetts Avenue. "You think Lisa will take the job?" She selfishly wanted Lisa with her when she returned to Cincinnati.

"She'd be crazy not to."

"I can see Lisa's point about being away from Frankie." Amy put her hand on Stacy's knee. "I'd hate to be away from you that much."

Stacy stared at her and sat up suddenly from her slouch. "Did they call you up?"

"No, no. I had a talk with Reed. He told me the Reds might be calling me up next month."

Amy stopped at a light.

"You'll be a trailblazer there like you are in the minors. You know that, right?"

"I guess."

"You guess? Amy Perry, you've already played a month with the Reds, but this time, it'd be for good."

"Nothing's for good, Stace. You have to work your ass off to stay there."

"Which you'd do, so don't try that with me."

Amy chuckled.

"What's so funny?"

"I love it when you get all fired up. It's that Irish temper in you."

Stacy raised her chin and looked out the window. "Keep it up, and you won't get your surprise when we get home."

"What surprise?"

"I'm not going to tell you, you big dufus. That's why it's called a surprise."

"Staaacy," Amy whined.

"I wished those guys on your team could hear you now."

"Pleeease."

"Oh, all right. It's black and skimpy."

"Skimpy?"

"Did I mention see-through lace?"

Amy punched her foot on the accelerator.

* * *

As promised, Lisa phoned Frankie after she landed in

Indianapolis the next day but waited until after she'd hired a limo. She held the phone away from her ear while Frankie complained about wasting money on a limo to drive her home.

"Why don't you leave the bar a little earlier than usual and meet me at the house?"

"I'll be there soon."

Thirty minutes later, the limo pulled into the drive behind Frankie's truck. Lisa handed the driver a tip, grabbed her bags, and entered the house.

"Frankie?"

"I'm back here."

Lisa followed the sound of Frankie's voice to the den. She poked her head around the corner just as Frankie was racking the balls on the pool table. Lisa strode to Frankie and gave her a quick kiss.

"I hope you're going to tell me you thought about it overnight and decided to take the job." Frankie struck the cue ball, scattering the balls, and knocking in a stripe.

Lisa went over to the rack and picked out a cue. "Mind if I knock in the solids?"

"Be my guest."

Lisa lined up her shot.

"You *are* taking it, right?" Frankie stood aside while Lisa moved around the table.

Lisa straightened from her shot. "I don't know…"

Frankie propped her cue against the table and sat on the worn leather couch.

"Set your cue down and march your little butt over here."

Lisa joined Frankie on the couch. "We have to decide if this move is right for us, not if it's right for me."

"But—"

Lisa held up her hand. "You seem to have this all figured out because the only person you're thinking of right now is me."

"This is an opportunity of a lifetime, Leese. I can't tell you to not do it."

"Yes, you can. You can because I love you enough to do what's best for our relationship." Lisa took Frankie's hand in hers. "Listen. Yes, it's a huge opportunity. But I'd never ask you to give up the Watering Hole. It's as important to you as this job would be to me. What we need to talk about is how we can be together as much as possible. I never want anything to come between us, especially something as inconsequential as a job."

"I wouldn't call this job inconsequential."

"You know what I mean."

"We need to work out the logistics, but I think we can do it."

"Remember how we were when I was in Chattanooga?"

"We had amazing reunions, though."

Lisa chuckled. "Yeah, we did."

"This is different. You'll be in Cincinnati, which is much closer than Chattanooga, and you can drive up to Indianapolis whenever you're free. I'll give Billie more control down at the Watering Hole, and I'll come to Cincinnati whenever I can."

Lisa pictured Billie behind the bar. "She does seem to love it."

"Just the other day she asked me if I'd consider letting her have more say in running the place, and this would be a perfect chance to give her a try. Maybe when you travel with the team, I can join you on some of those trips. It'd be fun going to the different cities, knowing you'll be there."

Lisa lowered her head. "Everything you're saying is true."

"But?" Frankie lifted Lisa's chin with her index finger.

"I'll miss you."

Frankie smiled. "Me, too. But you're made for this job, Leese. As for you and me, we'll make it work. Our love is that strong. I believe it. Don't you?"

Lisa kissed her. "Yes."

"And the salary?"

"Double my salary with Minor League.com and my freelance job at the *Gazette*, plus I'd get all the perks of traveling with the team and not paying for hotel rooms. The only thing I need to worry about if I take the job is finding a place in Cincinnati."

"You mean 'when you take the job.'"

"Guess I'll call them and tell them yes, huh?"

Frankie hugged Lisa. "I'm so damn proud of you. How about we celebrate tonight?"

"I have the Indians game to cover, but afterwards, maybe we can get Amy and Stacy to come over."

"That's another good thing, isn't it? Amy should get called up soon, and the two of you would be traveling together."

"It's one of the reasons they wanted me. They liked how Sarah Swift and I handled things with the steroid allegations and how I covered Amy's play last summer." Lisa checked her watch. "Shit. I'd better get ready to leave for Victory Field."

Frankie stood. "And I need to get to the bar. Billie's due in at five. I have some stuff I need to go over with her. Stacy should be at the game. She's off tonight."

"Good. It'll be fun to let both of them know I'm taking the job."

"When will you call New York?"

Lisa took off her suit jacket on their way back to the bedroom.

"I think I'll call them tomorrow. I have until Friday, but it's silly to make them wait. Besides, I don't want to give them a chance to change their minds." She undressed and walked to the closet to get a pair of jeans and her Minor League.com polo shirt.

Frankie stood behind Lisa and kissed her neck. She ran her fingers from Lisa's tight abdomen up to her stomach and cupped her breasts. Lisa drew in a breath. She thought back to when intimacy had been difficult for Frankie. Their fifteen-year age difference had never been an issue, but Frankie's mastectomy seven years before had left her afraid to accept Lisa's affection at first.

Lisa turned around. "If you keep doing that, I'll never get to the park."

"And this is bad, how?" Frankie gave her a crooked grin and pushed her against the closet door. "Can I at least have another kiss?"

Lisa moved her hand to the back of Frankie's neck and brought her mouth to Frankie's. They kissed, each fighting for dominance with her tongue.

Lisa pressed her forehead against Frankie's. "Jesus." She gave her another quick kiss. "Hold that thought, will you? I've changed my mind. I'll tell Amy and Stacy at the ballpark that I accepted the job. I don't want them hanging out here after the game. Tonight should just be the two of us."

"No argument from me."

* * *

Lisa took her customary seat in the press box next to Sarah.

"Why do you look like the cat that swallowed the canary?" Sarah asked.

"Probably because I have." Lisa plugged in her laptop.

"Do tell, Collins. Inquiring minds want to know."

"I can't."

"Bullshit."

At that comment, a couple of the other reporters who'd entered the press box looked their way.

"All good things come to those who wait or something like that," Lisa said.

"You're so full of shit that I don't know how your eyes are still hazel."

"I should be flattered. Sarah Swift noticed the color of my eyes."

"You know, if I'd known you go for older women, I'd have made my move years ago."

Lisa laughed loud and long. "You're good for my ego."

Sarah powered up her laptop. "At least I'm good for something. How's your wife, by the way? I haven't seen her at any games yet this year."

"She's been busy with the bar. We've meant to have you over again."

"Yeah, yeah, yeah. The story of my life. You know what they say about good intentions."

"We're not paving any roads. In fact, what are you doing Wednesday night?"

"Let me check my social calendar, and I'll get back to you."

The Indians ran out to their positions on the field. Lisa and Sarah grew quiet, taking in the scene below them. The Indians ace retired the Durham Bulls in order in the top of the first.

In the bottom of the inning, the Indianapolis second-place hitter lined a double down the right field line. Amy walked to the plate. The near-capacity crowd cheered when the announcer said her name.

Amy went through her ritual of unsnapping and snapping her batter's gloves. She checked the sign from the third base coach, then stepped into the batter's box. The first pitch was low and away. Amy laid off. The Bulls pitcher threw the ball down the heart of the plate. Amy smacked it on a line over the left field wall. The fans sitting on the grassy hill overlooking the field scrambled to get to the ball.

"I so wish I could do that," Sarah said while typing on her computer.

"Don't we all?"

The Indians coasted to an easy 8-1 victory. Lisa and Sarah entered the clubhouse for interviews. After Lisa got in a few questions for Amy, she stepped over to the next locker to get the pitcher's take on the game. She snagged a couple of quotes from Curt Reed and left for the press box. Sarah was already at her laptop.

Lisa sat down next to her and flipped open her computer. She pounded out her article and sent it through cyberspace.

"Have a good night, Sarah. I'll see you tomorrow."

"Take it easy, Collins," Sarah said, not looking up from her screen.

Lisa found Stacy standing outside the clubhouse.

"Hey, McCrady. How's it going?"

"It's going good."

"I can kind of tell. You haven't wiped that grin off your face since last July when you and Amy hooked up for the first time."

"Guess it's pretty obvious I'm in love."

"A little."

Amy exited the clubhouse, her brown curls in wet ringlets from her shower.

"Hey, Lisa. I understand you might have some big news for us?" Amy's green eyes sparkled with excitement.

"You can't keep a secret around here," Lisa said as she adjusted her laptop strap on her shoulder.

"We saw Frankie yesterday, but she said you hadn't decided yet."

Lisa walked toward the parking lot with them. "We talked about it when I got back today. I'll be taking the Major League.com job in Cincinnati."

"Yes!" Amy dropped her bag and embraced Lisa in a bear hug, pounding her hard on the back.

"Leave me with some semblance of lungs, will you?" Lisa laughed.

"Sorry. They'll probably call me up soon, and it'll be nice to see a friendly face in the press box."

"I agree with Amy," Stacy said. "It'll be good having you covering the games."

"You two will move down together then?" Lisa stopped in front of her car.

"Once I get the call, we'll scope out the apartments."

"Why not a condo or house?" Lisa opened the back door and laid her laptop on the seat.

"I'm superstitious, I guess," Amy said.

She's still humble, Lisa thought. Amazing.

"Aim, I think we can safely say once you get the call again, it'll be for good."

"You never know," Amy mumbled.

Lisa rolled her eyes. "I'll drop it. You two heading home?"

"I think we might stop at the Watering Hole for a beer first," Stacy said.

Lisa got into her car and powered down the window.

"Then tell Ms. Dunkin her better half is waiting for her at home in bed, will you? And be sure and emphasize 'bed.'"

"We'll pass on the information," Stacy said.

Amy tapped on the roof of the car. "Be safe, my friend."

"Always. See you tomorrow."

Chapter 3

Lisa and Frankie arrived in Cincinnati on Monday and found an apartment located on the river. The price was a little higher than Lisa wanted, but Frankie insisted on her taking it.

They had help with the gang from the bar in moving her essentials to Cincinnati. Lisa and Frankie shopped for furniture to fill out the rest of the apartment. They said their goodbyes until Friday when Frankie would join her for the weekend.

Thursday night, Lisa met with Ted Hillary to discuss Lisa's new job over dinner.

"Ted, it's nice to meet you," Lisa said.

Ted Hillary, a tall, thin man in his early forties, smiled as he took Lisa's offered hand.

Lisa slid into the booth across from him. "I appreciate you taking me under your wing for the next week or so."

"It's a pleasure, Lisa. I followed your articles while you were in Chattanooga and kept up on you in Indianapolis."

The waiter filled their water glasses and took their drink orders.

Lisa perused the menu. "Anything you recommend?" she asked Ted.

"If you're a meat eater, I highly recommend their New York Strip."

"You said the magic words." She set the menu aside. "What do you think of the team?"

"They're young, as you know. You've covered a lot of these guys in Indianapolis. I think they need to trade for a heavy-hitting left-handed bat. An outfielder, if you ask me. But of course, I'm not the GM."

"Doesn't mean you can't have a wish list."

Their server returned with their drinks and jotted down their orders.

Ted took a sip of his beer. "You're a first-rate reporter. You won't have any problems adjusting to the majors. Sure, the egos might be a little bigger, but it's still bat hits ball, ball flies to the outfield, outfielder catches ball."

"Not complicated at all when you put it like that."

"I think Amy Perry will follow right behind you."

"I wouldn't be surprised to see her next month."

"They have a platoon going on at first. They could use her bat there. Colston and Lawson are hitting a collective .200. They're good defensive players, but that's about it. I'm sure management's about ready to pull the trigger."

"It'll be something to see her back with the Reds. I believe once she gets here, she won't be leaving. She's too dedicated to her game not to stay in Cincinnati."

"From what I've seen of her, I agree," Ted said. "I caught the games when she was with the Reds spring training camp last season. She can hit. And field, too. I have to admit I was skeptical when I first heard of the Reds bringing her up through the instructional league and then on to Chattanooga. I know that makes me a male chauvinist." He looked over at Lisa. "Feel free to jump in and correct me, if I'm wrong."

Lisa cleared her throat. "Well, I—"

He laughed. "You're not hurting my feelings, Lisa. She made a believer out of me this spring."

The waiter brought their dinners. Conversation ebbed as they concentrated on their meals. After they'd finished, Lisa ordered a Michelob.

"You know Max Murphy from his days managing the Indians." Ted took another drink of his beer. "And like I said, you know a lot of the players from Indianapolis. I'll take you to the field tomorrow afternoon to meet some of the others. Then we'll go over my routine. It shouldn't differ from how you do things with Minor League.com. You'll still send the articles on to editors in New York."

They talked for a while longer over their beers before leaving for the parking lot.

"See you tomorrow at the ballpark," Ted said as he got into his car.

Lisa drove into her spot at the complex. She rode the elevator up to her apartment on the seventh floor. She let herself in and phoned Frankie as she walked over to the sliding glass window overlooking the Ohio River. The call immediately clicked over to voicemail.

"Hey, hon. Sorry I missed you tonight. I thought you might be home from the bar by now. Give me a call when you get in. I miss you like crazy."

She sank into the couch, laid her head back, and dozed off until her cell phone vibrated and awakened her.

"You sounded kind of down on your message. Everything okay there?" Frankie asked.

"No."

"What's wrong?"

"You're not here."

"Aww. I miss you, too, Leese. I'll see you tomorrow. It's not too much longer, right?"

"I guess I need to get used to not sleeping with you every night." Lisa punched the cushion of the couch in frustration. "Hell, I don't think I'll ever get used to it."

"You haven't even started covering the team yet. Give it a little time. How'd your dinner meeting go with the outgoing guy?"

Lisa heard water running in the background. "God, I wish I was there now. You're getting the water hot for your shower, aren't you?"

"Yes."

"Damn."

Frankie laughed. "We'll catch up tomorrow night."

"Promise?"

"Count on it."

"The meeting with Ted went fine. He'll get more specific tomorrow once we're at the ballpark." Lisa picked up a nearby throw pillow and put it on her lap. She imagined Frankie's skin under her fingertips as she ran her fingers over the embroidered design.

"I should arrive by ten tomorrow. I'll meet you at the apartment."

"To hell with waiting until tomorrow night."

"That's my girl."

"Yes, I am."

"I think I'll hit the shower. The bar wore me out tonight. We had two softball teams come in, and it was crazy."

"I'll see you tomorrow then. I love you."

"Love you too, Leese. Get a good night's sleep."

"I'll try. Night, Frankie."

"Night."

Lisa flipped her phone shut. She walked to the bathroom, stripped, and took a hot shower before climbing into bed. The extra pillow was a poor substitute, but she hugged it to her chest as she curled on her side. She stared at the shadows on the wall and wished she were about a hundred miles northwest in a ranch house on the south side of Indianapolis.

* * *

"What'd you think about the weekend series?" Ted asked while unplugging his laptop.

Lisa followed suit with her computer. Although she wasn't covering the games yet, she wrote the articles as if she were already on the job to get a handle on deadlines.

"Aside from Houston taking three out of the four games, I enjoyed it."

The late Monday afternoon sun warmed the press box. Lisa looked at the view below. She still had a difficult time accepting this was a permanent position—as long as her editors wanted her.

"We should be heading to the airport in about two hours," Ted said. "Does that give you enough time to get to your apartment and grab your bags?"

"I packed last night, so I'm good."

"We leave from Great American on the bus. You can park your car in the employee lot in the garage. It's safe."

Lisa thanked him and left for her car. She had about an hour to kill, so she called Frankie when she got to the apartment. Frankie answered on the first ring.

"Getting ready for your first road trip?"

Lisa heard low music playing in the background. Frankie usually worked on the books and orders on Mondays when the bar was dead.

"Got my luggage together. I need to leave for the ballpark in about an hour."

"This should be exciting."

"The Reds are in the middle of a ten-game run against Central Division teams. It's important even this early in the season not to get too far behind. They need to do better than they did in this Houston series."

"Did they win any of the other games? I didn't keep up after I drove back to Indianapolis Saturday."

"Yesterday. Morales pitched a four-hit shutout."

They chatted until it was time for Lisa to leave.

"I'll call you later tonight in Milwaukee. When will you be home?"

"I'm checking out of here earlier than usual," Frankie answered. "I should be home by ten."

"I'll call you around nine-thirty my time."

"That's right. Central Time up there, huh?"

"There and Chicago."

They hung up. Lisa drove to the stadium and parked in the garage as Ted suggested. Players and coaching staff were lugging their baggage to the bus. A couple of players tossed their bags on the ground by the open storage bins. Lisa fought the desire to call them on it and tell them to load their own frigging luggage. The driver stacked the bags in place. She put hers in an open space.

"Thanks," the driver said with a grateful smile.

"You're welcome."

Lisa hopped up the stairs to the bus and searched for an empty seat. She was about to sit next to Ted, but a familiar voice called to her a few rows back. She moved down the aisle and stopped in front of Max Murphy, the manager.

"Hey, Lisa. We haven't had a chance to chat since you accepted the job. Take a seat and chew the fat with me on the way to the airport."

She sat down in the open aisle seat.

"How've you been?" Murphy asked.

"Good. How do you like managing the Reds?"

"It's a challenge. I'm used to winning. After those championships in Indianapolis, I'll never get used to losing, which is a good thing."

"Finishing two games under .500 last year was a hell of an improvement for this team, Murph. Give it some time."

"I'd think you of all people would know that one thing a major league manager doesn't have is the luxury of time."

"With the talent you have on this team and with your skills, they'll come around. I have a feeling it'll be this year, too. Roberto Sanchez looked sharp in the starts I saw in Indianapolis. That kid has a wicked slider to go along with the heat."

"You got a good eye there, Lisa."

"You think he'll be called up soon?"

"I didn't say that."

"Right," she said with a knowing smile.

"Let's talk about you. A week from today, this baby will be all yours." He cast a quick glance Ted Hillary's way and leaned closer. "Nothing against Hillary, but you're in a different league when it comes to reporting."

Lisa knew her face was on fire.

"You sure you're not Irish, Lisa? You seem to have the same problem I do with showing your emotions."

"Jesus, Murph. Give me a break."

He laughed. "We'll get along fine like in Indianapolis. And Perry will get the call again soon."

"She'll stick this time."

He nodded. "No doubt. Too much talent not to."

They talked about Amy until the bus arrived at the airport and parked next to the chartered plane. It took about twenty minutes to get everything loaded and everyone boarded. Lisa sat by a window, grateful the seat remained empty beside her.

She peered through a break in the clouds and tried to guess when they flew over Indianapolis, but only an endless stretch of nondescript farmland lay below. After pushing her seat back, she fell asleep for the remainder of the flight.

Chapter 4

Amy finished with the last reporter. She still wasn't sure if she cared for the new Website beat reporter for the Indians, but it probably wouldn't have mattered if a Pulitzer-prize-winning journalist had taken over. She missed Lisa. Three weeks had passed. It seemed much longer.

The guys showered and left the clubhouse. Amy undressed, showered, and was about to leave for home. She'd taken two steps toward the exit when Reed's voice stopped her.

"Perry!" It looked like he was trying to maintain a scowl, but he broke into a grin. "My office please."

The blood pounded in her ears as she took a seat in front of his desk.

"Management called. You ready to face major league pitching again?"

"You know it, Curt."

"Go home, get your stuff together, and have a good night's sleep. They expect you at the ballpark in Cincinnati tomorrow afternoon. You'll start tomorrow night against the Mets." He stood and walked around his desk. "I won't give you another pep talk because you don't need it. Do what you've been doing. Concentrate on the game. You have strong support at home if the other shit gets in the way, right?"

"Yes."

"Good." He held out his hand. When she grasped it, he said, "Ah hell," and pulled her in for a hug, pounding her on the back a couple of times.

"Rake it in the show like you've been raking it in the minors, and you'll be fine. I'll try to make a game if our schedule will let me."

"I'd love to see you again."

"Don't go getting carried away. Grab your shit and hightail it out of here. I think you've got someone at home waiting to hear the news."

Amy paused at the door.

"Thanks, Curt. For everything."

He blinked, sniffed, and gestured toward the lockers. "Don't forget anything, ya hear?"

She gathered her equipment from her locker and shoved it into her bag. As she got to the door leading outside, she looked around the clubhouse one last time. Then she took her long strides to her car.

* * *

The apartment was dark except for the bedroom light shining down the hall. Amy heard the muted sound of the television. She dropped her gear and walked down the hallway toward the opened door.

Stacy lay in bed, propped up with pillows against the headboard. She set aside her latest lesbian romance purchase. "Hey, you look beat. I caught the highlights. You had a nice night at the plate."

Amy brushed her lips against Stacy's.

"Not bad."

"Not bad, my ass."

"Gosh, that's so lady-like for a femme."

Stacy smacked her arm before Amy left for the bathroom. She returned a short time later and retrieved her boxers and tank top from the dresser. As she dressed, she looked up and found Stacy watching her every move.

Amy pointed to the book. "She's still your fave, huh?"

Stacy picked up the book from the bed and set it on the nightstand. She turned off the television and flipped back the covers. "You're my fave. Come here." She patted the mattress.

"I love it when you get forceful." Amy climbed into bed.

Stacy reached behind her, dimmed the light, and snuggled into Amy's arms. "I could lie like this for the rest of my life and never get tired of it."

"The rest of your life, huh?"

"Yes," Stacy said with a sigh.

"I don't know…"

Stacy propped herself up on her elbow. "What does that mean? Don't you enjoy this?"

Amy looked at Stacy's face in the darkness. "Don't pout. It's not becoming."

"Amy Perry, what's wrong with you?"

"Let's put it this way. If you want to stay in bed the rest of your life, I guess you can't join me in Cincinnati tomorrow night."

"Cincinnati…" Stacy sat up suddenly and jumped on Amy, straddling her with her knees on either side of Amy's hips. "Oh my God! I can't believe you came home, undressed, got into bed, and didn't tell me right away." Stacy backhanded Amy's stomach.

"Oof. Damn, woman. Don't put me out of commission before I even get my next at-bat with the Reds."

"You're such a tease." Stacy stretched her body against Amy's. Her shoulder-length dark hair fell across Amy's breasts. "The sexiest, hottest tease a lover could ever hope for."

Amy kissed her, parting Stacy's lips and running her tongue inside.

"I'm not a tease," Amy whispered against Stacy's mouth.

"No?"

Amy easily flipped Stacy onto her back and climbed on top of her. She pressed her lips against Stacy's neck and enjoyed the low moan that vibrated against her mouth. She pushed up Stacy's T-shirt. Stacy squirmed as Amy sucked her nipple.

"Would a tease do this?"

"Yes… I mean no… I mean yes."

Amy grinned and brought her thigh between Stacy's legs to push against her panties.

"Which is it?" She kept up the motion, until Stacy parted her legs even more. "You like?"

"God, yes."

Amy pushed Stacy's panties aside and ran her fingers into her wetness. "You like more?"

Stacy moaned.

She watched Stacy's face. When Amy sensed she was close, she backed off a little.

Stacy whimpered. "Amy, please…"

Amy flicked her clit with her thumb as she slid two fingers deep inside. She let it build the way Stacy craved until Stacy tensed, and Amy brought her to a crashing climax.

After Stacy's breathing slowed, she captured Amy's mouth with a long, slow kiss.

Amy ran her fingers through Stacy's thick hair. "You're beautiful."

"You're not a tease. But you *are* the starting first baseman for the Cincinnati Reds." Stacy cupped Amy's breast and tweaked her nipple until it grew hard. "And you're all mine."

Amy lay back as Stacy gave her the same slow pleasure.

* * *

"Amy! Amy! Over here!"

Amy blinked as another flash blinded her. The Reds tried to treat this as a normal call-up, but the reporters and photographers didn't oblige. They descended on Amy as soon as she stepped out of her car at Great American. She made a move toward the entrance to the park but first had to run the gauntlet through about twenty members of the media.

"How's it feel getting the call again?"

"Are you ready to stay up this time?"

"Did you bring your partner with you, and do you anticipate it being a distraction?"

At the last question, Amy zeroed in on a short, scrawny reporter who appeared to be sixteen years old. She ignored him and pushed her way through the human maze. She finally reached the gate where a security guard opened it for her and held up his hand to the throng trying to push past him.

"This is far as you go, everybody." He closed the gate with a clang.

She heard his hurried steps behind her.

"Hey, Amy?"

She stopped and waited for him to catch up.

"Uh… my kid sister is one of your biggest fans. She asked me if… well…"

Amy set her bag down, reached in, and grabbed one of her batting gloves. "Don't suppose you have a pen or marker?" she asked him.

"As a matter of fact, I do."

She smiled when he whipped out a Sharpie from his front shirt pocket and handed it to her.

"Her name's Colleen."

"Can you turn around?"

Amy pressed the glove against his back and scribbled out, "To

Colleen, best, Amy Perry," in the palm of the leather. She handed it to him when she'd finished.

"Thanks, Amy. She already thinks you're the best. This?" He held up the glove. "She'll be a fan for life."

"Tell her to keep playing the game, because I'm assuming she plays, right?"

"Fast pitch softball. She argued to get on the boy's baseball team. You realize you started something, don't you?"

"Glad I could speed along the process," she said as she picked up her bag.

"Good luck tonight."

"Thank you."

Amy continued toward the rear entrance to the clubhouse. Another guard opened the door for her. She nodded at the bulky woman. The guard winked when Amy moved past her.

Guess I'd better get used to that.

"Amy, welcome back," Phil, the easygoing, rotund clubhouse and equipment manager, said as she entered the clubhouse. "Got your locker all ready. Right over here."

She followed him to a locker with a white nameplate above it, stenciled with "Perry 22" in red lettering. The Reds put her in between Nick Sanders, the veteran power-hitting third baseman, and Tim Rawls, the starting second baseman who'd made the team out of spring training. She'd not had much interaction with the two players the month she'd been with the team, so she still wasn't sure what kind of treatment she'd receive.

Phil watched her check out the other names.

"You'll like those two. They'll give you a fair shake."

Amy didn't respond, thinking, we'll see. She'd finished emptying out her bag when Max Murphy, dressed in street clothes, strolled toward her. He stopped at her locker.

"Good to have you back, Perry. Why don't you follow me, and we'll chat. I know you want to get out there for batting practice, but you have a few minutes."

She followed him to his spacious office.

"Have a seat." He took off his shirt and pulled down the uniform draped across a hanger on top of his door. "How you feeling?" he asked her as he finished buttoning the jersey and then sat down behind his desk.

"A little nervous but anxious to get going at the same time."

"That's good. The nervous thing should keep you on your toes.

The anxious stuff should keep you on top of your game."

"Hope so."

"Amy, I won't lie and paint some rosy picture about how things will be for you. You found out some of this last year when you were up for the month. You'll get cheers, you'll get boos, you'll catch crap from other players, and you'll have other guys tell you they're glad you got a shot. But you haven't been up since your press conference earlier this spring." His voice took on a more serious tone.

Amy clutched the arm of the chair a little tighter. She feared she was about to get a rebuke for announcing her sexual orientation before the Indians season opener. She'd only played the one month under Murphy.

"I expect I'll catch grief. I was aware of it when I held the press conference."

"Do you have a thick skin, and can you be hard of hearing?"

"I can be if I need to. Chattanooga wasn't exactly a cakewalk at first, but most of the other players accepted me eventually. That's all I ask—accept me or leave me alone."

"Good, good." Murphy ran his thick hand through his red hair. "I'll keep an eye on this team, and I'll step in if needed. But I can't control the other shit."

"I had my share of unruly crowds down in the south. I think I can handle it."

"Why don't you dress and take the field? If I remember, you like to get your batting practice in to where Donny had to yank you kicking and screaming out of the cage."

She laughed. "Hey, he should be happy I like to work on my hitting."

He stood up. "Don't give my hitting coach a heart attack on your first night back."

"I'll do my best for you," she said as she clasped his outstretched hand. "Always."

"I don't doubt it for a minute. Now go get suited up."

Other players had entered the clubhouse. A few of them looked in her direction. Nick Sanders sat in front of his locker, shirtless in his sliding shorts. He was a mountain of a man. Over six feet tall and all muscle. She moved in front of her locker. He glanced at her as he pulled on his socks. A lock of light blond hair fell across his forehead.

"Hey." He greeted her with a slight smile.

"Hey."

Might as well go for it, Amy thought. She lifted off her T-shirt but kept her jeans on as she put on a red undershirt over her sports bra. She'd discovered the guys weren't so nervous if she undressed in increments.

Sanders stood and lifted his uniform pants off the hangar in his locker. As he did, Amy tugged off her jeans. She pulled on a pair of sliding shorts that ended mid-thigh and clung to her muscles. She snuck a peek over at Sanders who remained facing his locker while he finished dressing.

Amy dressed in silence, accepting that he had nothing to say. She had her head down while looping her red belt through her uniform pants.

Sanders started to walk away but then stopped. "Anybody gives you any shit, tell me, all right?"

Amy looked up from what she was doing to meet his pale blue eyes.

"All right?" he repeated.

"Sure."

Shocked, she watched as he headed toward the tunnel to the field. The rustle of a newspaper caught her attention.

Phil sat in the corner with his feet propped up on another chair. He glanced over the paper, nodded slightly, and then went back to reading.

"I'll be damned," Amy said under her breath.

*   *   *

Lisa stood beside the batting cage as Amy sprayed line drives around the outfield. She got hold of one and bounced it against the left field wall.

"Picking up right where she left off, huh?"

Lisa turned at the sound of Sarah's voice.

"Jesus, Swift. You're like a jellyfish or something. I can't get away from you."

"I think the term you're searching for is leech. I'm like a blood-sucking leech."

"Thanks for clarifying."

Amy finished hitting. She took off her batting gloves, shoved them into her back pockets, and laid her helmet and bat by the cage before trotting to the outfield to do wind sprints.

"Check it out," Sarah said.

Lisa followed her line of sight to see Sanders jog to where Amy stood in right field. They bent over and started their sprints, side by side.

"That's refreshing," Lisa said. "And from a veteran."

"It's freaking amazing."

"Come on. Let's give the guys a break."

Sarah shot her an incredulous look. "You didn't just say that, did you? You can't tell me you expected her teammates to welcome her back with open arms."

"I don't know what I expected."

"I sure as shit didn't expect to see that." Sarah lifted her chin toward the outfield where Amy and Sanders now were doing their crossovers.

Lisa wasn't certain what she thought she'd see, but this was encouraging.

"If I tried to cross one leg over the other while running sideways, I'd fall on my ass," Sarah said while another player took his turn in the cage. "Have you had a chance to talk with her since she got in today?"

"No. I don't think she's been in town long."

Lisa's cell phone rang, and she read the display.

"This might answer some questions." Lisa hit Talk. "Hey, Stacy. How's the nervous wife?"

Stacy laughed on the other end of the line. "Nervous."

"An honest answer. When did you guys get in?"

"Late this morning. We planned to search for apartments but decided it'd be foolish when we can take our time tomorrow. So, we checked into the Hyatt, at least for the weekend. We're hoping you might have an idea on what's a good place to live."

Lisa thought about it. "I could help you out, but if you want to live on the river, where I'm at is nice. They have six-month leases, too."

"Sounds good, Lisa. Maybe I'll see you later after the game."

"Talk to you soon."

Lisa clipped her phone back on her belt.

"Couldn't help but overhear," Sarah said. "I'm glad you all remained friends. Amy will still need that. Hey, how's Frankie taking this job change and your move?"

"Better than I am," Lisa said.

Sarah stared at her. "Why don't you and I have a beer later after the game?" They agreed on a nearby bar.

They joined the other reporters when Amy trotted toward the

dugout. Amy slowed her step as they converged around her.

"Glad to be with the Reds again, Amy?" an ESPN reporter asked.

"Yes. I'm looking forward to learning more about the game from Murphy."

"Do you feel any added pressure or has it lessened some for you?" Sarah asked.

"I think the only pressure I feel is pressure I put on myself to be the best I can be."

The reporters had a few more questions for Amy before they dispersed. She walked over to Lisa and Sarah.

"How're you really doing, Aim?" Lisa asked.

"I'm ready to go out and play baseball."

"Stacy said you need some help finding a place."

"Can you show us around?"

"I told her you may like where I'm at. Six-month leases, too."

"We'll talk later."

Lisa clasped her hand in a buddy shake. "Good luck tonight."

Amy trotted into the dugout. Lisa and Sarah left for the press box.

The capacity crowd roared when the Reds took the field and Amy assumed her position at first base. Lisa spotted Stacy below, seated in the second row up from the Reds dugout.

After a quick top half of the inning, the first two Reds batters reached base in the bottom half. The Mets pitcher, Mike Allison, paced behind the mound and rubbed up the baseball while the announcer boomed out Amy's name. Amy read the signs from Pete Servace, the third base coach, did the usual unsnapping and snapping of her gloves, and stepped into the batter's box.

The first pitch clipped the outside corner of the plate for a called strike.

Allison checked the runners and toed the rubber as he stared in for the sign. He curled into his windup before unleashing a ninety-two-mile-an-hour slider down and in. Amy whipped her bat around and lined it over the third base bag. It rattled down in the left field corner. Both runners scored easily. Amy raised her head as she rounded second. The left fielder fumbled the ball for an instant. She kicked on the afterburners and heeded Servace's sign to slide. She slid headfirst into the bag with the third baseman tagging her on the back.

The umpire threw his hands out. "Safe!"

Amy stood and called for time. She stepped off the bag to brush the dirt from her uniform while the crowd roared. The next batter, Sanders, flew out to center field, deep enough to allow Amy to tag up and score.

The Reds remained ahead, 3-2, heading into the top of the ninth. The Reds closer, Danny Lopez, got two quick outs but walked the next two batters. The pitching coach strolled out to the mound, but no one was warming up in the Reds bullpen. The meeting ended when the home plate umpire broke up the conference.

Lopez threw two out of the strike zone to the Mets cleanup hitter. He checked the runners and fired a fastball over the inner half of the plate. The left-handed hitter pulled the pitch down the first baseline. Amy dove and snagged the ball on one hop. From her knees, she tossed it to Lopez who covered the bag for the final out.

Lopez smacked gloves with Amy. The players lined up, and she followed Lopez down the line, getting high fives from each teammate.

Sarah and Lisa picked up their reporters' notebooks and rode the elevator down to the clubhouse. They huddled with the other reporters stacked three deep around Amy's locker. Amy answered each question with the same professionalism she'd shown in Chattanooga and Indianapolis.

* * *

Lisa sat down across from Sarah.

"I already ordered you a Mich. Hope that wasn't too presumptuous of me," Sarah said.

"Of course it was," Lisa deadpanned.

"Tough shit," Sarah said with a grin.

The waiter brought their beers over and asked if they wanted to order anything.

"I think we're just having a couple of these tonight." Sarah held up her bottle. She waited for the server to leave their table. "How are you and Frankie really? And be honest."

"We're good."

"But…"

Lisa picked at the label on her bottle. "I didn't think it'd be this damn hard to be away from her. I mean, I did, but I didn't. We talked about it before I took the job, but it's just now hitting me."

"How's she about your being away?"

"She's handling it all right. She's keeping busy at the bar. She'll be in St. Louis next weekend. I'm driving up to see her after Wednesday's game and staying with her on our off-day, so that's two nights we'll be together."

Sarah took a sip of her beer. "I'm going to tell you something about my five-year relationship." She gave Lisa a look. "And, yes, I'm capable of having a relationship."

Lisa held her hands up in defense. "Hey, I didn't say anything."

"You didn't have to," Sarah said. "Mary and I met at a newspaper awards ceremony. She was and still is a reporter for the *Seattle Times*. Hell of a good one, too. We struck up a conversation over drinks. I had to leave that night to cover the National League divisional playoffs. After the World Series, I called her. We got together again in Seattle and started dating. Everything was good. The next spring, we bought a condo, got two dogs and an aquarium. You get the picture."

Sarah paused a moment. "The longer I was away from her, the more I missed her. The more I missed her, the more I resented our time apart. So much so, that when we got together, I argued with her the entire time about how much I missed her. She asked me if I thought she should give up her job. I told her, 'Yes. I make more money than you do. It only makes sense.' As you might suspect, everything went downhill from there. We broke up two summers ago."

"I'm sorry, Sarah."

Sarah blinked away tears. "I'm not telling you this to give you the story of my love life." She leaned forward. "I'm telling you because you need to get over your damn self and accept this is how things will be. Don't make the same mistake I did, Lisa. Lose your insecurities and frustration of being apart. You're both big girls. Sit down with Frankie again and talk this out until you get everything in the open. Your relationship's worth it."

"I know it is."

Sarah took a long pull of her beer. "Good. I don't want to give you a lecture every week."

"Wouldn't want that." Lisa hid her smile behind the lip of her bottle.

Lisa drove back to her apartment and sank into the leather recliner. She punched in the Watering Hole number.

"Yeah?" Billie, the manager, shouted over the din.

"Is Frankie around?"

"Let me hunt down the boss woman for you."

Frankie came to the phone a few minutes later. It was much quieter on her end.

"Hey, hon. In your office?" Lisa asked.

"Yes. I wanted to be able to hear you without the noise out there. How'd Amy do?"

"Played like the Rookie of the Year I think she'll be."

"Doesn't surprise me."

Lisa picked at her jeans. "Frankie, have I told how much I love you?" Her voice broke.

"Hey, is everything all right?"

"It is now."

Chapter 5

Lisa heard the demonstrators before she saw them at the Busch Stadium entrance in St. Louis.

"God hates fags! God hates fags!"

She rounded the corner in her rental car, narrowly avoiding two women and a man sprinting across the street. The woman held a sign scrawled with crude, red letters, "Homosexuality is an abommination against God."

"Can't even spell," Lisa muttered. She maneuvered around the group of about fifty people and drove a little farther to the press lot. While stepping out of the car, she spotted a news crew and an ESPN cameraman videotaping everything. She walked toward a red-faced Sarah Swift.

Sarah glared at the mob. "Fucking assholes," she said as Lisa drew closer. "Make that fucking bigoted assholes."

"I wondered how long it'd take. I didn't think it'd be Amy's first road trip."

"Think she'll be able to handle all of this?" Sarah motioned behind them at the demonstrators. She and Lisa showed their press passes to security to enter the stadium.

"Would you be?"

"Hell no, but she had to know this could be the fallout when she held that press conference before opening day in Indianapolis."

They walked out into the open stadium with its bright red seats and view of the city skyline—including the Arch, clearly visible, that stretched beyond the outfield wall.

"This is one gorgeous place to play baseball," Lisa said.

"Were you listening to me?"

Lisa noticed they seemed to be the only members of the press there when they sat down in seats behind home plate. The grounds crew was hosing down the infield. She inhaled the glorious smells of a ballpark. The pungent aroma of grass and dirt tickled her nose.

"Hello? Collins?" Sarah leaned forward so that Lisa had no

recourse except to meet her eyes.

"I heard you. And to answer your question, yes, Amy was very aware of what could happen by coming out. We had a good talk. She and Stacy discussed it at length before Amy made her decision."

"Do you know if she's caught any flak so far?"

"I know of some letters she received in Indianapolis. But for every negative letter she received, she'd get one from a gay teenager or from parents of gay kids applauding her for her honesty and courage."

Lisa's cell phone rang. She smiled when she saw the number. "Hey, Frankie. You're awake?" She glanced over at Sarah who rolled her eyes.

"I've been awake for an hour but have been basking in the afterglow." Frankie made a loud yawning noise.

"Glad I could be of assistance in helping you relax."

"You can assist me anytime you like." It sounded like Frankie stifled another yawn. "You know, this has been like a vacation for me. First, you spend two nights in Indy, and then we drive down to St. Louis to be together for the weekend. Thank you for that."

Lisa took her phone up the stairs to the concourse for more privacy.

"When you take the taxi here, be prepared to get pissed off the closer you get to the stadium." Lisa relayed details of the scene she came across when she arrived.

"Shit," Frankie said. "That didn't take long."

"No, it didn't."

"Are you going to talk to Amy about it?"

"The rest of the press might've already gotten to her. She's not made it here yet."

"Stacy's in town, right?" Frankie asked. "She mentioned coming down to catch the series."

"I think she should be here by now. What'd you two decide about the job at the Watering Hole?"

Lisa heard banging sounds on Frankie's end of the line.

"I told her she had a job there in any capacity as long as she wanted. If it means she can't work except when the Reds travel, that's fine. Told her she could work in the winter, too. I have a feeling, though, they'll have a condo or house bought in Cincinnati by that time." Another bang assaulted Lisa's eardrum. "Shit!"

"What's wrong?"

"Didn't think the coffeepot would get hot that fast."

"Be careful, Ms. Dunkin. Those hands are valuable commodities."

Frankie laughed. "Listen, I'll take a shower and be there before the first pitch, shortly after seven."

"You can pick up your ticket at the will-call window. You're sitting next to Stacy."

"See you soon."

Lisa shut her phone and stomped back down the steps to where Sarah had her face tilted toward the sun. She waited for Sarah to acknowledge her presence.

"You're in my light, you love-struck goofball."

Lisa sat down next to her. "I won't argue. You're right. I'm still love-struck."

"Really?" Sarah asked. "I never would have guessed."

"Thanks again for talking to me last week. Frankie and I had a heart-to-heart and worked out everything. Seems she was feeling insecure as well. We're good now."

"As I knew you would be. And yes, I'm jealous."

"You'll find someone, Sarah."

Sarah's expression grew sad. "No. Mary was the one."

"How do you know?"

"Trust me. She was."

Lisa let it drop. "Back to what we were talking about. Sometimes it won't be easy for Amy, but Stacy will be such good support for her."

"And of course there's you. You're the best friend she has, you know?"

"I'll be there for her as much as I can be."

Sarah smacked Lisa on the thigh. "How about we visit the vendors' stands and see if we can rustle up some tomatoes or something equally mushy. Then we'll go up one level and drop them on some unsuspecting, ignorant, pompous, far-right dipshitters."

"As tempting as that sounds, I think I need to keep this job for longer than a few weeks."

"You're always so practical, Collins."

* * *

From the backseat of the taxi, Amy saw the gathering in front of the stadium.

"Do you want me to find another way in?" the driver asked.

Her face grew hotter with anger as she read the various signs. "No," she said, her voice tight. "Drive past them."

"Hey! There she is!" one skinny guy shouted. The crowd surged toward the car with the cameramen and photographers in hot pursuit.

"You sure?" the driver asked.

"In fact, stop right by the gate. I'm getting out."

"You're what?" The cabbie swiveled toward her in disbelief.

"I said stop."

He didn't have much of a choice. The crowd blocked the way.

Amy paid him, grabbed the door handle, and swung the door open.

"Do you think that's a good—"

She didn't hear the rest of his words.

"Go back to whatever hole you crawled out of!" one man snarled.

"God condemns you for what you are!" a woman shouted. A small child stood beside her.

Amy looked down at the boy, and her blood ran cold. He held a sign that read in very neat red print, "Fags Will Burn in Hell."

She pushed through the throng as the cameras clicked around her. Without warning, a stocky man jumped out in front of her. He was slightly over six-foot tall; Amy stood almost at eye level with him.

"You and your kind disgust me," he said.

"My kind, as in first basemen?"

"You know what I mean."

The gates opened behind him, and two security guards grabbed him by each shoulder.

"Step aside, sir, or we'll place you under arrest," one of the guards said.

"Arrest me?" the protestor shouted. "Why not arrest her? She's the pervert."

"Step aside." The guard with the crew cut moved in front of the man and put his hand on his chest.

The man glowered first at the officer speaking and then at the other officer. "Fine."

Amy started for the gate as they pushed him aside. She heard a disgusting sound behind her, and a wet, sticky substance struck her neck.

"I spit on you just as God spits on you!"

She whirled around. "Your idea of God and my idea of God

don't mesh. The God I know doesn't hate or spit on anyone."

The security guards shut the gates with a loud clang. Amy kept walking.

"What do you know of God?" she heard the man shout. He followed the words with a string of obscenities.

"Yeah, and God talks like that, too," Amy said through clenched teeth.

The security guards fell in beside her.

"Why didn't you have the taxi drive you in?" the younger one asked her.

"Because I won't let a bunch of bigots intimidate me."

"Let us do our job, Ms. Perry." He yanked a handkerchief from his back pocket and handed it to her.

She used it to wipe the back of her neck. "Sorry. I didn't mean to make your jobs more difficult." She held out the handkerchief to the guard.

"Toss it in the trash. I don't need any reminders of that asshole."

They reached the back entrance to the clubhouse. The other guard unlocked the door. "Hope the Cards kick your butts tonight," he told her. His smile softened his words. "And I hope you have a good game."

* * *

Lisa was about to step onto the field to interview Max Murphy when her cell phone rang again.

She flipped the phone open. "Hey, Stacy. Did you need help getting to the stadium?"

"Is Amy on the field?" Stacy sounded frantic.

"No. The players haven't made it out yet. Why? What's wrong?"

"I'm watching ESPN. They're running a tape of what happened minutes ago there in front of the stadium."

Lisa's stomach dropped. "What happened?"

"Amy got shoved around some, and they were shouting at her. And this one guy fucking spit on her."

Lisa was already jogging over to the Reds dugout to enter the clubhouse. "Try not to worry. I'll check on her and have her call you."

"I've been trying to reach her, but she must have turned off her phone."

Lisa heard the tremor in Stacy's voice.

"It'll be all right, Stacy."

"Tell her to call me."

Lisa hung up and hurried down the dugout steps.

* * *

Amy ripped off her T-shirt and grabbed a bar of soap. On the way to the sink, she snatched a washcloth and towel. She soaped up the washcloth and scrubbed the back of her neck. No matter how hard she scrubbed, it felt like the glob of spit was still there. She looked in the mirror over the sink and saw the raw emotion imprinted on her face.

"Fuck!"

After hurling the towel and washcloth into the laundry bin, she stomped to her locker. She tugged her red-sleeved undershirt over her head. She took off her jeans and was looping her uniform belt when a hand touched her shoulder. Amy turned.

"Lisa," she said. "Didn't hear you come up behind me."

"Stacy called and told me what happened."

"How'd she know?"

"She caught it on ESPN."

"Crap. I don't want her worrying, and she must be or she wouldn't have called you." Amy finished shoving her jersey into her pants.

"She wants you to call her."

Amy lifted her phone from the shelf of her locker. "Damn it. Forgot to turn it back on."

"What happened?"

"I'm assuming you saw the same jackasses out front when you arrived."

"I almost hit a couple of them with my car."

"I got out of the taxi before we drove through the entrance."

"Amy, why would you do that? You don't know what some of these fanatics are capable of."

"I did it because I wanted to show them I'm not scared. Tell me what's wrong in that?" Anger boiled over again, and she hated she was taking it out on Lisa.

"I can understand why you did it, but you need to be careful. Did one of them assault you?"

"If you want to call spitting on my neck assault, I guess he did. He was maybe a couple of inches taller than me, six-two at the most. I could have taken him."

"Maybe you could have, but the nut might have had a gun or a knife. You don't know with these people. It's not worth it, Aim."

Some of her anger dissipated with Lisa's words. "That's pretty much what the guards told me, to let them do their jobs."

"Keep that in mind, will you? I don't want anything to happen to you. There's someone else who's worried sick. Think of her, too."

Amy stared down at her feet. "I know." She felt Lisa's hand on her shoulder and raised her head.

"We all love you," Lisa said. "You sure you're not too shaken up?"

"I'm fine."

"Give Stacy a call. I'll see you after the game."

Amy phoned Stacy, and she picked up on the first ring.

"Are you okay?" Stacy sounded breathless.

"Pissed off, but okay. Scolded, but okay." Amy dropped into the chair facing her locker.

"Scolded?"

"Lisa."

"If she told you to be more careful next time and not jump out of taxis into a mob, then I agree with her one hundred percent."

Amy smiled. "Feisty little Irishwoman."

"Macho jock. I'm taking a shower, and I'll be at the park soon. We can talk more about this later."

"I'll see you on the field."

Amy lifted her cleats out of the bottom of the locker and was lacing them when Nick Sanders lumbered in.

"Christ, Perry. You ever hear of waiting for security?"

Amy glanced up at Sanders scowling at her.

"I've been reprimanded by my best friend, my partner, and the two guards. I think I get it now. And good Lord, does everyone watch ESPN in the afternoon?"

"One of the guards talked to me on the way in." He tossed his bag down with a thump and flipped his chair around so that he straddled it to face Amy. He leaned his elbows on the back, his expression more serious. "This isn't funny."

Amy sat up in her chair to face him. "Did I say it was?"

He looked like he was about to say something else but must have thought better of it. "Try to be more careful. You haven't even been up that long. Wouldn't want to lose our first baseman after only a few games."

"That's all I'm good for? Playing first base?" Amy asked, glad the mood had lightened.

He stood up and unbuttoned his cotton shirt. "Eh. You're useful when a group of us needs to get seated when all the tables are taken at a restaurant."

"Gee, thanks." She grabbed her glove and made a move to pass him.

He gripped her arm. "Next time, Perry, wait for security."

"I will."

Amy's cleats clacked loudly in the tunnel that led up into the dugout. She emerged from the shade of the tunnel and squinted as the sun greeted her full force.

Phil was laying out towels along the dugout bench.

"Hey, Phil, do we have shades?"

He reached behind him and grabbed a pair of sunglasses out of a container. "Here." He tossed them over.

"Sweet." She admired the dark, mirrored lenses, slid the glasses on, and pushed them against her nose.

"Looks like you belong now." Phil brushed past her to shove batting gloves into their corresponding shelves with the helmets.

She grinned. "I know. I'm a nerd."

"Nah. You're a rookie," he said as he went back to his equipment.

Amy was about to trot out onto the field to take some infield practice but stopped when she saw Dan Taylor, the Reds GM, approaching.

Well, shit, she thought. How many more lectures can I get on this?

"Amy, I understand there was an altercation out front between you and some demonstrators. If this ever happens again, please wait on security. We don't want to see you hurt. You've already shown this organization how you can handle pressure situations, and I have no doubt you can handle this as well. But let security do their jobs."

"I'm sorry. It won't happen again. Several people have helped me see I handled today's situation badly."

He raised his eyebrows.

She recounted to him the advice from everyone, including Stacy.

He chuckled. "I need to meet your partner sometime."

"I'd like that, and I know she would, too."

"Try to get past this and focus on the game."

"Yes, sir."

Amy took infield practice before trotting in for her turn in the cage. Sanders hit a long fly ball to left that bounced off the facing of the upper deck. He set his bat aside, took off his helmet, and pulled off his batting gloves.

"Try and beat that, Perry."

He'd already jogged past her to third base before she could reply.

She hit line drives around the field while attempting to ignore the photographers, huddled as closely together as possible to avoid getting hit by a ball.

* * *

In the first inning, the leadoff and second-place hitters flied out. On her walk to the plate, Amy ran through what she'd studied about the Cardinals pitcher, Bobby Tinders. Likes to come inside and jam right-handed hitters. Throws a slow curve when he gets ahead in the count. Teases you with breaking stuff in the dirt.

She was concentrating so hard that the roar from the sold-out stadium crowd didn't register until she stood in the batter's box. The pitcher paced behind the mound while the cheering increased in volume. Amy backed away from the plate, unsure of what to do. When she'd been with the Reds last September, she'd received some cheers from opponents' fans, but nothing like this.

"You'd better tip your hat or we'll be here all night." The umpire glared at her from behind his mask.

Amy barely raised her batting helmet before settling back into the box.

The first pitch was a high and tight fastball. She shifted out of the way. The next pitch caught the outside corner of the plate for a strike. Tinders threw her another hard fastball that she lined foul by third base.

Behind in the count. Time for the slow curve.

The next pitch dipped toward the outer half of the plate. Amy dropped her bat and lined it between first and second for a solid base hit. The crowd cheered again as she rounded the bag.

Tom Jeffries, the first base coach, put his hand on her shoulder and leaned in to tell her to watch for the quick toss from Tinders for a pick-off attempt. It wasn't until Jeffries stepped away that it sunk in she was standing next to Albert Pujols.

He put his foot by the bag in preparation for pick-off throws. "Nice hitting."

She managed to stutter out her thanks. Get a grip, she thought. You belong here just as much as he does. Amy strayed off a few feet, but dove back in when Tinders flipped the ball to Pujols. He slammed his glove against her shoulder. Amy stood up and brushed off the dirt while watching for the sign from Servace, the third base coach. She edged a little farther away from the base after getting the sign for the hit-and-run.

As Tinders started his move toward home plate, she took off toward second. She ventured a quick peek to see if Sanders made contact. He lined the ball toward the left field gap. Amy chugged around second and picked up Servace's signal as she drew closer to third. He gave her the go sign by frantically pinwheeling his arm. The toe of her cleats barely hit the bag when she rounded it for home. Mark Roberts, in the on-deck circle, tossed his bat aside, fell to his knees, and motioned to slide by slapping the dirt.

The catcher loomed ahead with his body blocking the plate. The ball hadn't made it into Amy's periphery yet. She slid into the catcher's shin guard, but on instinct, reached over and swiped the plate behind him before he tagged her shoulder.

"Safe!" the umpire bellowed.

The catcher jumped to his feet and fired the ball to third base, but Sanders slid in ahead of the throw.

Amy stood and limped toward the dugout. She took the congratulatory hand slap from Roberts as she passed him. Murphy smacked her hand when she came down the steps. Most of her teammates greeted her with high fives. Only two players, both veterans, ignored her by remaining seated at the end of the dugout.

The Reds lost the game in extra innings, 4-3. Amy filed into the clubhouse with the rest of her teammates. Just like in Indianapolis, she wished she could simply strip down and step into the shower. Instead, she went to her locker where the reporters had already camped out. She saw Lisa and lifted her chin in her direction.

Questions bombarded her before she reached her locker, and they weren't about the game.

"Amy, what happened outside the stadium this afternoon?"

"Do you have any comment about the demonstration?"

"Do you think this is something you'll have to face in every city?"

She answered the first question.

"I got out of my taxi and tried to enter the stadium. I had a little difficulty with one of the demonstrators." With all of them, she added silently.

Other reporters fired off more questions, but the reporter wasn't finished.

"What was said?"

"He expressed his opinion about my sexual orientation, and I disagreed with him." She responded to the reporter from the *St. Louis Post-Dispatch*. "My comment is I'm happy with who I am. I'm a baseball player who—"

"A female baseball player," the reporter said.

"I'm aware of that." Amy swallowed her impatience. "I'm a female baseball player who happens to be gay, and, again, I'm not ashamed of who I am."

She met Lisa's eyes as she said this. Lisa smiled.

"And as for if I see this at the other ballparks… I won't know until I get there. I'll be a little more careful in how I handle it if it happens again."

"You seemed to be reading Tinders pretty well tonight with your three hits."

Amy turned toward the voice she knew so well.

"I only wish I hadn't popped out with guys on second and third in the eighth," she told Lisa.

She took a few more questions before the reporters moved on to other players or departed for Murphy's office. After grabbing a towel, she sat down and wiped her face to get rid of some of the grit and grime while awaiting her chance at the showers.

A reporter stood at Sanders's locker. Sanders answered his questions, but it was obvious to Amy that Nick wanted the guy to leave. Nick had struck out in the eleventh with the tying run at third.

The reporter finally finished with his last question.

Sanders began stripping off his uniform. He turned his back on her as he removed his sliding shorts, athletic cup, and jock strap. He wrapped a towel around his waist and grabbed a folded towel and soap.

"You're a good hitter, Perry."

"I sure wasn't in the eighth."

"It happens. I'm fucking pissed off I struck out in the eleventh, but I got to have a short memory about this shit, same as you. You should be proud of how you handled everything tonight. You concentrated on the game and didn't let that other crap affect you."

"It affected me, Nick, but I tried to set it aside while I played."

He stared down at his towel and twisted it in his hands. Then he met her eyes. "You should still be proud. Not everybody can do what you do." He didn't wait for a response as he turned and walked toward the showers.

Chapter 6

Lisa pushed through the front door at the Watering Hole. Billie was washing glasses behind the bar. Val, one of the servers, was wiping down the tables.

"Look at what the cat dragged in." Billie grinned, which made her deep dimples even more pronounced.

Lisa mockingly checked around her. "I don't see any damn cat."

"I sure miss you around here, chief. I know you needed to take that job, but it's been lonely since you left."

"Oh, come on, Billie. You have the girls beating down your door."

"I don't know about that." Billie looked like she was about to have an "aw shucks" moment, which for Billie would be a minor miracle.

"You haven't heard?" Val shouted from the other side of the room. "Billie's been dating the same woman for three months now."

"Wait." Lisa thought back. "Is it the little redhead?"

"Her name's Alexis," Billie said.

"You mean to tell me the great Casanova, the woman who's been breaking hearts in Indy for the past three years, is settling down?"

Billie blushed.

"Oh my God. Is that a blush?"

"Shut the fuck up, Lisa. I can't help it. She's got my heart."

She scrutinized Billie's appearance. She still had short-cropped hair, but she'd let it grow out to about an inch. Her T-shirt wasn't as tight as the others Lisa had seen her wear, and she now sported a bra.

"It wears well on you, my friend."

"You think so?"

"Yes, I think so. Congratulations."

"Thanks." Billie beamed. "Guess you're looking for the boss. What are you doing in town, by the way?"

The Reds had wrapped up a ten-game road trip, the longest one they'd have in June. She'd flown in late the night before to Cincinnati and decided to wait until the next day, Thursday, an off-day, to make the drive to Indianapolis. She'd spend the day and night with Frankie before driving back down to Cincinnati in the morning.

"Off-day for the Reds. Day home for me."

"She's in the office."

Lisa hurried over to the door and knocked. Then she tried her best to imitate Billie's voice.

"Hey, boss. We need more Jim Beam from downstairs."

"Get your ass in here, Leese."

Lisa laughed and opened the door.

Frankie stood up and rushed to her for a kiss.

"I've missed you, too," Lisa whispered.

"Please tell me you're off until tomorrow like you told me."

"Today, tonight, and I leave tomorrow morning for Cincinnati."

"I can think of a lot of things to do between now and tomorrow."

Lisa draped her arms across Frankie's neck. "What kinds of things? Tiddlywinks? Marbles? Stuff like that?"

Frankie brought her mouth close.

"What I have in mind has nothing to do with kids' games."

She captured Lisa's lips and plunged her tongue inside. Lisa moaned. She didn't hear the door open behind them until someone cleared her throat.

"Um, boss?" Billie said. "Before you go, I need you to check the register. The tape thing isn't working right, and you know how I can't figure that shit out."

Frankie smiled at Lisa. "We'll pick this up again soon."

While Frankie tinkered with the register, uttering an occasional obscenity, Lisa tried to hide her impatience by playing a game of pool.

Fifteen minutes later, Frankie had the tape feeding through the register and they could leave. Lisa drove her new Sebring into the driveway. She got out of the car as Frankie parked her truck behind her.

"How about getting reacquainted?" Lisa asked.

Frankie let Lisa lead her into the house.

They walked to the bedroom. Lisa unbuttoned Frankie's shirt and pushed it down from Frankie's shoulders. Frankie stepped back and took off her prosthetic bra. Lisa brushed the scar with the back of her hand and bent over to press her lips against it while caressing

Frankie's breast. Frankie's breathing hitched. Lisa kissed her way over to Frankie's nipple.

They finished undressing, never losing eye contact. Lisa eased Frankie onto the bed and dipped her hand below. Feeling how ready Frankie was made Lisa even wetter. She brought her mouth back to Frankie's nipple as she moved in cadence with Frankie's body. When she knew Frankie was close, she rose up and stared down at her.

"Look at me, Frankie."

Frankie's dark-brown eyes held Lisa's as Lisa entered her. She felt Frankie close around her fingers as she thrust deep inside, gliding with the rhythm of Frankie's hips. Frankie tensed and cried out her name.

Lisa lay beside her to catch her breath, but Frankie didn't give her the chance. She moved on top of Lisa and pressed her lips into her neck, slowly kissing a trail down Lisa's body. Lisa opened her legs wider and clutched the sheets as Frankie's mouth found her. When she captured Lisa's clit between her lips, Lisa's hips rose off the bed. Frankie held her tighter with one hand and pushed her fingers deep inside, stroking her until Lisa exploded into her orgasm.

"God, Frankie," Lisa moaned and grabbed Frankie's hair as the waves of her climax washed over her.

They made love until exhaustion claimed their bodies.

Lisa held Frankie in her arms. "Every time I'm with you, I realize how much I miss you."

Without saying another word, she pushed Frankie onto her back and pressed her mouth into the sensitive underside of Frankie's breast. Her fingertips slid down Frankie's abdomen on her journey below. Frankie raised her hips, but Lisa suddenly stopped.

She brought her hand back up to Frankie's breast and probed where her lips had been. Cold fear coursed through her when she felt a lump.

"What's wrong?" Frankie asked.

"There's a..." Lisa struggled with the word. "There's a lump, Frankie. Have you felt this before?" She took Frankie's hand and placed it where she'd touched.

"I don't feel—" Frankie stopped short. She sat up.

Lisa joined her. She glanced at Frankie and wondered if her own face registered as much fear.

"I did a check two weeks ago. This wasn't there." Frankie swallowed. "It wasn't there, Leese."

Lisa held Frankie's hand.

"We'll make an appointment with the doctor. Let's call her today and try to get you in tomorrow. I want to be there."

Frankie began shaking.

Lisa wrapped her arms around Frankie as she tried to take away her fears. "It'll be okay."

"How do you know?" Frankie whispered. "This is how it started last time."

Lisa kissed her hair and felt a wet drop hit her arm. She looked down at Frankie.

"Oh, baby, don't cry." Hot tears trickled down Lisa's face as she squeezed her eyes shut.

Please, God. Please let her be okay.

* * *

They held hands in the doctor's waiting room. Frankie had called first thing in the morning, and the scheduler had squeezed her in between appointments. It meant waiting longer—an hour had passed since they'd taken their seats—but Lisa didn't care. She also didn't care when she arrived in Cincinnati that day. The most important part of her life was right beside her.

A middle-aged man sat across from them. He stared at Lisa. Then his gaze dropped to their clasped hands and back up to Lisa's eyes.

She stared back at him until he looked away.

The door opened. A nurse propped it ajar with her hip while she read from a chart. "Francine Dunkin?"

They followed the nurse into the hallway of the exam rooms. She took Frankie's weight and led them into an empty room. She placed the blood pressure cuff around Frankie's bicep and turned on the machine. Lisa stared at the cuff as it expanded and stretched against the Velcro, feeling herself tense just like the cuff. The machine released the air.

"A little high today, 160 over 85."

"I think it's nerves," Frankie said quietly. "I've never had a problem with my blood pressure before."

"It happens sometimes." The nurse scribbled down the reading. She walked over to the examining table and lifted a gown from a drawer.

"Remove everything from the waist up and put this on so that it opens in the back. Dr. Hodges will be in soon."

Frankie undressed, slipped into the gown, and sat down on the examining table. She stared straight ahead while Lisa tapped her foot against the tile floor.

A knock at the door interrupted the silence between them.

"Come in," Frankie called out.

Dr. Hodges, dressed in a white lab coat, peeked around the door before stepping inside and closing it behind her. She seemed young. Too young, Lisa thought. She was probably about Frankie's height of five-four, her auburn hair falling to her shoulders. She extended her hand to Lisa.

"Hello. You must be Frankie's partner. I'm Pat Hodges."

Lisa stood and took her hand.

"Hi, Doctor. I'm Lisa."

Dr. Hodges turned to Frankie. "I understand you found a lump?"

"We found it last night and called right away," Frankie said.

"Why don't you lie back?"

Frankie scooted farther back on the table. Dr. Hodges yanked out the end of the table so Frankie's feet didn't dangle off the edge. She asked Frankie to raise her arm and began her physical exam, not speaking until she found the lump. Dr. Hodges furrowed her brow. "Have you had any discharge from your nipple?"

"No. I haven't noticed anything. I did a thorough exam two weeks ago, and it wasn't there."

"It feels like it might be two centimeters." Dr. Hodges continued moving her fingers in circular patterns until she felt under Frankie's arm. "Nothing here. That's good." She moved to the other side of the table and examined Frankie's scar. She probed under Frankie's right arm as she had her left. "Everything feels normal." She patted Frankie's shoulder. "Why don't you sit up?" She held her hand out for Frankie to grab and helped her to a seated position.

Dr. Hodges sat down on the stool and wheeled so that she was between Frankie and Lisa.

"I'll make the call to get you squeezed in Monday for a sonogram and a core needle biopsy. Be prepared to wait awhile since this is last minute. I'll push to get the pathology results by Wednesday."

"And then what happens?" Lisa asked as her stomach clenched in anxiety. She held back asking about the urgency in the scheduling of the tests.

"Let's just wait until we get those results, okay?"

Lisa wanted to shout, no, it's not okay. This was her partner, and she wanted immediate answers.

Dr. Hodges stood. "I'll write up the paperwork for your sonogram. Why don't you get dressed and wait out front for my assistant to bring it out to you? I'll call you with the results next week." She squeezed Frankie's shoulder. "Try not to worry. I know that's not an easy thing to do, but we're on top of this. Remember that."

After the doctor left the room, Frankie dressed. They retrieved the paperwork from the front desk. On the drive home, Lisa attempted to engage her in conversation about staying positive, but she only received one- or two-word responses from Frankie.

*   *   *

"Please come to Cincinnati with me and spend the weekend, Frankie. I think it's something we need."

"I can't. With Pride tomorrow, the bar will have a big weekend. You know that." Frankie stood up from the dining room table and carried her dirty dishes to the sink to rinse them off.

"But I want to be with you."

Frankie spun around. "My job is as important to me as yours is to you." Her sharp tone took Lisa by surprise.

Lisa studied Frankie's face. *She's scared.*

"I understand. I've never said otherwise."

"Then quit asking me to give up this weekend."

Frankie flipped on the hot water. She banged the door open to the cabinet underneath the sink and picked up the box of dishwasher soap.

Lisa eased behind her and put her arms around Frankie's waist. "I'm scared, too, sweetheart."

Frankie tensed, bracing her hands against the counter. "Isn't it time for you to leave?"

Lisa backed away. "Ye-yeah."

Frankie turned to face her. "I'll talk to you after the game, right?"

"Sure. Like always."

Frankie kissed her. "You should go so you're not late," she said with a weak smile.

"I'm sorry I won't be here."

"I'll be all right."

She searched Frankie's face for some warmth but found only a

distance she'd never seen before. She left the kitchen for the front
door and expected Frankie to follow her, but when she reached the
door, she found herself alone. "I'll talk to you tonight," she called out
as she picked up her suitcase.

"Be careful."

Lisa tossed her suitcase into the backseat and started the Sebring.
She watched the blinds for movement, but there wasn't any.
Unsuccessful in her attempt to shake off Frankie's coldness, she
drove toward the on-ramp to the interstate.

Chapter 7

Amy stood in the batting cage and tugged her helmet down a little more to shade her eyes against the sun. "Fire me in some good ones, Wally," she told the bullpen pitching coach on the mound.

"You get it the same as everyone else, Perry. It's up to you what you do with them."

At least he's an ass to everyone else, too. She lined one up the middle. It banged against the protective fence that stood between Wally Enders and a fat lip from a line drive.

"You've made your point," he shouted at her. "Hit this shit." He tossed in a knuckleball, the pitch he'd been notorious for during his years of playing in the majors.

She swung wildly at it and missed.

Wally snickered.

Sanders, standing beside the cage, laughed.

"You think that's funny, Sandy?"

"Uh, no, not funny at all."

"Quit bitching, you fucking baby." Wally lobbed a medium-speed fastball toward home plate. "There you go," he said in a sing-song voice.

Amy timed it and smacked the ball into the left field seats.

"Much better," Amy called out.

"Yeah, yeah."

Wally tossed her another. She lined it over the first base bag. After fifteen minutes of hitting, sweat dripped down her forehead and into her eyes. Using her shirt sleeve, she wiped away the perspiration and left the cage.

"Thanks, Wally."

He bowed low. "Any time, your highness."

What a sexist jerk, she thought while removing her batting gloves.

"Let a man show you how it's done, rook," Sanders said before hitting the next ball against the left center wall.

Amy spotted Lisa standing off by herself. Lisa was staring at her shoes with her hands jammed into her jeans pockets. She remembered this pose from when they'd dated. Something was wrong.

"Hey, Lisa." Amy grabbed a nearby towel and wiped her face before approaching her.

"Hey, Aim."

Amy waited until she drew closer before speaking again. "Anything wrong? You seem kind of down."

Lisa wouldn't look at her at first. Amy decided to wait her out until she finally met Amy's eyes.

"It's Frankie," Lisa choked out in a hoarse whisper.

An involuntary shudder ran down Amy's spine. "Why don't we go over to the dugout?"

They sat down together on the wooden bench.

Amy touched Lisa's arm. "Tell me."

"You have to promise me something. I'll understand if you share this with Stacy, but you have to promise me it goes no further. No one at the bar can know about this."

"You have my word." Amy braced for the worst.

"We found a lump yesterday in Frankie's breast."

"Oh, Jesus."

"We saw her doctor first thing this morning. They're doing a core needle biopsy Monday, and we should get the results by Wednesday."

Amy squeezed Lisa's hand.

"I'm so sorry."

Lisa bit her lower lip. "I'm so fucking scared, Aim."

"I know you are. How's Frankie holding up?"

Lisa gave a humorless laugh. "She's shutting down and, in the process, shutting me out."

"I'm sorry." Amy realized she could think of little else to say, almost like repeating the same words when offering sympathy to someone who'd lost their loved one.

"She's never been that cold toward me in all the time I've known her. I'm not sure how to take it."

"And like you, she's probably very scared."

"You think I don't know that?" Lisa stopped. "God, listen to me."

"I'm your friend. You don't need to hide how you're feeling with me."

"I'm afraid she'll keep shutting me out, and I don't know what to do."

"It's easy for me to say, but try to think the best. It might be nothing."

"But she's had this before."

Amy didn't miss Lisa's refusal to say "cancer."

"It doesn't mean it'll be the same thing again."

"Yeah?"

Lisa's expression was so vulnerable. Amy wanted to hold her to make it all go away, but that part of their relationship had changed forever.

"Yeah." Amy tried to sound as confident as possible in her response.

"Say some prayers, will you?"

"I already have."

They stood, and Amy enveloped her in a hug.

"I'd better get out there and do my job," Lisa said. "I'll catch you later in the clubhouse."

Amy watched as Lisa went behind the batter's cage to the visitor's dugout and shook hands with the Rockies manager. She couldn't help but think that at that moment, baseball seemed so small.

* * *

"Glad you could grace us with your presence."

Lisa ignored Sarah's comment while plugging in her laptop.

Sarah studied her. "You look like you didn't get any sleep last night."

"That's probably because I didn't."

"Shit, woman, you two are like freaking rabbits."

"It's not what you think." Lisa's tone was sharper than she intended.

"I'm sorry. I didn't mean anything by it."

Lisa nodded.

The teenage trumpeter below began the opening bars to the national anthem. Lisa kept her eyes on the field to avoid facing Sarah.

After the final notes rang out, Sarah asked, "What's wrong?"

"I can't talk about it now."

The innings passed quickly. Both pitchers tossed a good game, with the Reds prevailing, 2-0. Lisa followed the other reporters to the elevator that took them to the lower level. They filed out for the clubhouse.

She interviewed the Reds pitcher and Amy, who had singled in one of the runs. Amy answered her questions with hushed words, almost as though she feared she'd shatter Lisa's fragile psyche if she spoke any louder.

Lisa finished her Reds interviews with a trip to Max Murphy's office. She then made a quick jaunt over to the Rockies clubhouse to ask their manager about his decision to yank the starter with two on and two out in the bottom of the eighth. The game had been scoreless at that time.

After her last interview, she sat in front of her laptop and mixed the quotes into the article she'd started during the game. She fired the article off to her editors, finishing at ten-thirty. With her notes gathered and her laptop shoved in its case, she left for her car. She opened her cell phone before she started the car but shut it after making the decision to wait until she arrived home.

When she got into her apartment, she stepped out onto her balcony facing the Ohio River and tried to draw some peace from the lights of the dinner boat below that twinkled and reflected onto the calm, black water. She called the bar first, thinking Frankie might still be there.

"Yeah!" Billie yelled into her ear.

"Billie, it's Lisa. Is Frankie around?"

"Hang on." Lisa heard Billie shout for Val. "The boss lady still here?" The muffled response was inaudible. "We think she left for home about an hour ago. She told Val she wasn't feeling well."

Lisa jumped to her feet. "What's wrong with her?"

"I can hardly hear you, man. It's fucking nuts tonight."

"Never mind."

Lisa hung up and hit speed dial for their home number. "Come on, come on. Pick up the damn phone."

"Hello?"

Frankie's voice sounded strained.

"Are you all right? Billie said you went home sick."

"Damn it. I didn't tell Val that. I said I had a headache and was tired. There's a difference."

Lisa was about to argue with her but refrained. "Are you feeling any better?"

"I walked into the house five minutes ago. I still have a headache, and I'm still tired. How'd the Reds do?"

"I'd rather talk about you."

"And I'd rather not, so I guess this will be a short conversation."

"Don't shut me out, Frankie. I'm fucking scared, too." Silence greeted her words. "Frankie?"

Frankie sighed. "I know you are, but it's not you who's facing the possibility of losing another breast. It's me."

"Shouldn't we wait until we get the results before you talk like that?" Lisa cringed at her words. She knew she'd been thinking the same worst-case scenario.

"Let's face it, Leese, the odds aren't good for these kinds of things."

"But—"

"Look, I'm tired. I need to take some Tylenol and try to get some sleep. Tomorrow will be crazier than today. You know we sponsor Pride, and we'll be down at the American Legion Mall. I'm sure you're probably tired. You tossed and turned enough last night."

"I'm sorry if I kept you awake."

"I wasn't sleeping anymore than you were. Listen, get some rest. I'll do the same. I won't be able to talk to you tomorrow or tomorrow night."

"I can call in the morning."

"No. I'll be out of here by six."

"I can call before—"

"I'll talk to you Sunday after the game. Give me a call when you're on your way home."

"I… I love you." Lisa heard sniffling on the other end.

"Love you, too."

The line went dead before Lisa could say more. She flipped the phone shut and stared out at the water where a tugboat pushed a barge under the bridge. She sank down into her chaise lounge and laid her head back, not even bothering to wipe away the tears streaming down her face.

*   *   *

"Do they know anything yet? I mean, could the doctor tell anything by feeling the lump?" Stacy asked when she left the bathroom for the bedroom.

"Lisa said the doctor couldn't tell. They won't know anything until after the biopsy next week, if even then."

Amy lay in bed propped up on pillows. She watched Stacy,

dressed only in her panties, go to the dresser and take out an oversized T-shirt. Amy's gaze dropped to Stacy's small, firm breasts. A thought flashed through her mind. *What would I do if the same thing were to happen to Stacy?* Her answer came fast. *It wouldn't matter.*

"What are you thinking about?" Stacy walked over to the bed, leaned over and switched off the light before climbing in beside Amy.

"You're sure you want to know?"

Stacy snuggled in closer. Amy draped her arm around Stacy's shoulders.

"I do."

"That if, God forbid, anything like this ever happened to you, it wouldn't matter to me."

Stacy slipped her hand under Amy's sleeveless T-shirt and cupped her breast. "Me neither," she said softly. She caressed Amy's breast until she moved her fingers over to the other one and cupped it then dropped her hand to encircle Amy's waist.

"I can't imagine what Frankie's going through," Stacy said. "It's already happened once. And her ex left her because of it, running off with one of their friends."

"I didn't know that." Frankie's behavior was beginning to make more sense. "Lisa said Frankie's been shutting down around her."

"They don't even know for sure yet."

"After what you've told me, it's almost like Frankie's preparing for the worst and thinks that if she distances herself now, she can deal with Lisa leaving her later."

"We both know that's not going to happen."

"But when you're scared, you don't think clearly." Amy thought of Lisa, and her heart went out to her—to both of them.

"I… I don't know what I'd do if anything ever happened to you."

"Aw, come up here."

Stacy moved on her side to face Amy.

"Nothing's going to happen to me, sweetie."

"Promise?" Stacy's dark eyes searched out her own.

"Promise." Amy kissed her.

"Mmm. Nice," Stacy said against her lips. She shifted to face the other way, and Amy spooned her as they fell into a peaceful sleep.

Chapter 8

Lisa drove to Indianapolis Sunday afternoon. When she'd called from the road, Frankie told Lisa she'd be busy at the bar until late that night, so Lisa should just go home and wait for her there. Lisa dropped off her bags at the house and drove to the Watering Hole.

A large crowd greeted her when she entered the bar. Rainbow Mardi Gras beads around everyone's neck and the raucous din clued Lisa that these were Pride celebrants.

She searched for Frankie, finally spotting her behind the bar. Frankie saw her at the same time and waved.

Lisa pushed her way through the throng.

"Thought I told you I'd see you at home," Frankie said.

Lisa glanced around at the crowd. "When can you can leave?"

Frankie made a face. "Does it look like I can leave anytime soon? I need to stay until late. Maybe ten or so. Go home, Leese. You look beat."

"But—"

"Frankie, I need a Long Island," a frazzled-looking Val said as she plunked her empty tray down.

Frankie left to make the drink.

Someone shoved Lisa from behind.

"Oops, sorry."

Lisa turned around. A tall, curvy brunette gave her the once-over.

"Hell, maybe I'm not so sorry. You're cute," the woman said.

"And she's taken, Tammy," Val told her.

Frankie set the Long Island on the tray while keeping her eye on Lisa and Tammy. "There's your drink, Val."

"Thanks, boss." Val shot one more look Tammy's way before heading back into the crowd.

"You're sure you're taken, sweetie?" Tammy ran her fingertip down Lisa's arm and back up again.

"Yes, very taken," Lisa said with a scowl.

"Well, alrighty then." Tammy searched the crowd again, and her face lit up with recognition. "Rose!" she shouted at a nearby woman. "Where've you been?" She latched onto Rose's arm and walked away.

Lisa was about to say something to Frankie, but she'd already moved to the other end of the bar.

More than a little frustrated, Lisa pushed and shoved her way back outside. She stood there for a few seconds, taking deep breaths of the smoke-free air. Then she walked to her car and drove home.

*   *   *

Lisa glanced up at the clock. Ten-thirty, and Frankie still wasn't home. She struck the cue ball as hard as she could. "Like this is going to help." The balls scattered across the table.

With each stroke she made, she tried to relieve the tension coiled in her shoulders. She was down to only the eight-ball and leaned over to take a tricky shot.

"I've seen you make that one before."

Lisa jumped, and the cue slid against the bottom of the cue ball. The ball flipped up in the air, thunked down on the table, and came to rest several inches from the eight-ball. She turned to Frankie, who stood in the doorway to the den.

"Jesus, don't scare me like that." Lisa carried the cue to the rack and thought about what she wanted to say. But when she turned around, the doorway was empty.

Lisa caught up with Frankie walking down the hallway to the bedroom.

"Frankie, we need to talk."

Frankie stopped and turned around, her dark eyes sparked with anger. "I swear to God, Lisa, if you say that to me one more time, I'm going to scream."

Lisa took a step backwards. "I'm… I'm sorry."

Frankie continued into the bedroom. "Don't be sorry. Just leave me alone so I can take a shower to get rid of this stench of smoke." She snatched up her nightshirt and a fresh pair of panties before going into the bathroom.

Lisa undressed and went to the guest bedroom to shower. When she came into the bedroom, it was dark, and Frankie was already under the covers. She was on her side with her back to the door.

Lisa got into bed and stared at the ceiling, afraid to break the tension that infused the room. She'd just closed her eyes when Frankie spoke.

"Did you think she was pretty?"

Lisa opened her eyes. "Who?"

"That woman at the bar. The one who came on to you."

Lisa sighed. "I didn't even notice."

Silence.

"Well, she was," Frankie finally said.

Lisa moved onto her side and placed her hand on Frankie's shoulder. "Hey." She gently pulled her shoulder so that Frankie lay on her back. Lisa saw the glimmer of tears in Frankie's eyes. "Where did that come from?"

Frankie shook her head.

"I'm not letting you off that easy, Frankie. Do you honestly believe I even think about other women?"

"But she was younger and…"

"And she's not you, okay? I love you and only you. Period." Lisa started to kiss her, but Frankie turned back onto her side. "You do believe me, don't you?" Frankie didn't answer. "Frankie?"

"Yeah," Frankie said in a muffled voice.

Lisa thought of saying more. But Frankie's up-and-down moods and her sudden outbursts of anger prevented Lisa from taking the chance. Instead, she wrapped her arm around Frankie's waist and held her.

* * *

The next morning, they both were quiet as they got ready to go to the hospital. They sat down in the waiting area. Dr. Hodges had been right. They had to wait almost two hours before the technician called for Frankie. Lisa picked up a magazine and flipped through the pages, not even seeing the type or the photos. She finally tossed it onto the table in frustration.

An hour later, Frankie emerged grim-faced. On their way to the car, Lisa tried to draw out any information from her.

"Frankie—"

"I'm fine. Let's just go home."

Lisa gave up trying to get Frankie to talk. She hated that she had to leave for Cincinnati for the night's game and wished she could take the week off—take off as long as she needed—until she knew Frankie was well. Back at the house, Lisa gathered her belongings, hoping Frankie would say something—anything—but silence was her only offering. Lisa grabbed her keys, and Frankie walked with her to the door.

Lisa bent down to kiss her. "I wish I could stay at least until Wednesday for the results."

"No. You need to do your job, and I need to do mine, Leese. I'm not putting my life on hold for this." Frankie opened the door. "Have a safe drive to Cincy. Call me when you get there."

"All right." Lisa hugged her, but Frankie barely returned the embrace.

When she got onto I-74, she cranked up the radio, not wanting to think or speculate on anything else other than that night's pitching matchup.

*   *   *

Wednesday morning, Lisa had dried off from her shower and had just started dressing when her cell phone rang. It was Frankie.

"Did Dr. Hodges call?"

"Yes." There was a long pause. "They think it's some sort of lesion. I can't remember the name of it. But the pathology came back as indeterminate. Because they didn't have a definite answer on the makeup of the cell tissue, Dr. Hodges has scheduled surgery to remove it."

Lisa sat down on the bed and held her head in her hand. "When?"

"Next Monday morning. She had an opening and wanted to get me in as soon as possible."

Lisa felt the fear roll over her. "I'll be there. What time?"

"Lisa, I can do this on my own. You have a game that night, right? You don't need to be here and then rush back to Cincinnati."

She couldn't believe what she was hearing. "You're kidding, right? Please tell me you're kidding."

"No. I know how important—"

"Don't even say it, Frankie. This job is not my life. You are."

Frankie sighed. "All right. I have to be at the hospital at six. They have to do a wire localization before the actual surgery. The wire helps guide Dr. Hodges to the lesion."

"I'll drive home after the game tonight so I can be with you."

"What? No. No way. You're not going to be driving

back and forth to babysit me."

"It won't be like that, and you know it."

"No, Lisa. Monday, I agree to. But I don't want to see you until Sunday after the game."

Lisa knew it was fruitless to argue when she heard the flat finality in Frankie's voice.

"I don't like it, but I'll do it."

They hung up. Lisa held back a sob as she finished dressing.

"I can't lose it. Not yet."

Chapter 9

Lisa tried to concentrate on doing her job, but she was distracted. She'd only spoken with Frankie twice since Wednesday morning. She worked the games, numb to everything around her as she interviewed players and coaches and wrote her articles. Amy gave her sympathetic looks during their interviews, but Lisa couldn't bring herself to talk about how lost she felt.

After Sunday's game against the Pirates, she drove home. She and Frankie shared a silent dinner. When they finished, Frankie excused herself to play a game of pool. Lisa left her alone.

Later that night, Lisa stirred awake and reached beside her only to find cool sheets. She sat up and peered through the darkness. Frankie was in the rocker by the window at the foot of the bed. Moonlight streaming into the room from the raised blinds cast shadows across her face.

"Frankie?"

Frankie stared out the window. "I'm over here."

Lisa got out of bed and stood beside the chair. She caressed Frankie's cheek. Frankie didn't pull away, but she also didn't lean into the touch.

"How long have you been up?" Lisa asked her.

"An hour, maybe two. I don't know."

"Why don't you come back to bed, and I'll hold you? We can talk."

"I don't want to talk. How many times do I have to tell you that? Go back to bed and try to get some sleep."

Lisa knelt beside the chair and took Frankie's hand in hers. "Please," she whispered.

Frankie looked like she was about to argue some more. "As long as we don't talk." She let Lisa lead her to the bed.

Lisa drew her close once they'd gotten under the covers. Frankie's body was tense in her arms. Lisa stroked her hair until

Frankie's breathing deepened. She brought her lips to her ear. "I love you," she whispered, hoping the words would find their way into Frankie's unconsciousness.

Frankie murmured something in her sleep and burrowed even more into Lisa's shoulder.

* * *

After they parked, Frankie registered at the outpatient surgery desk. She answered the typical insurance questions and signed the forms. They walked down the hallway to surgery. Lisa waited in a small partitioned room while they took Frankie upstairs for the insertion of the wire.

A nurse wrenched the curtain open, startling Lisa, and brought Frankie back into the room to settle her into the recliner. She scanned Frankie's chart and asked Frankie a few questions before leaving them alone again. A surgical nurse came in and asked most of the same questions before the anesthesiologist came in to talk to Frankie.

After another short wait, Dr. Hodges entered. "Frankie, how are you feeling today?"

"Scared."

Lisa tried not to let it bother her that Frankie spoke that one word so easily to her doctor, but not to her.

Dr. Hodges patted Frankie's leg. "We'll get this taken care of so there are no more questions." She looked at Lisa. "I imagine you're feeling the same way."

Lisa's eyes burned with unshed tears. She could only nod in answer.

"I'm not sure what you've been told, Lisa. This procedure won't last long. The prep time is almost as long as the actual surgery. We'll be done in about an hour but will need to keep her in anesthesiology recovery until we can clear her. It might not be a bad idea if you want to walk around, maybe grab a cup of coffee. Frankie, I'll give you two a minute and then send in the nurse to bring you back. I'll see you shortly."

Dr. Hodges pulled the curtain aside and left.

"Why don't you do what she said and get a cup of coffee?" Frankie asked. "No use in having you waiting here all that time."

Lisa rose and leaned over to kiss Frankie softly on the lips. "I love you. See you soon."

She tried to shake her feelings of uneasiness and helplessness. In the vending area, she put a dollar in the machine and watched as the cup dropped down and coffee filled the container. She blew into the cup, took a sip, and checked out her surroundings, thankful she was the only one in the small room.

Twenty minutes passed. She tossed out her cup with the remaining dregs of coffee. The desk attendant nodded as Lisa passed her on the way to the prep room. The recliner was gone. She sat down in the chair, and fatigue flooded every bone of her body. She drifted off to sleep.

The sound of the curtain drawing back awakened her. A nurse pushed Frankie in on a gurney. She checked the fluids leading into Frankie's IV and gave Lisa a gentle smile before leaving them alone.

Lisa tried not to balk at the sight of Frankie's pale face. Frankie's eyes fluttered open.

"Hey." Lisa leaned over and kissed her forehead.

"They're done?" Frankie asked in a hoarse voice.

Lisa noticed a cup and a small pitcher of ice chips on the table beside the gurney. She poured ice into the cup and held out the plastic spoon while Frankie took some chips into her mouth.

"Yes, they're done," Lisa said. "I guess Dr. Hodges will be in soon."

At those words, the doctor drew back the curtain. "How are you feeling, Frankie?"

"Like I just woke up."

"We were able to reach the mass and the surrounding tissue. It was, as we suspected, a mucocele-like lesion. I've sent it off to the lab, and I'm pushing to get the results by Friday."

"What's a muco… muco…" Lisa gave up trying to pronounce it.

"Mucocele-like lesion. They're mucous-filled lesions that are rare. But because of Frankie's history, it's good we excised it."

"Could you tell from what you removed if it's…"

"No, I can't. We have to wait for the pathology report. In the meantime, let's try to stay positive about this." She pinned them with an earnest stare. Then she addressed Frankie. "I'll call you before noon on Friday."

"Thank you, Dr. Hodges." Frankie managed a weak smile.

"You two take care."

The nurse brought a bottle of juice for Frankie. About an hour later, she was alert enough to leave. On the drive home, Lisa glanced at Frankie, who was looking out the window. She put her hand on Frankie's thigh and waited for Frankie to place her hand on top. But

Frankie didn't return the touch.

At the house, Frankie walked to the bedroom, undressed, and put on a nightshirt. "I think I need to rest," she said while slipping under the covers.

"I'll call my editors to tell them I won't be there tonight."

Frankie frowned. "No, you won't. The only reason I agreed to you being here this morning was because I knew you'd still have time to make the game. You want to do something for me? You want to help? You go to that game tonight. It's not like this was major surgery."

Lisa recoiled at her harsh tone. She saw the determined set of Frankie's jaw and decided not to push it.

"Then I'm staying for a couple of hours to make sure you're okay."

"You don't have to—"

"I'll be over there in the rocker. I won't disturb you, Frankie. Let me at least do this, all right?"

Frankie lay back on the pillow.

Lisa sat down in the rocker. She watched Frankie sleep and fought the urge to burst into tears.

* * *

"Will they have her bunt here?" Sarah asked.

Lisa stared down at the field, not really watching the Wednesday night game against the Phillies.

"Lisa?"

"Murphy's kind of unpredictable about these situations. With the way Amy can handle the bat, I'm guessing he'll call for the hit-and-run instead of bunting."

As the words left Lisa's mouth, the runner at first sprinted toward second and the second baseman moved to cover the bag. Amy hit a single in the spot the Phillies player had just vacated. The runner rounded second and beat the throw to third.

"There you go. Hell, you could manage this team, Collins."

Sanders hit a long fly to score the runner from third.

"How are things with you?" Sarah asked.

Lisa almost lied, but she needed to talk to someone.

"Can we go out for a beer after the game? Or maybe you can follow me to the apartment where it's quieter."

"We'll go to your apartment."

The game ended with the Phillies pounding the Reds pitchers for a 10-2 win. Lisa and Sarah conducted their interviews, finished up their stories, and walked out to their cars.

Sarah chuckled as Lisa put her laptop into the backseat.

"What's so funny?" Lisa asked.

"That." Sarah pointed at the Sebring. "I've never been in the lot when you finished up, and it's the first time I've seen it. Guess I planted some ideas in that little brain of yours in Phoenix."

"I liked your rental car while we were there. What can I say?" Lisa climbed into the driver's seat. "Follow me?"

They arrived at the gated complex. Sarah parked in a visitor's space. She followed Lisa inside, where they took the elevator to the seventh floor.

"Michelob?" Lisa asked after they entered the apartment.

"Like you'd offer me anything else."

Lisa brought out two opened bottles of beer from the kitchen and handed one to Sarah. "How about we go sit out on the balcony? It's a nice night."

Lisa lit a couple of citronella candles on the railing. They sat next to each other in the chaise lounge chairs and sipped their beers for several minutes.

"It's Frankie," Lisa told her.

"What's wrong?"

"We found a lump in her breast."

"Christ, Lisa, that sucks."

"She had surgery Monday morning. We're supposed to get the results Friday." Lisa hesitated. "I've never told you this, but Frankie had a mastectomy seven years ago, which makes this even scarier."

"How'd this surgery go? Did the doctor say they got it all?"

"According to Dr. Hodges, it went well. She said she removed the lesion and some of the surrounding tissue."

"And how are you two handling it?"

"Me? I'm a mess, trying not to think of everything that could be wrong. I've tried to stay focused, but I'm scared as hell."

"And Frankie?"

"That's what I wanted to talk to you about, Sarah. She's completely shut me out. She even argued with me about missing any of these games. Rather than adding more stress, I did what she asked and drove back Monday afternoon."

"You haven't been able to talk at all?"

"No. She won't share her feelings with me. I think she's afraid

I'll leave her like her previous partner did. Sherri left Frankie after Frankie's surgery. While she was in her first treatment of chemo."

"Jesus."

"Tell me about it. What can I do?"

"Just what I told you last time. Keep talking."

"How do I talk to her when she doesn't want to talk?"

"Keep at it."

"Easier said than done."

"Have you told her how all of this is affecting you? The cutting you off?"

Lisa stared at her bottle. "No. I told her I was scared but nothing more."

"You love her, right?"

"You know the answer to that one."

"Then quit tiptoeing around her, sit her ass down, and *make* her listen."

* * *

Thursday afternoon's game turned into a fifteen-inning marathon. Lisa didn't get on the road until seven-thirty. The team would be leaving directly from the ballpark for the airport for their trip to Washington, D.C. Lisa made arrangements for a flight from Indianapolis the next day that would get her there in time for the evening game against the Nationals. While driving to Indianapolis, she thought about what she'd say to Frankie.

During the game, Frankie had left her a message to wait until morning to make the drive home. She called Frankie back at the bar to let her know she was on her way. Frankie either couldn't or wouldn't take the call, but Lisa told Billie to be sure Frankie knew she'd be on the road shortly. A darkened house greeted her when she arrived; Lisa wondered if Frankie had gotten the message.

She unlocked the door and noticed a candle flickering through the sliding glass door in the back. Lisa saw Frankie's silhouette in the darkness. She set her overnight bag down and walked through the house. She slid the door open, hoping she didn't startle Frankie. But Frankie didn't turn around.

"I told you to stay in Cincinnati tonight."

"Frankie, we need to talk."

"And for the hundredth time, I told you I don't want to."

Lisa took a deep breath and then released all of her frustration.

"Well, you know what? I do. It isn't all about you. This involves me, too. I've been out of my mind with worry and not only about the possibility of you having cancer again."

Frankie opened her mouth to speak, but Lisa cut her off by slashing her hand in the air.

"You wait and listen. You've been shutting me out since this started. You're assuming the worst, which I get. What I don't get is you not talking to me, Frankie. I'm your partner, damn it, and this affects me. I feel like I'm losing you in this. That you have no faith in me."

Frankie stood up and tilted her head to meet her eyes. What Lisa saw there was a mixture of anger and fear.

"You've never lost a breast to cancer, have you? You've never had to endure radiation and chemo, have you? You've never been so sick from the chemo that you wished you'd die." Frankie's voice rose with each word. "You don't know how you'll react if I have to have another surgery. You could have the same reaction as Sherri when you see the results and the fucking hole they leave in my chest."

Lisa gripped Frankie's shoulders.

"I love you. I love *you*. Don't you believe me? I'm telling you this now, and I'll tell you again tomorrow morning, regardless of what Dr. Hodges says. I'm not leaving you. You couldn't get rid of me if you tried. We're going through this together, whether you want to or not. I'm here today, just like I was yesterday, and just like I'll be tomorrow and everyday for the rest of our lives. And if you don't believe that, then what are we doing together, Frankie? Tell me."

Frankie's eyes shimmered in the candlelight, and she took several shaky breaths.

"Tell me," Lisa choked out as tears streamed down her face.

"Oh, God, Leese, I'm so sorry," Frankie cried.

Lisa took Frankie into her arms. She held her tight as Frankie's body shook with sobs.

"I'm scared, and I took it out on you," Frankie said between sobs.

"Shh." Lisa kissed the top of Frankie's head.

"I love you so much, and all I saw in my nightmares was the look on Sherri's face after the surgery. I'm sorry I ever doubted you."

Lisa cupped Frankie's face in her hands and used her thumbs to wipe away her tears.

"Please. No more apologies. We'll get through this together. But don't ever doubt my love for you. I'd never hurt you." She pressed her lips softly to Frankie's.

Frankie deepened the kiss.

"Let's go to bed." Lisa took Frankie's hand and led her into the house.

* * *

The next morning, Lisa sat beside Frankie on the side of the bed. She held the portable phone in her hand. When it rang, she turned to Frankie. "Ready?" she asked.

Frankie reached for the bedside phone as Lisa clicked on the portable. "Hello."

"Is this Frankie?"

"Yes, Dr. Hodges."

"I'm on the line, too, Doctor." Lisa held out her other hand for Frankie to grasp.

"I'm glad, Lisa, because we have good news. There was no sign of malignancy or atypical cells. Completely benign."

Lightheaded with relief, Lisa squeezed Frankie's hand.

"You're sure?" Frankie asked.

"Yes. Everything's clean, including the surrounding tissue we tested. I'd like to see you again in a week to check your incision. Once it's healed completely, we'll take another mammogram. Why don't you call to set those appointments after you and Lisa celebrate the good news? I like making these phone calls."

"And I like getting this kind of news." Frankie smiled at Lisa.

"I'll see you next week."

"Thank you for everything, Dr. Hodges," Frankie said.

"Yes, thank you," Lisa chimed in.

"You're welcome. Take care."

They hung up. As Lisa clicked off the phone, she began sobbing. Everything she'd held inside—her fears about the cancer and their relationship—all of it came flowing out of her.

"Come here." Frankie pulled her close.

Lisa buried her head into Frankie's shoulder and cried even harder.

Frankie stroked Lisa's back. "I love you, Leese."

Lisa allowed herself to cry, secure in Frankie's arms.

As Lisa quieted down, Frankie pulled out a tissue from the box on the bedside table. She dabbed Lisa's eyes and wiped her nose.

"I'm sure I'm a sight right now," Lisa said and sniffed.

"You're beautiful." Frankie tossed the tissue into the trashcan. She turned to kiss Lisa with the tenderness that Lisa knew so well.

When they pulled out of the embrace, Lisa asked, "Do you mind if I give Amy a quick call? She'll want to hear the good news."

"Sure. And when you're done, why don't we go celebrate at our favorite restaurant before we get you to the airport?"

"Flapjacks?"

"Where else?"

Chapter 10

"Where are you playing tonight, sweetheart?" Thelma, Amy's mom, asked over the phone.

"We're in San Diego." Amy fell back on the bed. *God, she sounds so weak,* Amy thought. "Mom, will you be honest with me?"

"I'm always honest with you."

Not when you don't want me to know how sick you are.

"What did the doctors tell you when you saw them last week?"

There was a slight hesitation, which was all Amy needed to confirm that her mother was holding back information.

"Dr. Graham told me I have congestive heart failure."

Amy drew in a breath. "That's bad, isn't it?"

"He's given me medication to help, and I'm fine."

"But—"

"Don't worry about me, young lady. You concentrate on that hitting of yours. You've started to drop that back shoulder some. Don't think I haven't noticed."

Amy laughed. "You always knew what I was doing wrong in my hitting."

"Outside of that partner of yours, I'm your biggest fan. I'd think you'd know that by now."

"Yeah, I do," Amy said softly. She closed her eyes as a rush of memories flooded over her.

"Well, if I'm not mistaken, figuring the time it must be there in San Diego, you need to leave for the ballpark."

"Yes, ma'am." A tear trickled down the side of Amy's face. "I love you, Mom."

"Love you too, honey. Now go out there and show them how it's done."

After they hung up, Amy wiped her eyes and stared at the ceiling. She sighed as she stood up and left the hotel room for the lobby.

* * *

Amy looked at the third base coach in confusion. What the hell? She shook her head slightly. They both called for time, and Servace trotted toward her.

"Thought you knew that one, Perry," he said as he leaned in with his mouth next to her ear. "Hit away after showing the bunt."

She was about to tell him she was up on the signs, but the home plate umpire was fast approaching. The runner took his lead at first with no outs. Tied with the San Diego Padres in the top of the eighth, Amy was sure Murphy would have her move the runner over with a bunt. The Padres had thought the same thing. The third baseman and first baseman had charged toward home with the first pitch.

I can do this. I'm hot and tired. I wish I were home, or I wish Stacy were here. I'm worried about my mom. Come on. Throw me a frigging fastball. I don't care where. I'll hit it.

The pitcher granted her wish. A fastball on the far outside corner of the plate. She lunged at the ball, barely connecting, but managing to get enough of the ball to bloop it over the charging first baseman's head and into shallow right. The runner hustled around second and pulled up at third.

The first base coach smacked her on the butt when she came back to the bag.

"Way to go, Perry."

Amy took off her batting gloves and shoved them in her back pockets. She watched Servace run through the signs before taking her lead. The Padres pitcher did the typical fake-the-throw-to-third-and-then-first trick that rarely worked. Amy stepped back on the bag. She took her lead again when the pitcher moved to the rubber and went into his stretch.

Nick Sanders hit a sharp two hopper to the second baseman.

Amy charged toward second, intent on breaking up a double play. She hooked into the shortstop, who was covering second. It was a clean slide, but she upended him enough to cause an errant throw to first. The runner scored from third, putting the Reds on top 5-4.

She trotted to the dugout and accepted the congratulations of her teammates. She sat down on the bench next to the hitting coach.

"Nice job with the bat," Donny said around the thick wad of tobacco jammed into his right cheek.

Amy struggled to pay attention to the rest of the inning as she replayed in her mind the conversation she'd had with her mother.

Rawls, seated beside her, shoved her glove into her stomach.

"Wake up, Perry. Time to go back to work."

She ran out onto the field with the rest of the infielders. As she tossed the ball across to Sanders, she thought again about how much she missed Stacy. She didn't think it would be this bad—it was only her second month up with the Reds. But on these road trips, not having Stacy beside her each night in bed hurt more than she could have ever imagined.

The lead-off batter came to the plate before further thoughts intruded. The Reds reliever shut down the Padres in order for the bottom of the eighth. Lopez came on in the bottom of the ninth to close out a 5-4 win.

She joined her teammates in gathering their equipment in the dugout. Everyone was jovial entering the clubhouse. On the heels of a six-game win streak, the Reds stood only three games out of first in the Central Division.

Amy answered the reporters' questions thrown her way. As they dispersed, Amy called out to Lisa before she walked away. "Could we maybe get together for dinner after my shower?" she asked her.

"Sure. Sarah told me about O'Leary's Steakhouse and Irish Pub not too far from the hotel we're staying in."

"Do you mind if only the two of us go out?"

"Not at all. Everything all right?"

"I just wanted to talk with my best friend."

"I'd like that."

* * *

Amy took a taxi to the pub. She spotted Lisa waving her to a table by the window.

A few people stared at her when she passed by their tables. She noticed their expressions of recognition and caught bits and pieces of their conversations.

"…Perry that plays for the Reds?"

"…the woman who's the Reds first baseman?"

Amy sat down in the booth across from Lisa. Before she could even say hello, the waiter was there with their water and asking for drink orders. She chose a Foster's while Lisa ordered a Coke.

"How's Frankie? It was so good to hear the news it was benign."

"She's doing fine. Back to working like nothing ever happened.

Her mammogram came back clean, so she's in the clear until she goes back in three months for a follow-up appointment."

The waiter brought their drinks. "Are you ready to order?"

"If you could give us a minute, I haven't had a chance to check out your menu yet," Amy said.

"Sure. Take as much time as you need."

"Efficient, aren't they?" Amy asked after he left them.

Lisa glanced at the bar. "I might be wrong, but I think you're getting the star treatment."

Amy looked that way. The two bartenders, their server, and a man who was probably the manager focused on their table.

She sighed. "Damn it."

"It's not so bad being a big superstar baseball player, is it?"

Amy glared across the table.

Lisa held up her hand. "Only kidding."

The server materialized again out of nowhere. "May I take your order?"

"Hamburger. Medium well. And fries." Amy handed him the menu.

"You're sure you don't want to try our prime rib? It's our specialty."

"Nope. Hamburger is fine."

"But we—"

"Hamburger."

"Yes. Of course." The waiter at least had the sense to look embarrassed. "And you, ma'am?"

"The same." Lisa handed over her menu as well.

After he left, Amy said, "I wanted to snatch my menu back and smack him over the head with it."

"Now, now. They're only trying to make sure you're treated right."

"Whatever." Amy took a long drink of her Foster's and set the glass down. "It's my mom."

"What's wrong?"

"Remember how her health hasn't been that great?"

"Yeah, I do. She was only able to attend your debut game last September."

"I talked to her before the game tonight. The doctor has diagnosed her with congestive heart failure." Amy picked at her napkin. "My Aunt Charlotte has stayed at the house since my mom's health started deteriorating after my dad died, and I feel better knowing that. But still…"

Lisa squeezed Amy's restless hand.

"I hate that I can't visit with her very often," Amy continued. "I mean, I knew how involved this would be once I got into the majors, but I still don't think I was prepared for the constant grind. And it's only the end of June."

"Being away from Stacy doesn't help matters any either, does it?"

"How'd you know?" Amy stopped herself. "Right. I'm sure you miss Frankie as much as I miss Stacy."

"We're in the same boat here."

"Should we have gone for careers as accountants? Or teachers? Or, I don't know, zoo attendants?" Amy managed a crooked grin.

Lisa laughed. "I can picture the two of us cleaning out the chimp cages."

They talked about the series and Cincinnati's six-game winning streak.

Their server brought their meals. He also had another Foster's on his tray and set it in front of Amy.

"I'm not ready for my next one yet," she told him.

He motioned to a table across the bar where three women sat. A blonde held up her drink in salute to Amy. The woman's gleaming white teeth cut through the dimmed lighting.

"She asked what you were drinking and ordered it for you."

"I don't want—"

He'd already left the table.

"Fuck," Amy said.

"First time for you?"

"No. The last time, I was out with Stacy. Can you believe it?"

"Yes, I can. People want a piece of stardom and, hell, Amy, you are attractive. Unfortunately for these women, you're taken. Lock, stock, and barrel."

Amy took a bite of her burger. "You should've seen Stacy when the drink came to our table in Cincinnati. Ever hear the expression 'got her Irish up'?"

"I take it Ms. McCrady let her views be known?"

Amy snorted. "I had to hold her back from running over to the other side of the bar and smacking some woman in the face."

"I would like to have seen that. But back to what we were talking about, the good thing is, you'll have an off-day when we get home. The Reds don't play until the next evening. That'll give you some quality time with Stacy. And you have the All-Star break coming up soon. You can visit your mom then, right?"

"Stacy and I have already told her and Aunt Charlotte we're coming in for the four days, so we're expecting some homemade meals."

"You better enjoy the break this year, because next year, you'll be *on* the All-Star team."

Amy was about to take a drink. She stared at Lisa. "You're crazy."

"Crazy, hell. You're batting .294 since they called you up with eight home runs and twenty-one RBIs. Trust me, Amy. You'll make the team. I'm not saying you'll start. Pujols will have a lock on your position for a long time, but you sure as shit will get picked by the coaches to be on the team."

"We'll see. In the meantime, it'll be good to get back to Stacy and then visit my mom the next week. My two favorite women."

"Hey, what about me?" Lisa asked.

"You're my favorite best friend."

Lisa laughed. "Finish your burger so I can take you back to your room. You look beat."

* * *

The team's plane didn't land at the Cincinnati airport until after midnight. Amy rolled her luggage behind her and hefted her bag of equipment higher on her shoulder. She scanned the pickup area for a taxi. She phoned Stacy when she landed and told her to stay home. No use in her driving this late.

Amy was about to flag down an available cab when she saw their gold Chevrolet Equinox rounding the corner. Stacy stopped the SUV and hopped out of the driver's seat.

"Hey." She kissed Amy lightly on the lips. "There'll be a more thorough welcome home later."

"It's so good to see you. God, I've missed you," Amy said after they placed her luggage in the back.

Stacy pulled into the lane to exit the airport and merged onto Interstate 275.

"I've missed you, too." The headlights from the car driving behind them reflected onto the rearview mirror, cutting a swath across Stacy's face. "You guys had a fantastic road trip. I can't believe you're only a game out now. Houston's tanking."

Amy tilted her seat back. "Don't worry. They'll still be there at the end. They have the pitching."

"The Reds have pitching *and* you and Sanders."

Amy turned sidewise on the seat to get a better look at Stacy. "I'm so lucky to have you as a partner."

Stacy met her eyes before focusing again on the road. "Where'd that come from?"

"You're always pumping me up, even when my ass is dragging."

"We'll get you home and into bed. Thank God you have an off-day tomorrow."

Amy stroked Stacy's thigh with her fingertips. "I don't plan on sleeping when we get home. At least not right away. I hope you got a nap in today."

Stacy smiled. "What do you know? As a matter of fact, I did this afternoon."

* * *

Lisa fell onto her back with a huff. "It's so nice to have sore muscles for all the right reasons."

"Leese, anytime you want sore muscles, let me know," Frankie said. "I'll be more than happy to accommodate."

"Yeah?"

"Now why would you doubt that?"

"I didn't say I doubted it. I was only thinking it'd sure be nice to have you on one of these road trips. It's too damn long to be without you."

Frankie took Lisa's hand and kissed her palm. "It can be arranged."

"What do you mean?"

"Having Billie take care of the bar those days I took off for the surgery and recovery helped me realize she's more than capable to manage the bar on her own for longer stretches of time. She told me she's happy doing it. And I found I wasn't missing it as much as I thought I would. I think I'm ready to step back and let Billie take over full-time management."

Lisa sat up. With the move, the sheet fell away to expose her breasts.

"Damn, Leese, how can I have this conversation with you looking like that?"

Lisa drew the sheet to her neck. "But, Frankie, the bar's your baby. You've owned it for how long now? Twenty-five years?"

"Almost. And it's not like I'm selling the Watering Hole. I'm only stepping back and letting someone else who's younger and has a bit more stamina than I do take care of the everyday running of the place."

"You sound like you're ancient. You're only fifty-one. I'd hate to have you give up something because of…"

"Because of…"

"Me."

"Don't put this on yourself. This last scare made me realize what I had in my life and what matters the most to me. I don't want to be standing behind the bar one night, look around, and realize I'd missed out on spending the best years of my life with the woman I love. I want to see you happy, and this job makes you happy. It's time for me to move on to the next stage of my life, and I'd like nothing more than to share it with you."

Overwhelmed, Lisa grabbed hold of Frankie and held her tight. Through her tears, she said, "I love you, too."

"We'll keep the house in Indy," Frankie said. "What about here?"

"I'm happy with this apartment, aren't you?"

"Yes, except for one thing."

"What's that?"

"Where the hell are we going to put a pool table?"

Chapter 11

"What are you and Stacy doing for the Fourth tomorrow?" Nick Sanders paused from his task of rolling down his socks.

Amy unbuckled her belt. "We wanted to take in fireworks later after our afternoon game. I don't know where, though."

"Why don't you guys come over to my house? I live in the Heights with a fantastic view of the river where they'll shoot them off. We can do a barbecue in the back before they start."

"Are you sure we won't be cramping your style?"

"What do you mean?" Sanders stood up and joined Amy in unbuckling his belt. He tugged his jersey out from his uniform pants.

"Come on, Nick. I'm sure you have at least one hot babe who'd love to have you to herself for the evening."

"I see. You're saying I'm a playboy." He challenged her with a raised eyebrow.

"Well…"

"Yes?"

"It's kind of hard not to think that when you're photographed with one of the most beautiful women in the world."

Nick ignored her comment. "Why don't you check with Stacy about tomorrow night?"

Amy hesitated.

"What's your problem?"

"Nothing. I was wondering how comfortable your date will be around two lesbians."

"Let me worry about it."

"Okay. I'll ask Stacy and let you know tomorrow."

* * *

They pulled into the long drive and entered the code Nick had given them for the gate.

Stacy whistled. "Would you look at that."

Amy stared in awe at the sprawling brick mansion. "Nice, isn't it?"

Stacy nudged her with her elbow. "Think about it. We can have a place like this one day when you get your big contract."

"Do we even want a place like this?" Amy asked as she drove through the opened gates.

"No, but it's still fun to say the words."

They got out of their SUV and walked up the stairs to the huge wooden door.

Stacy pointed. "I bet if you hit that button, it'll sound like the bells of Notre Dame."

Amy pushed the doorbell. Stacy wasn't too far off. Heavy footsteps stomped across the floor inside.

"Has to be Sanders," Amy said. "He can't tread anywhere lightly with those size thirteens."

The door flew open and a handsome man with dark curly hair and deep blue eyes stood there.

Maybe he invited another couple, Amy thought.

The man, who was a few inches taller than Amy, extended his hand.

"Amy Perry, wouldn't mistake you for anyone else." He turned to Stacy. "You must be her partner."

"Yes, Stacy McCrady."

"I'm Ryan Fisher, Nick's—"

"Husband." Nick came up behind him, draped an arm around his shoulders, and kissed him on the cheek. Then he looked at Amy with amusement. "Hell, rookie, you act like you've seen a ghost. Aren't you going to introduce me?" He tilted his head toward Stacy. "We've never met."

"Su-sure. Stacy, this is Nick Sanders."

"I kind of knew that." Stacy smiled and took Nick's outstretched hand. "I think you might've thrown Amy for a loop."

"Stacy. You're going to tell me you suspected?" Amy asked as they entered the foyer.

"Well, no."

"Then why not include yourself? It threw you for a loop, too, right?"

Nick and Ryan laughed.

"You two are cute," Ryan said. "Come on out back to the deck. We got lucky. It's cooled since the sun went down, and there's a breeze coming up from the river."

They followed Ryan and Nick to the wooden deck where four cushioned chairs sat around a smoked-glass table. A large pool, complete with a diving board and slide, was perpendicular to the deck. The backyard sprawled in each direction, encircled with a privacy fence with solar lights lining the top.

The instant Amy and Stacy sat down, a yellow Labrador sprinted toward them, his tongue hanging out the side of his mouth.

Nick bent over, picked up a rubber ball, and flung it to the far reaches of the yard. The dog took off. "Buster likes to run."

"I guess he does, since that's your patented throw from behind the bag," Amy said. "You about break my hand sometimes with that throw."

"What can I get you all to drink?" Ryan asked.

"A Coke or Pepsi if you have either," Amy said.

"We have both."

"Pepsi."

"Pepsi it is. And for you, Stacy?"

"Pepsi's fine."

Buster sprinted back with the ball and dropped it at Nick's feet. "Last one, big guy." He heaved another long one before sitting next to Amy.

"What, Perry? All of this take you by surprise?" His light blue eyes sparkled with amusement.

"Does Ariana Montegue know?"

He gave her a sly grin.

Amy's mouth fell open. "You're shitting me. Ariana's gay? She's one of the highest-paid models in the world."

"Amy, Amy, Amy. You disappoint me with your stereotypes."

"Quit drooling there, sport," Stacy said, slapping her on the arm.

Ryan came outside with a tray of drinks. He set the Pepsis in front of Amy and Stacy and handed Nick a Budweiser. Seated next to Nick, he took a sip of his bottled water. "Let me guess. By the looks of things, I'd say you told them about Ariana."

"How long have you and Ryan been together?" Stacy asked.

"Six years now. We met in New York after Ryan spilled a drink all over my brand new Armani suit."

Ryan blushed. "What'd you expect? Seeing you in the flesh kind of did a number on me."

"Ryan was our waiter at the Four Seasons Restaurant. He ran to get a washcloth and was about to load it down with club soda and rub my crotch with it.”

Ryan’s complexion deepened an even darker red.

Nick smiled. “I grabbed his hand and told him, ‘I can get this.’”

“And,” Ryan said, “he gives me this intense stare with those fucking gorgeous eyes of his.” He returned Nick’s smile. “That’s when I knew.” He motioned at them. “How’d you two meet?”

“Amy was dating someone else when we first met. I was attracted to her, but I was and still am good friends with the woman she was dating. So, I waited.” Stacy held Amy’s hand. “She was well worth the wait.”

Amy brought Stacy’s hand to her lips.

“Time to get the grill going, studmeister. I’ll go grab the meat.” Ryan poked Nick’s shoulder as he walked by. “Don’t even think of commenting on that last statement.”

Nick prepped the gas grill. In no time, hamburgers, franks, and four medium-size steaks were sizzling enticingly.

Stacy picked up the ball to play with Buster out in the yard. Ryan joined her. Amy watched Buster sprint back and forth between them with the ball in his mouth.

“Go ahead and ask,” Nick said. “I know you want to.”

“It’s none of my business.”

Nick regarded her for a few seconds and then flipped a burger. “It is your business, Amy. You’re my friend, and I have no problem talking with you about it.”

“Okay. I get the need to stay closeted. I’ve been there myself. But what about Ariana? Why go that far?”

“Because it’s what the fans and the media expect. The fewer the questions, the better. If I’m not dating Ariana or someone like her, things get said. Trust me. I don’t want to deal with that shit. So, I put it out there for them.”

Amy listened to Stacy’s gentle laughter and watched as she and Ryan chased after Buster.

“I bet you’re wondering how Ryan feels.”

“Well, yeah.”

“He understands that by handling it the way I do, I don’t take heat from my teammates or any opposing players. I don’t have to answer any questions from the media. And by dating Ariana, there’s no need to be with a different woman in each city. It’s better for her, and it’s better for me. Ryan and I are monogamous, and we’re happy.” He looked up from his task.

“Your friendship and what you think of me mean a lot to me,” he said softly. "You put yourself out there by revealing who you are. I can't help but feel guilty when I'm around you for staying in the closet. I can understand if you question how I live my life."

"The sad thing is, I do understand. You're a man playing a professional sport dominated by macho men. It fucking sucks you have to live this way."

"Thank you for that even if you don't mean it."

"Nick, I never say anything I don't mean, especially when it concerns good friends."

Stacy and Ryan walked over.

"We're starved, he-man, where's our meat?" Ryan grinned.

Nick waved the tongs at him. "You'll get yours. Be patient."

"Promises, promises."

* * *

The fireworks were spectacular as they flashed overhead and were mirrored below on the Ohio River. Just past midnight, Amy and Stacy drove home. Amy let Stacy sleep undisturbed in the passenger seat until they arrived at the gated apartment parking lot.

"Hon, we're home." Amy nudged her awake.

Stacy stretched, then looked around with a groggy expression.

Amy got out of the SUV and opened the passenger door.

"Come on, sleepyhead."

She led Stacy to the elevator and down the hallway to their apartment.

They went to separate bathrooms for their showers before dressing in their nightclothes and getting into bed.

Stacy snuggled into Amy's arms. She moved her hand under Amy's sleeveless T-shirt and did circles with her fingertips on her stomach. "A penny."

"A penny?"

"For your thoughts."

"I was thinking about the differences between Nick's situation and mine."

"Does it bother you that he's not out?"

"No. I told him the same thing. He was worried about what I thought."

"Which is?"

Amy blew out a breath. "I think male professional athletes are under so much scrutiny and pressure to be super tough guys, that

                    Chris Paynter

there can be no question they're heterosexual. I told him it sucks, and I get it. But I wish…"

"You wish?"

"That life was fair and all this other bullshit was unnecessary."

Stacy continued to stroke Amy's stomach. "Try not to let it get you down." She leaned up on an elbow. "Give me a kiss, woman."

"Ooh. Demanding, aren't we?" Amy smiled as her lips met Stacy's.

"Damn straight."

Amy groaned against her mouth. "You're going to pay for that."

"Go for it, Perry."

Chapter 12

"Where you headed for the break, Collins?" Sarah wrapped up the cord from her laptop and shoved it into her case.

"Frankie's at the apartment waiting on me. We're driving down to the Turkey Run Inn in Indiana for the next three nights. Then we're driving back to Indianapolis on Wednesday to get more of Frankie's stuff together to bring down."

"What do you mean bring down?"

"Frankie's decided to have another employee take over management of the bar. She's coming to Cincinnati to live during the season and will travel with me whenever she can."

"You're shitting me. Wow, I know how much she loves her bar."

"We've talked it out. After her recent health scare, our priorities changed."

"Good for you."

"It is." Lisa gathered her things. "You doing anything special?"

"My job. I'm flying into Detroit for the All-Star game festivities tomorrow and covering the game for *Baseball Weekly*." A trace of loneliness flickered across Sarah's face.

"Maybe when we get back to town, we can have dinner Thursday night. Will you be back then?" Lisa asked.

"I should get back to Cincinnati Wednesday morning. I'd love to have dinner with you and Frankie. Are you sure she won't mind?"

"Why would she mind?"

"I don't know. What's that expression, 'three's a crowd'?"

"Whoever said that didn't have you as a friend. Trust me. You're more than welcome at our place. We can fix some steaks. It's a mini-grill out on the balcony, but it still gets the job done."

"Give me a call Wednesday around noon, and let me know the time. I'll be there. Have a good break."

"You, too, Sarah."

* * *

"Ready to go?" Lisa asked as she entered their apartment.

Frankie emerged from the hallway and carried their luggage to the front door.

"I'd say you are. Let me take this"—Lisa held up her laptop case—"to the den, because I'm sure not taking it to Turkey Run."

They piled two bags into Frankie's truck and started the drive to west central Indiana.

"I've been looking forward to this all week," Lisa said.

"I think I've been looking forward to this all summer."

Soon, the drone of the tires on the pavement was too much for Lisa. She dozed off and didn't awaken until they pulled onto the Crawfordsville, Indiana, ramp. She sat up in her seat and rubbed her eyes.

"Sorry, Frankie. Didn't mean to conk out on you."

"You needed it. You've been going almost nonstop since you accepted the job."

Frankie turned onto the state highway that took them to the back roads leading to the state park. "How are Amy and Stacy doing, by the way? I know Amy's still playing well for the Reds, but how about their relationship?"

"They seem to be fine. Amy told me they were flying into Kansas City right after the game this afternoon. They plan to stay at Amy's mother's house until Thursday morning. I think they both need it. Her mom hasn't been feeling well, either. Amy and I had dinner in San Diego a couple of weeks ago. She's still trying to adjust to life in the majors with all the traveling. Especially being away from Stacy."

Forty-five minutes later, they paid the park entrance fee and turned into Turkey Run Inn's parking lot.

"That's a welcome sight," Lisa said.

Frankie parked, and they took out the luggage.

"Brings back memories every time we come here, doesn't it?" Frankie asked with a smile.

"What's this? Our fifth time?"

"I think so."

They walked toward the entrance.

"I remember when we came here for the first time last fall," Lisa said. "God, the leaves were spectacular."

"Not as spectacular as the two of us in bed."

Lisa chuckled. "True."

They checked in and walked through the great room with the huge fireplace. The inn was rustic. The rooms came with modern conveniences, like televisions, but they rarely watched TV when they stayed.

They squared everything away and then stood staring at each other.

Lisa stepped toward Frankie and gave her a kiss. "That's for your patience." She kissed her again. "That's for your selflessness." She brought her mouth to Frankie's once more, delving her tongue inside until Frankie moaned. "And that's for your love."

They discarded their clothing and climbed into bed. They made love in a rush at first, but then they slowed and took their time. Lips to skin, hands to soft places only the two of them knew, they made love until darkness enveloped the room.

"I'm so glad we came here," Lisa whispered.

"Me, too, Leese. Me, too."

* * *

The plane landed a little too hard for Amy's liking. Of course, it could have been the smoothest landing in the history of flight. She'd never think so. She hated flying, which was a real pain since she had to do it several times a week for more than half the year.

"You can release me from the death grip now," Stacy said.

"Sorry." Amy let go of Stacy's hand.

With a grimace, Stacy flexed her fingers. "It's what I'm here for."

Their luggage was among the last to bounce onto the conveyor belt. Amy lifted the two suitcases, set them down, and released the handles. "I'm so thankful for whoever came up with this clever invention."

"Here, give me mine, you grouser." Stacy grabbed the handle and wheeled toward the exit.

"Now, now, darling. It's all right you decided to bring three weeks' worth of clothing for a three-day visit."

Stacy stopped in front of Amy so abruptly that Amy almost collided with her. Stacy turned, and scowled. "You're pushing it."

"I'm sorry," Amy said with a grin.

"Come on, *rookie*. Let's get our rental car."

They got the keys for their car and waited for the shuttle to take them to the parking lot. Only one other couple was taking the shuttle with them, so the driver jumped down and helped with their luggage, lifting the bags up the steps.

"Where were you fifteen minutes ago?" Amy said under her breath as she sat down next to Stacy.

Stacy elbowed her in the side.

"Ow!" Amy rubbed her ribs in mock pain.

"Oh, give me a break. I barely touched you."

The shuttle dropped them off at the parking lot. They found their car and loaded the luggage once more.

Amy adjusted the driver's seat for her long legs. "A very short person drove this last. Maybe you should be driving." She felt Stacy's stare and looked over at her.

"You know, for this to be a pleasant getaway, you sure aren't starting off on the right foot."

"Admit it. You love me."

Stacy glared at her before she cracked a smile. "More than you'll ever know. Let's go see your mom and aunt. I'm sure they'll be waiting for you on the porch until you pull into that long drive."

It was an hour's drive to Lecompton from Kansas City. They talked about a lot of things—the Reds, Nick Sanders and his partner, Frankie's decision for Billie to take over management of the bar.

Amy called her mother from her cell phone as they neared the old two-story home. Stacy had been right. Amy's mother, Thelma, and Aunt Charlotte stood on the porch, waiting.

Amy put the car in park and got out. Her mother appeared frail, and her color wasn't good. As always, she'd dressed sharply. Today's outfit was a pair of gray slacks and a soft-blue cotton blouse. She was wearing the ever-present silver necklace with a locket. She'd worn the locket every day since Amy's father died. It held a photo of Amy and her father, taken when Amy was four.

"You made it," Thelma, said with a smile.

"Hi, Mom." Amy stepped onto the porch, bent down, and hugged her. Her mom made a move to pull away, but Amy held her longer. "Missed you."

"Missed you, too, honey."

Amy leaned back and looked into her mom's green eyes. Her hair was grayer now, her face lined with more wrinkles than Amy recalled. "Are you getting enough rest?"

"I'm fine." Thelma flashed Amy a warning look. "Let me see

Stacy." Her mom held her arms open. "Come and give me a hug."

"Hi, Mom."

Amy and Stacy greeted Aunt Charlotte with an embrace.

"I'll get the bags," Amy said.

Her mom grabbed her arm. "Come inside and have some lemonade first. Your bags aren't going anywhere."

They followed Thelma and Charlotte into the foyer. Amy lifted her nose in the air.

Her mom patted her on the arm as she passed her on the way into the living room. "Yes, Amy, there's some chicken in the kitchen. I fried it earlier today. I figured you'd be hungry, regardless of what time you arrived."

"May I?" Amy asked.

Thelma laughed and motioned toward the kitchen. "Make sure you bring out enough for Stacy."

Amy made a beeline for the fridge and reentered the living room with a plateful of chicken. She set the plate down on the coffee table in front of Stacy.

"Good Lord, Amy," Aunt Charlotte exclaimed. "Can you eat all of that?"

"Aunt Charlotte, I think you know the answer to that one by now." Stacy reached for a chicken leg and took a bite. "This is delicious, Mom. As always."

Amy grabbed a piece, closed her eyes, and savored her mom's cooking as the chicken melted in her mouth. "Mom, you're the best."

"Humph. I see what got you here. My cooking."

"How've you been feeling?" Amy asked.

"Fine. I'm fine." Thelma stood up suddenly. "How about that lemonade? I'm sure you want some, Amy. Stacy?"

"Yes, please."

Amy waited for her to leave the room. She asked Aunt Charlotte in a lowered voice, "How is she really?"

"Not well. She tires easily, usually in the late afternoons and evenings. The doctor started her on a new medication last week, which seems to tire her even more."

"Have you been able to talk her into selling this place? It's too big."

Her mom stood in the doorway leading into the kitchen, her brow furrowed in a frown. "It was fine for your father and me, and it's fine for us." She brought Amy a glass of lemonade and handed one to Stacy. "This is my home, honey. I'm not leaving."

"But, Mom, maybe—"

"End of discussion."

Stacy put her hand on Amy's knee and squeezed.

"Yes, ma'am," Amy said.

They drank their lemonades and chatted for over an hour until Amy felt the effects from the flight and the earlier game. Her fatigue must have shown.

"I imagine you're both tired," Thelma said. "I've made up your bed in your old room."

"Thanks, Mom."

Stacy took her hand. "Come on. Let's get our luggage."

"Night, Mom. Night, Aunt Charlotte."

"Good night, dear," her mom said. "We'll see you in the morning."

Amy and Stacy retrieved their bags and climbed the creaky stairs to the second floor. They traipsed down the hallway to the last door on the right. Amy flipped on the light and looked around the room. Everything had remained the same since the day she left home, except her mom had added more clippings to the bulletin board about Amy joining the Chattanooga Lookouts and then the Reds.

"Gosh, I'm never sure what to do in this room. Do I genuflect?" Stacy asked.

Amy swatted her on the head.

"Hey!"

"You're such a smart-ass sometimes. Who gets the bathroom first?"

"I'll let you go first," Stacy said. "You take so long."

"Now you're definitely being a smart-ass."

"Go, and don't use up all the hot water."

Amy grabbed her toiletries, panties, and night clothes. She tried to hurry, just to prove Stacy wrong. She was glad they'd talked her mom into putting in a shower. Her mother had tried the "it's too expensive" trick, but Amy stopped that excuse by paying for it herself.

She dried off and walked back to the bedroom. Stacy was reading the clippings with a slight smile.

"Your mom's so proud of you, as she should be," Stacy said.

Amy looked over Stacy's shoulder at the article she was reading. It was a printout of one of Lisa's articles written during Amy's season with the Lookouts. She thought back to when her mom had insisted on purchasing a computer after finding out Lisa would cover Amy the entire season. "I have to keep up with you since I can't be there," her mom had said.

"Lisa knows how to write, doesn't she?" Stacy said.

"Makes me sound better than I am, I think."

Stacy turned to face her and cupped Amy's cheek. "Which is impossible." She kissed Amy gently. "Time for my shower. I'll be right back."

Amy switched on the bedside lamp and turned off the overhead light. She lay with her hands behind her head and stared up at the shadows on the ceiling. A few minutes later, Stacy reentered the bedroom and closed the door. Her still-wet hair appeared black now. She sat next to Amy on the edge of the bed and began brushing her hair.

"Let me." Amy held out her hand.

Stacy handed her the brush. Amy tucked behind Stacy and stretched her legs on either side of Stacy's hips. She ran the brush through her silken strands, marveling at the softness. After several strokes, she set the brush on the bedside table and pressed her mouth against Stacy's ear.

"I love you," she whispered.

A shudder ran through Stacy's body. She turned toward Amy and stared at her lips. "Kiss me."

Amy began the kiss lightly, but it soon became more passionate. She lay back and brought Stacy with her so that Stacy straddled her body.

Stacy pulled Amy's T-shirt off with a quick tug.

"I know we're at your mom's," Stacy whispered as she stared at Amy's breasts. "But, God, I want you. I want to feel you." She took off her shirt and then pressed her body against Amy's. "Can we do this quietly?" she asked with a grin.

"Yes," Amy said before Stacy took her nipple in her mouth. She arched her back at the contact.

"I'm taking you fast, because I think you're ready, aren't you?" Stacy pushed her hand under Amy's panties.

Amy bit her lower lip to stifle a cry as Stacy ran her fingers through her wetness.

"Oh, you're so, so ready." Stacy thrust inside of Amy. "This is what you want, isn't it?" she whispered before lowering her mouth back to Amy's breast.

When Stacy brought her thumb to Amy's clit and began her steady stroking, Amy knew she couldn't last much longer. Stacy swallowed Amy's cries with her mouth when Amy shuddered with a thundering orgasm.

As Amy came down from her climax, Stacy moved to lie beside her.

Amy waited for her breathing to return to normal. "You're amazing."

Stacy patted her stomach. "That'd be you."

Amy sighed in contentment.

"I feel the same way," Stacy said and snuggled closer.

* * *

Amy awakened in the middle of the night with tears rolling down her cheeks. She turned to Stacy who had flipped onto her stomach in her sleep and was facing the other way. Amy's fuzzy mind tried to grasp at the last tendrils of her dream. But as hard as she tried, she only remembered the lingering sadness.

Chapter 13

"Have you prayed to God for forgiveness today?"

"God asks you to repent!"

The middle-aged man with his face pressed against the fence spouted off a passage from the Bible.

Amy walked with the security guards on the other side of the fencing at Kansas City's Kauffman Stadium. What was that expression? she wondered. You can never go home again? She'd hoped they could slip into Kansas City, Missouri, enjoy the accolades of her neighboring home state crowd, and avoid facing the wrath of Reverend Phillips's fanatical congregation from Topeka.

But no such luck. And she hated it. Her mom and aunt would be at the game this afternoon. It would mark the first game her mom had been able to attend since last fall. With the interleague play, the Reds were facing the Royals for the first time in three years.

She hurried along with the two guards toward the back entrance.

"May God have mercy on your soul!" a woman shouted at her as she entered the clubhouse.

She thanked the guards and continued down the long hallway, still thinking about her mom and aunt. She'd paid for their suite at the Hilton President in downtown Kansas City. Amy fended off her mother's objections about the price of the room. Her mom and aunt had insisted they were capable of driving to the game and then driving home, but Amy wouldn't listen to their arguments. Stacy had helped persuade them to stay.

"Hi, Donny," Amy said when she saw the batting coach.

"Hey, Amy. Everything okay?"

"Oh, same ol' same ol' out there tonight. I guess it's to be expected in this neck of the woods with Phillips's church not too far away."

He shook his head. "Fucking jerks."

She pulled off her T-shirt. She was always one of the first to arrive. Not because she didn't like undressing in front of the guys, but because she loved to get to the park as early as possible. It felt like home.

Amy thought about the pennant race. Entering late July, the Reds were still in the hunt, much to the surprise of the majority of the pundits, except for Lisa who'd predicted the Reds would be in the thick of the Wild Card race. But the dog days of August were fast approaching, and the Reds were in second place, three-and-a-half games out of first behind the Houston Astros and tied for the Wild Card with the Rockies. The Giants, with their young arms, were running away with the divisional title in the West, as were the Mets in the East.

Amy tugged on her sliding shorts. She sat down, rolled up her socks, and gave one a pat. They'd be dirty and sweat-stained by the end of the game.

As she was pulling on her uniform pants, Tim Rawls, the affable second baseman, entered the clubhouse.

"Hey, Perry. I see your fan club camped out in front of the stadium again."

"They're still trying to save my soul."

"Your soul needs as much saving as my Grandmother Deidre's. Considering I think she's a saint, that's saying a lot."

"Thanks, Tim."

"What are you thanking this little nerd for?" Nick Sanders asked as he playfully shoved Rawls when he passed by.

"He's all right by me, Nick."

"How much did you pay her to say that, Rawlsey?"

"What, Perry? Twenty-five bucks?"

"That'd about do it."

She finished dressing and left for the batting cage. Nick followed her into the tunnel leading up to the dugout.

"You okay?" he asked.

"Why wouldn't I be?"

"Amy…"

She waited for him to catch up. "It bugs me, Nick, so, no, I'm not okay. Especially knowing my mom has to see and hear this stuff when she has a ticket to the game. With the freedom of speech thing, they can have their protests, even if it's so many feet away. But my mom loves me. She doesn't like hearing that crap."

He put his hand on her shoulder. "Hang in there. Concentrate on the game."

She met his eyes. "Wouldn't it bother you?"

He dropped his hand and focused on something above her head. "It does bother me."

She started to walk away.

"Amy."

She stopped.

"You still understand, right? How it's different for me?" He searched her face.

She hesitated. It was only a slight hesitation, but it was long enough to give away her feelings rendered raw by the demonstration in front of the stadium. "I do, Nick." His expression told Amy that he didn't believe her.

He opened his mouth to say more, but the trainer's voice from the clubhouse stopped him.

"Yo, Nick. Time to tape up that hamstring."

"Coming!" he shouted.

She hurried up into the dugout, glad to end the conversation.

* * *

Amy had a good night at the plate. She'd struggled to concentrate, but knowing her mom and aunt were there to see her play had spurred her on. After the game, Stacy and Amy met them in their suite. Amy called for room service.

They dug into the food spread out in front of them on the table.

"Pass me a couple of those packets of salt, please," Amy said to her mom.

When Thelma reached for the salt, Amy didn't miss the tremor of her hand.

"How are you feeling, Mom?" she asked, already knowing what the stock response would be.

"I'm fine, dear. You worry too much." Thelma put her quavering hand out of sight on her lap and used her other hand to raise her fork.

After dinner, Amy stood and stretched. "I'm sorry, but I need to get back to the room to rest."

Thelma and Charlotte rose from the chairs, and they hugged.

"Love you, Mom," Amy whispered before trying to end the embrace. This time, her mom wouldn't let her pull away.

"I love you too, sweetheart. You keep playing the game, you hear? Don't let those nutcases get to you. You belong in that uniform. Your dad would be so proud." She cupped Amy's face in her hands.

"Don't you ever be ashamed of who you are and never forget how much your dad loved you and how much I still do. Promise me."

Amy's throat tightened. "I promise. I'm not sure when I'll see you again. We're flying out west for a nine-game road trip, but I'll call you."

While walking down the hallway, Stacy reached for Amy's hand. Amy held it even tighter as they entered the elevator.

* * *

"That kid has a hell of an arm, doesn't he?" Sarah punched the keys on her laptop.

"They said he'd be something special coming up, and he hasn't disappointed." Lisa watched the action below as Brennan, the young southpaw for the San Francisco Giants, went into his windup. He followed up his ninety-six-mile-an-hour fastball with a slow changeup. Rawls, the Reds second-place hitter, swung early and didn't come close to the ball. He carried his bat back to the dugout while shaking his head.

"Care to make a little wager on how Amy handles him?" Sarah asked. "I say she doesn't even sniff a hit."

"You're on. How about you buy me a steak dinner after the game at Ruth's Chris? I heard the one here in San Francisco is supposed to be one of the best in the country."

"Good God, Collins, when you wager, you wager."

"Cold feet?"

"No, but I expect the same dinner deal from you when I win this."

Amy strode to the plate, went through her batting glove ritual, scuffed her front toe in the dirt, and took a couple of practice swings.

The first pitch was an inside fastball that tied her in knots. She tried to check her swing but couldn't. Brennan threw a sharp-breaking curve on the next pitch. Amy took a big swing but missed.

"Ready to pay up?" Sarah asked.

"Just wait."

Brennan reared back with a high leg kick and fired his hardest fastball of the night—a ninety-seven-mile-an-hour pitch to the outside part of the plate. Amy lunged and lined it past the diving first baseman. It rattled around in the cavernous right field corner. The right fielder raced over, but the ball took a tricky hop. Amy rounded second and made it to third easily with a stand-up triple.

With a smug grin, Lisa said, "I can smell that steak now and taste it as it melts in my mouth."

Sarah sighed. "Guess you'll have no mercy on me and my measly paycheck."

"Oh, save it for someone who might fall for that line of bullshit."

"You don't believe me? You wound me with your distrust."

"I'll give you a break."

"I'm off the hook?" Sarah asked.

"Hell no. I thought we could share a cab on the drive to Ruth's Chris."

"You're such a bitch."

Lisa continued watching the play below. Nick Sanders lined an 0-2 pitch up the middle, almost taking off Brennan's head in the process. Amy trotted home and picked up the bat as she crossed the plate.

"I think they're starting to time his fastball," Lisa said.

"That's the thing about these young pitchers. They have it going through five innings and look like they might be the next Cy Young. In the sixth inning, they implode."

The next batter knocked a single into left field. Sanders stopped at second.

The Giants pitching coach sauntered out to the mound as the relievers began loosening in the Giants bullpen. Brennan remained in the game. Three more runs scored before the manager made the trek out onto the field and signaled for the right-hander.

The game got a little tighter in the bottom of the eighth but ended with the Reds on top, 6-4.

Lisa followed Sarah to the elevator that took them down to the clubhouse. They filed in behind the other reporters and spread out to interview the players.

Lisa stood behind the group interviewing Amy and closely observed her as she answered each question. She seems down about something, Lisa thought. The writers dispersed.

Lisa waited for Nick Sanders to leave for the showers. Amy faced the locker and started undressing.

"Hey, is everything all right?" Lisa asked.

No response.

"Aim?"

Amy sat down in the chair in front of her locker and sighed, keeping her back to Lisa.

Lisa came around the chair to face her. "What's wrong?"

Amy still didn't say anything.

Lisa squatted down and placed her hand on Amy's knee. "You can tell me."

"It's... it's my mom again. She's not doing well at all." Amy was clearly fighting back tears.

Lisa waited for her to compose herself.

"Stacy and I saw her and my aunt when we were in Kansas City," Amy said. "But only for the one night. They drove back to Lecompton the next day. I told you about her heart." Amy rubbed her eyes. "I'm so worried, Lisa. I feel helpless not being there."

"Have you talked to Murphy about it? Can you maybe ask for a special leave or something?"

"No. For one thing, my mom wouldn't like me taking off. She wants me to keep playing. And this isn't an easy job to take time away from, you know? We're thin at my position right now, what with Colston on the fifteen-day disabled list. I've called her every night. She sounds so weak."

"Hang in there, Aim. I guess Stacy couldn't make this trip?"

"Not this one. She's covering for Billie this week at the bar."

"I'm sure if you need Frankie to, she'd be happy to cover for her. She didn't make the trip, either."

"Stacy still enjoys working there, even though it's not as much as she used to. I didn't want to take it away from her."

"You can tell her you need her."

"I know," Amy said quietly.

Lisa stood up. "You've got my number if you want to talk. Call if you need to, no matter the time."

* * *

"Shit, Collins. Did you have to order the most expensive steak on the menu?"

"Since you're paying, yes." Lisa took a drink of her wine. She rarely drank wine, but if someone else was paying, what the hell. Her mind returned to her talk with Amy in the clubhouse. She didn't realize Sarah had asked a question.

"Lisa?"

"Sorry. What'd you say? I think I'm tired. This road trip's dragging me down."

"I know what you mean." Sarah cut into her steak and took a bite. "You were right. There's nothing like these steaks." She waved her fork at Lisa. "What I was asking was how do you see the Reds matching up against LA this week?"

"I think the pitching has held together for the season. Roberto Sanchez's stuff has been electric since they called him up. If he can keep going, and if Fowler and Granderson can come through with top games again, I think they have a good opportunity to at least take two out of three from the Dodgers. They'd go home with a 6-3 road record for this trip. Not bad. Not bad at all."

"You're looking smarter and smarter with your predictions at the beginning of the year. I remember the *Sporting News* reporter razzing you when he saw who you picked to finish first in the divisions and that you had the Reds in there for the Wild Card hunt."

Lisa swirled her wine before taking another sip. "Kind of nice being right sometimes."

"Don't get a big head."

Lisa laughed. "Frankie wouldn't let that happen."

Lisa's filet mignon was so tender it only took one pass of her steak knife to cut into it. She tried to enjoy the savory juices, but the image of Amy's worried expression was still fresh in her mind. She said a silent prayer.

* * *

The sun broke through an overcast sky at Dodger Stadium. Lisa and Sarah stood chatting while they watched the players go through their wind sprints and crossovers.

"I think she has a legitimate shot at Rookie of the Year, don't you?" Sarah asked.

"The only one I think is her competition is Bill Wilkins from the Marlins. He's had a decent year so far. What's Amy up to now? Isn't she batting .293 with fifteen home runs and fifty-three RBIs? And that's since May 15?"

"Why are you asking me, you stats geek? You know everything by memory. I have to look the shit up."

Lisa's cell phone vibrated on her side. She unclipped it and looked at the display. *Stacy.*

"Hi, Stacy. What's up?"

"Lisa..." Stacy started crying.

Lisa's chest constricted. "Oh, God. It's Amy's mom, isn't it? Is she... is she..."

"No. She's still alive, but it's bad. Really bad. I just got off the phone with Aunt Charlotte. Thelma collapsed at home an hour ago. They rushed her by ambulance to the hospital, and she's in ICU. Amy needs to get there as quickly as possible. She's probably in warm-ups for the game, so I knew I couldn't reach her. Can you tell her, Lisa? And ask her to call me after you talk?"

Sarah looked over at her with upraised eyebrows. Lisa shook her head and turned away.

"Sure. I'll have her call as soon as I talk to her. Are you okay?"

"No," Stacy choked out.

"I'm sorry, Stacy. I hate that you're alone."

Stacy let out a breath. "I'll feel better after I talk to Amy. And when I see her."

"Let me get her now."

She got off the phone and turned around. Amy was walking toward the dugout. Lisa headed toward her. Amy had just stepped down the stairs when Lisa called out to her.

"Oh, hey, Lisa." Amy's expression changed. "What's wrong?"

"Amy, let's go into the clubhouse."

The color drained from Amy's face. "What is it? Tell me."

"It's better if we talk inside."

They walked in silence except for the "clack clack" of Amy's cleats on the concrete floor.

"Why don't we have a seat?" Lisa said.

They sat down on a nearby couch.

"Amy, I don't know how to say this other than to just say it. I just got off the phone with Stacy. Your mother's in critical condition at the hospital. An ambulance rushed her there after she collapsed at home an hour ago."

"Oh, God," Amy cried. "Oh, God, I was so afraid this would happen."

Lisa put her arm around her shoulder. Amy pressed into her and sobbed. Lisa waited until Amy had recovered enough to talk.

"I… I don't know what to do," Amy said with a sniff. "How do I get there?"

"Let me go get Murphy and tell him what's going on." Lisa held out her phone. "Why don't you give Stacy a call?"

Amy started crying again. "I'm not sure I can talk to her."

"It's okay, Aim. She'll understand."

"But what about flight arrangements?"

"Like I said, I'll talk to Murph. I'm sure he'll get management involved to set up everything. Don't worry about any of that, okay?"

Amy nodded. She stared at Lisa's phone.

Lisa squeezed her shoulder and left for the tunnel. Before she made it very far, she heard Amy say, "Stacy? Oh, God…"

Lisa closed her eyes when she heard Amy's ragged sobs.

Chapter 14

Amy grabbed her bag from the overhead bin and resisted the urge to shove everyone out of the way in the aisle of the plane so she could make a quick exit.

She walked out of the concourse and searched for Stacy, whose flight should have landed two hours earlier. Passengers hurrying to their gates bumped into Amy, but she bounced off them, barely noticing. She searched for Stacy in the area they'd agreed to meet and saw her a few feet away.

Stacy took Amy into her arms and held her tight. "I love you." She reached for Amy's hand. "Come on. I had time to reserve a car."

The shuttle drove them to the parking lot. Stacy popped the trunk of the car to put her bag inside. "Here. Hand me yours."

Amy felt as if she were in a trance and unable to move. Stacy lifted the bag off Amy's shoulder. After placing the luggage in the trunk, Stacy led Amy to the passenger seat and opened the door. She got into the driver's seat and buckled up. "Put your seat belt on, honey."

Amy numbly reached for the belt and buckled it.

On the drive to Lecompton, Stacy took Amy's hand that rested on the console and let that be the extent of interactions between them. She exited off the interstate. They entered Lecompton, and she slowed to a stop at the light.

"You'll have to help me, Amy. I don't know where the hospital is."

Amy gave her directions, and they parked. She struggled to put one foot in front of the other as they walked to the ICU. She tried to ignore the overpowering smell of antiseptic rising up to her nose. She hated hospitals. She'd visited this hospital only one other time, and it was in a similar situation. They'd rushed her father there after a heart attack. Amy remembered she'd finished a Bandits game when her cell phone went off in her equipment bag. It was her mother. As soon as she heard her voice, Amy knew it was bad. The same sense of dread settled on her now and grew heavier and heavier with each step.

They stopped at the ICU desk. The woman explained that only two people could visit at a time. If Amy would like to visit, she'd have to send her aunt out to the waiting area before Stacy would be allowed in.

"You go see your mom," Stacy told her. "I'll wait until Aunt Charlotte comes out."

Amy didn't move.

"Go, sweetie. Your mom's waiting for you."

Amy entered the restricted area and passed the nurse's station in the center of the circular room. Machines hissed and beeped all around her. She took a moment to compose herself before she opened the door. Her aunt sat on a chair facing the bed. She got to her feet and met Amy halfway into the room.

Amy engulfed Charlotte in her arms, pressing her aunt's head under her chin. Charlotte shook with quiet sobs.

Aunt Charlotte's eyes were red and swollen. "I'm glad you made it. They say she doesn't have much longer. Why don't you sit down and hold her hand? She'll know it's you."

"Stacy's in the waiting area. Can you send her back so she can see her?" Amy managed to choke out.

"Yes, honey. Now go sit down."

Amy inched nearer to the bed as quietly as possible, almost as if entering a church service after the sermon had started. She picked up the chair and set it next to the bed. She studied all of the machinery surrounding her mom, as well as the IV going into her hand and the oxygen tube in her nose. Her mom's graying hair lay pressed against the pillow, encircling her face like a halo. *She looks so old.*

Amy sat down and took her mother's hand in hers. "Mom," she whispered, "please don't leave me." She heard the door behind her click open, and she felt a familiar touch on her shoulder.

"I can't lose her, Stace." Amy began crying.

Stacy brought another chair over and set it beside Amy's.

They were alone for some time until a nurse entered. Amy glanced up at her as she checked the bag of fluid leading into the IV. The nurse gave her a sympathetic smile and wrote down readings from the monitor. She left as quietly as she'd entered the room.

"Sweetie, why don't we go downstairs and get something to eat?" Stacy said. "Your aunt should be in the waiting room now. I sent her down to the cafeteria when I came back."

"I don't want to leave her."

"When's the last time you ate?"

Amy thought about it and realized she hadn't eaten since that morning. Her stomach growled as a reminder.

Stacy stood up. "Come on. We'll tell them at the nurse's station where we're going. And we can let Aunt Charlotte know she can come in again."

Amy reluctantly agreed. Taking Stacy's hand, she allowed her to lead them out into the ICU waiting area.

"Aunt Charlotte, why don't you sit with Mom for a while? I need to get Amy to eat something. We'll be up as soon as we finish."

They rode the elevator down to the first floor and visited the deli connected to the cafeteria. Stacy ordered two sandwiches, as if understanding Amy couldn't make any decisions. They finished their meal and took the elevator up to the fourth floor again.

"You go in with your aunt. I'll wait."

Amy reentered the room. Charlotte was sitting in the chair she'd placed at the head of the bed. When Amy entered, she got up and took the other seat.

"You don't need to move, Aunt Charlotte."

"Come sit next to your mother." Charlotte motioned to the chair.

Amy sat down and held her mother's hand, so tiny and frail within her own. She touched her lips against it. "I love you, Mom," she whispered.

Thelma's hand twitched, and her eyes opened. They were cloudy and unfocused at first, but then, it was as if she realized who was there. She smiled, weakly squeezed Amy's hand, and drifted off again with the heart monitor continuing its steady rhythmic beat.

Amy's eyelids grew heavy. The time change was getting to her. She must have nodded off when a touch on her shoulder awakened her. Her aunt was gone. She looked behind her and saw Stacy standing there.

"Why don't we go to the house and come back in the morning?"

"No," Amy said with an even tone.

"But, sweetheart, you have to be exhausted. It's eleven-thirty."

"I can't leave, Stace."

Stacy's expression softened. "Okay. I'll sit with you then."

"You don't have to."

"I want to be with you," Stacy said as she sat down.

"Where's Aunt Charlotte?"

"I sent her home about an hour ago. She isn't in the best of health, either, and needs to get some rest." Stacy looked at Thelma. "Has she been awake at all?"

"Briefly. I was holding her hand. She squeezed my hand and opened her eyes, but it didn't last long."

Stacy brushed her fingers through Amy's hair. "You're a good daughter, Amy Perry."

"I don't know about that."

"Well, I do. Your mom does, too."

Amy leaned forward and kissed her mom's forehead. She held her hand again and stroked the top with her fingers. Stacy settled back into her chair. The methodical hissing and clicking of the machinery surrounding the bed was too much of a hypnotic serenade to overcome. Amy succumbed to her exhaustion, laid her head on the bed, and fell into a restless dream.

* * *

She was fifteen years old with her parents leading her to a baseball field. She glanced up at her dad. He still had an inch on her height, but at five-eleven, her mother told her not to be surprised if she made it to six feet after all. She'd grown three inches in the past three years.

"You wait with your mother while I discuss this with Coach Mitchelson," her dad told her.

Amy had already talked to the Perry-Lecompton High School baseball coach. Unsuccessfully. The high school didn't have a girls' softball team, so she thought she'd try out for the baseball team. Coach Mitchelson didn't want to hear how well she played fast pitch softball. "It's not the same," he'd said. "Not even close."

She and her mother hung back as her dad marched over to the diamond and talked to Mitchelson. At first, it sounded like a pleasant conversation. But soon her dad's voice rose, and his face reddened in anger.

"Oh, dear," her mother said. "I think your father needs my help, don't you? Why don't you join me?"

Amy followed her mom who sauntered up to the coach as if she was about to ask him to dance.

"Coach Mitchelson, hello, I'm Thelma Perry, Amy's mother," she said with a smile.

The coach blinked as he shook her outstretched hand. Amy's father had the same dumbfounded expression.

Her mother telegraphed a look to her father that said, "Don't interrupt me."

"I think what my husband's trying to explain is that our daughter is a talented fast pitch softball player. If you'll allow her to show you her skills, I'm sure you'll find she's as good as some of these players on your baseball team, if not better." Her mom gestured to the boys out on the field who were watching with interest.

"Mrs. Perry—"

"It's Thelma." Her mother's eyes twinkled in the sunlight, and the dimples deepened as her grin widened.

The coach swallowed hard. "Thelma. I think you can understand my dilemma. We've never had a girl play baseball for Perry-Lecompton High School. Never." He repeated the word louder as if to emphasize how right he felt the policy was.

"Ah, but you can set a precedent. And you can be known as the coach who first took a chance on Amy Perry."

"But—"

Her mom touched his arm, her hand lingering there.

"You need to let her show you how well she can play. That's all we ask. After that, if you don't think she's talented enough, we'll walk away. No arguments."

He opened his mouth to say something else, but Thelma didn't let him.

"This one chance, Coach Mitchelson." She held up her index finger.

He rubbed his forehead, which made the bill of his cap tilt back at a crooked angle. "But we stop this when I say so. And I'm still saying it won't work." He spoke the words like a man who thought he was still in control.

"Of course," Thelma said.

"All right, Amy. Let's see what you got."

After Coach Mitchelson had watched her hit and field for thirty minutes, he walked over to her parents with Amy trailing behind.

"I'll have to give it to you. She's a damn fine ball player. But I'm telling you again, we've never done it before, and I can't allow it now. I'd have to let more girls try out. That ain't gonna happen."

Amy's father started arguing with him again.

Thelma pulled Amy away. "Come on. Let's go back to the car and wait on your dad."

Amy turned back to watch her dad's face redden again as his voice rose. "I don't think I'll get to play, Mom."

Thelma put her arm around Amy's waist.

"You're not giving up on this, Amy. They can't deny your talent. It may take some fighting. It may even take you going in front of the school board."

Amy started to pull away, but her mom held her close.

"I know how hard it is for you to talk in front of people, sweetheart. But this is the time for you to shine."

"You really think so?"

Her mom squeezed her waist. "Mark my words."

* * *

A persistent beeping awakened Amy.

The door banged open, and two nurses flew in.

Amy jerked awake and tried to comprehend what was happening.

"Mom?" She watched in horror as one of the nurses started compressions on her mother's chest. "Mom!"

Stacy grabbed Amy's arm and pulled her away from the bed. Amy jerked out of her grasp.

"Mom!"

A doctor entered the room. "Get them out of here," he said as he rushed past them.

The other nurse ushered them into the hall.

She and Stacy watched through the open door as the nurse continued CPR and the doctor ordered more medications.

"She's flatlined. Give her another round of Atropine."

Time stood still for Amy. More CPR. More frantic, controlled movement.

Minutes later, Amy heard the doctor's order. "Stop CPR." He checked the monitors, shook his head, and looked up at the clock. "I'm calling it. One-thirteen."

He talked to the nurses before he turned toward the doorway and met their eyes, his mouth creased in a grim line. He joined them in the hall.

"I'm sorry. We did all we could, but her heart was too weak."

"No!" Amy wailed. She slumped hard against the wall and slid to the floor. "No!"

Stacy knelt down and hugged her, but Amy tried to push away. "She can't be gone, Stacy. She just can't be."

Stacy held her tight as Amy sobbed into her chest.

"I'm so, so sorry." Stacy rocked her and kept repeating, "I'm sorry, honey. I'm so sorry."

* * *

Amy and Stacy drove to the house where Aunt Charlotte met them at the door. Stacy had called her from the hospital. Amy could tell Charlotte had been crying.

After they hugged, her aunt said, "She's not suffering anymore, Amy. She's struggled so hard these past few months."

"I feel like I missed out on so much. I wish I could have been here. I wish…"

"Why don't we all go inside? It's been a long afternoon and night."

When they entered the living room, Amy's gaze fell upon the family photos. The pictures taunted her with their smiles of captured moments in the past. Amy put her face in her hands and sobbed. An arm encircled her waist, and she caught the faint whiff of Stacy's shampoo.

"Come on. Let's get you upstairs."

Stacy led her to her bedroom and helped her to the side of the bed. She undressed Amy and pulled her nightshirt over her head. Then she gently pushed her back onto the mattress.

"Don't leave me." Amy was about to sit up, when Stacy placed her hand on her chest.

"I'm right here, but I need to undress."

Amy lay back onto the pillow, and after getting into her nightshirt, Stacy slipped under the covers beside her.

"Hold me," Amy pleaded.

Stacy pulled her into her arms.

Amy grabbed Stacy's nightshirt and gripped it in her fist.

This time when she drifted off to sleep, there was no comforting dream of her mother rising to her defense.

* * *

Amy awakened and tried to focus on the objects hanging on the walls. Confused at first, she realized she was in her bedroom at her mom's house. Then she remembered why she was there. She gasped and bolted upright.

Stacy put her hand on her back. "I'm here, Amy."

Amy needed to feel something—anything—other than the terrible emptiness strangling her heart. "I want you to make love to me," she whispered.

"Are you sure?"

"Please."

Stacy touched her lips to Amy's for a soft kiss. They undressed, and with her strong arms, Amy lifted Stacy on top of her. Stacy pressed her body against hers and kissed her again. She used light touches and caresses to bring Amy to the edge.

When Amy climaxed, she began crying and covered her face with her hands.

"I didn't get to say goodbye," she sobbed. "I fell asleep and didn't get to say goodbye." She turned away from Stacy.

Stacy moved behind her and put her arm around Amy's waist.

"I believe she knew you were there," Stacy said and gently squeezed her. "*You* have to believe that."

"But I fell asleep."

"Honey, you were exhausted, both physically and emotionally. You still are. There was nothing wrong with you sleeping."

"That's easy for you to say. You still have your mom." Amy regretted the words as soon as they left her mouth. Stacy stiffened behind her and then withdrew. Amy rolled back over. "God, I'm sorry. I didn't mean it, Stace."

Stacy's eyes glistened in the dim light. "You're hurting."

Amy wiped away a trailing tear from Stacy's cheek. "That still doesn't give me the right to lash out at you. I'm sorry."

"Why don't you try to get some rest? These next few days will be stressful."

"Can you hold me again?"

In answer, Stacy opened her arms and enveloped Amy in the comfort and security that she needed.

Chapter 15

Lisa fumbled for her cell phone in the early morning darkness of her hotel room. She looked at the digital clock: 4:30. It's never good to get a call this early in the morning.

She tried to focus on the number on the display but couldn't read it. Clearing her throat, she flipped open the phone. "'lo?"

"Lisa?"

"Stacy?" She swung her legs over the side of the bed.

"I hate calling you this early. What is it? Four-thirty there?"

Lisa tensed.

"Amy's mom passed away early this morning."

"I was afraid that's why you were calling," Lisa said. "How's Amy?"

"About how you'd expect. She's still in bed. I wanted her to get a little more sleep before we tackle the arrangements. She was exhausted when she arrived and even more so after last night."

"Have you called Cincinnati's management?"

"Yes. I just got off the phone with them. She's taking the ten-day bereavement leave from the team."

It would take a lot longer than ten days, Lisa thought. "What do you need me to do?"

"I wish you were here now. Amy could use a good friend, but I know you can't leave your job."

"I'll get there when I can. Frankie and I will be there for the services. Keep me posted."

"Sure."

"And Stacy?"

"Yes?"

"Tell Amy we love her and we'll keep her in our prayers."

"I'll tell her, Lisa. I'll talk to you soon."

Lisa closed the phone and got up to use the bathroom. After she finished, she called Frankie.

"Hey," Frankie said. "Missing me so much you're calling me at four-thirty in the morning your time?"

Lisa didn't say anything.

Frankie's tone sobered. "It's Amy's mom, isn't it?"

"She passed away early this morning. I guess Stacy must've already filled you in that they admitted her mom to the hospital."

"She called me last night to let me know Val would take over for her. Billie's due back later this afternoon from her vacation. I feel bad for Amy. Poor kid. Did Stacy say how she was doing?"

"Stacy told me she's about how you'd expect."

"Didn't you tell me her dad passed away a few years ago?"

"Yes. This is going to be tough."

"We're attending the services, right?"

"As soon as Stacy lets me know about the arrangements, we'll fly in for the funeral."

"If you get to talk to her, tell her we love her, and she's in our prayers."

"That's what I told Stacy to tell her. Listen, I'll make my flight arrangements and let you know when I'll land in Kansas City. Then you can reserve your flight so we can meet up there to get a rental car."

"All right. In the meantime, why don't you try to get a little more sleep?"

"I don't know if I can after that phone call. I can't quit thinking about Amy and how I felt when my mom died. Like I said, this is going to be one of the hardest things Amy's had to go through."

*   *   *

Lisa handed the driver her money and jumped out of the taxi. She tugged her laptop case higher up on her shoulder and walked to the gate at Dodger Stadium. She showed her press credentials to the guard.

After setting up her laptop in the press box, she went back downstairs to seek out Max Murphy on the field. She caught sight of his red hair amidst the entire Reds team. She walked closer but stopped at a respectful distance and listened to what he was saying to the team.

"Amy's mother passed away last night. She'll be on bereavement leave for ten days or even longer. I've told her to take as long as she needs. It'll put us in a hurt because we need her bat and defense, but family comes first." He made eye contact with each of them. "I'm asking you to pick up the slack and give even more than what you've been giving this season. We're still in the thick of this thing. I don't want to let up."

"Have funeral arrangements been made yet?" Nick Sanders asked.

"No. Unless it's on an off-day, none of us will be able to attend."

"I'd like to go to represent the team," Nick said.

"I don't think we can have that."

"Fine me. Bench me. Do whatever you have to do. I'm going."

Murphy waved the rest of the players away. "You all get to working out."

Lisa maintained her distance. Nick glanced at her, but Murphy hadn't noticed her yet.

"Listen, I know you and Amy are good friends, Nick—"

"Very good friends."

"But I can't have two of my best hitters out of the lineup," Murphy said.

"It's one game, skip."

"I don't think I need to remind you one game can be the difference between making and not making the playoffs. Don't you remember the tiebreaker games these past couple of years? Those teams were tied at the end of 162 games. One more win would've gotten them in."

"Then you can fine me," Sanders said. "I want to be there for her."

Lisa awaited Murphy's answer.

"All right. I'll let Dan Taylor know you're going. I'll take the heat if he gets mad."

"I appreciate it." Nick lifted his chin at Lisa. "Hi, Lisa."

"Hi, Nick."

Sanders trotted to the outfield to join the other players.

Murphy turned to her. "Sometimes, I hate this fucking job."

"I didn't mean to eavesdrop. I came over to talk about Amy. I didn't know what you were discussing with the team."

"You'll be there, right?"

"My partner and I plan to fly in, if only for the funeral. Sounds like that's what Nick wants to do, too."

"Do you know what an ass I felt like telling him he couldn't go? I'd like to be there myself." He pounded his fist against his thigh. "Fuck."

"I'll let her know how much you wanted to be there. She'll understand."

The pitching coach approached them.

"Guess I'd better get to work," Murphy said.

"Good luck. I'll talk to you after the game."

Lisa took the elevator up to the empty press box. She stood at the open window and stared down below as the grounds crew began grooming the field. She thought about how much she still missed her mom. It had been eleven years, but the pain still felt fresh in her heart.

* * *

Lisa and Frankie took the Lecompton exit off I-70. Frankie studied the directions.

"You go through two lights and make a left at the next one."

Lisa followed Frankie's instructions.

"At the second stop sign make a right, and the funeral home should be half a block ahead on the left."

Lisa turned the car. What she saw in front of them made her slow to a crawl. A group of about one hundred protesters stood across the street from the funeral home with state troopers lined up in front of them. Lisa read their signs.

"Fags Go to Hell!"

"God Hates Faggots!"

But one sign stood out above all others, and the man carrying it blasted the words through the bullhorn he held to his mouth. "Your Sin Did Your Mother In!"

He repeated the words until a chant rang out from the crowd as the others joined him.

"Oh, Jesus." A wave of nausea hit Lisa.

"Goddammit." Frankie reached for the door handle.

Lisa grabbed her arm. "Frankie, don't. It won't do any good. These are Reverend Phillips's followers, and they're not going to change."

She made the left into the funeral home drive and parked. She tried to ignore the hateful words shouted across the street as she and Frankie neared the funeral home entrance.

Standing there was Nick Sanders. He stared across the street with his face flushed.

"I know, Nick," Lisa said. "It's horrible. Were they out there when Amy arrived?"

"One state trooper told me they've been camped out front since six this morning. I guess they wanted to make sure they were at the funeral home when she arrived with her aunt and Stacy. I want to go over there, grab that fucking bullhorn, and shove it down the asshole's throat."

Lisa put her hand on his arm and felt him tremble.

"I'm glad you were able to make the funeral. This is my partner, Frankie Dunkin. Frankie, this is Nick Sanders."

They shook hands.

He glanced across the street one last time. "Sorry about my behavior, but Amy doesn't need this crap."

"You don't have to apologize to us," Lisa said.

Nick led them inside to the guestbook where Lisa signed their names. They walked a little farther down the hall to the last room. It looked as though all of Lecompton turned out for Thelma Perry's funeral. Amy's manager from the Bandits, Marge Tompkins, and her ex-teammates stood together in one corner.

Nick helped push their way to the front where Amy and Stacy stood near the open casket. Nick touched Amy's shoulder.

As soon as Amy saw Lisa, she burst into tears. Lisa went to her and held her while she cried. Lisa tamped down the sobs that threatened to escape. She looked at Nick just past Amy's shoulder. He had tears in his eyes.

"I'm sorry, Aim. She was a good woman."

Amy embraced Frankie. After they greeted Stacy, Amy led them to the casket. Photos lined a small table nearby. Lisa bent over to get a closer look. There was one of her parents with Amy wearing a baseball uniform with "Kaws" and the mascot across the chest, probably taken when she was in high school. Lisa recognized another photo of Amy's first game as a Cincinnati Red last fall.

"She loved you very much and was so proud of you, Amy. I'm glad she got to see you live your dream." Lisa ran her fingers over the glass frame as she thought about her mom.

"I guess you saw them out front when you arrived," Amy said with her jaws tightened.

"I'm so sorry you had to go through that. It's horrible. Couldn't the police make them leave?"

"No. They told me it's the First Amendment and freedom of speech, just like the demonstrators at the stadiums. They have to stay so many feet away from the entrance, which is why they're allowed across the street."

An elderly couple walked over to Amy.

"Excuse me. I need to talk to them," Amy said.

Lisa took a seat beside Frankie and Stacy in the front row of chairs.

"She seems to be holding up all right," Lisa whispered to Stacy.

"I don't think it's hit her yet." Stacy smiled at a woman Lisa recognized to be Amy's aunt. Lisa remembered seeing her at the Kansas City Royals game. "You've met Amy's Aunt Charlotte?"

Lisa and Frankie stood up. "No, I haven't." She extended her hand. "Hi. I'm Lisa Collins, and this is my partner, Frankie Dunkin."

"Stacy's told me what a good friend you are to Amy, Lisa. You'll need to watch over her when she returns to baseball."

"Yes, ma'am."

Everyone took their seats. The minister, a short, balding man began the service. Lisa didn't pay much attention as she became lost in the memory of her mother's funeral and the loneliness she felt. She glanced over at Amy, Stacy, and Charlotte.

Amy has family, and she has us.

Lisa looked at Nick, seated at the very end of their row.

And she has a good friend on the field.

* * *

After the graveside services, Lisa and Frankie lingered by their rental car until Amy, Stacy, and Charlotte walked over to them. Nick had already said his goodbyes to Stacy and Amy and left for the airport.

"I'm sorry we can't stay any longer, Aim. I need to get back to Cincinnati for tonight's game."

"I understand. You'll never know how much it means to me that you came." Amy's eyes glistened.

"We love you and wouldn't be anywhere else. I guess you'll be back the end of next week?"

"I told Murph I'd make it in for the Houston series."

"I'll see you then. Keep in touch if you need anything."

They embraced each other before going to their cars.

On their drive to the airport, Frankie said, "You'll need to keep an eye on her. I think she'll be a lot like me in how she'll handle this."

"What do you mean?"

"Remember how I shut down when we found the lump in my breast?"

Lisa thought about it for a moment and agreed that Amy could react the same way. "You're right. It might not hit her until she gets back to playing ball."

"She'll need you then."

"Stacy will be there."

"But you're her best friend, Lisa. She might break down in front of you before she does her own partner."

Lisa only hoped she could be the friend Amy needed if that time arrived.

Chapter 16

Amy sat on the picnic table in the backyard and stared at the long green field that stretched out in front of her. Her parents owned seven acres, which was one of the things she'd worried about for her mother. How would she keep it up? Thelma had solved that problem by hiring the neighbor's son to mow the lawn with his riding mower.

Stacy was inside going over paperwork with Aunt Charlotte. Amy had sat with them for a while but became overwhelmed and told them she was heading outside for a few minutes. That was over an hour ago.

Birds landed on a nearby bird-feeder. Her mom loved to feed the birds. Her mom loved a lot of things about life.

Now she was gone.

Amy learned about finality when her father died. She'd never thought death would make another unwanted visit so soon.

"It's not fair."

She jumped down and trudged to the back of the property where her parents' land ended and the farmer's property behind them began. She almost stumbled over an old Frisbee and picked it up. She flipped it in her fingers a few times, bent her knees, and flung it as far as she could. It floated through the air like a slow-moving flying saucer until it landed several yards away.

"Not bad for an old lady."

Amy spun around.

"I'm sorry, sweetie. I didn't mean to startle you." Stacy cupped her hand over her eyes as she gazed up at Amy. "How are you doing?"

"I'm surviving."

"Are you sure you're ready to fly back to Cincinnati tomorrow morning? Didn't they say to take as long as you needed?"

"They did. But I have to do something other than sit around thinking about it. I never thought I'd say this, because I always figured it was bullshit whenever I heard an athlete say it, but I think she'd want me playing ball. I still remember her telling me to play the game as we were leaving the hotel room in Kansas City. I had a feeling it would be one of the last times I'd see her."

Amy looked away from Stacy toward the setting sun skirting the tree line in the distance. "How's the paperwork coming?"

"Okay. Aunt Charlotte and your mom had discussed what her wishes were. She'd told your aunt she'd put them in the will. One thing she requested was the selling of the house and for you and Aunt Charlotte to split the money."

"I don't want the money. I want her back." Amy felt like she was about to cry again.

"Are you sure you don't need a little more time? I can call—"

"No." Amy almost shouted the word and hated herself when she saw Stacy's hurt expression. "I'm sorry. I don't mean to take it out on you, but it seems like that's what I'm always doing. I just don't know—"

Stacy stopped her from saying more by placing her finger over Amy's lips.

"Remember I'm your partner," Stacy said softly as she searched Amy's face. "That's all I ask. You can talk to me."

"I'll try, Stace."

* * *

"Hey, Perry. Sorry about your mom, man."

Rawls watched while Amy lined balls around the outfield. He was the first player she'd seen since entering the stadium.

"Thanks." She grunted when she hit the next ball down the left field line and over the wall.

"How you doing?"

She didn't look up. "I'm all right."

"Hang in there," he said and left for the outfield.

Nick carried three bats to the cage and leaned them against the netting.

"You okay?" he asked while putting on his batting gloves.

She sighed and gestured to Wally. "That's enough."

"Get your ass in there, Sandy," Wally yelled at Nick.

"Well?" Nick asked as he stepped into the cage.

"I won't lie. It hurts like hell, Nick. I thought coming back to the team would help, but I'm not so sure."

"Give it some time," Nick said. He hit a long fly ball that banged around in the left field seats. "You just got back."

"We'll see."

"One thing that should help is concentrating on keeping up with the Rockies. I don't know if you noticed while you were gone, but we've dropped seven out of eight and are now three games out in the Wild Card chase."

"I noticed." She answered a little sharper than she intended.

He glanced over at her.

Amy tugged off her batting gloves and stuffed them in her back pockets. "Catch you later." She jogged to the outfield grass and dropped to the ground to loosen up. She bent one leg back, stretched the other out in front of her, and touched her hand to the toes of her cleats. She caught a whiff of the mowed grass and smiled. No matter how many times she smelled it, freshly cut grass always brought back memories of her high school days. She had a dream back then that one day, she'd be right where she was—stretching out as a member of a major league baseball team. As fast as the nostalgic memory materialized, it dissolved like a mist with the knowledge that her mom was no longer on the earth to share it with her.

Amy blinked back her tears, got to her feet, and began her wind sprints.

* * *

From her vantage point in the press box, Lisa studied Amy going through her warm-up routine in the outfield and didn't hear Sarah enter the box.

"Have you talked to her since she got back?" Sarah asked.

"No. Stacy called to let me know they were in town, but Amy hasn't talked to me yet. Stacy said not to be surprised if she doesn't call."

* * *

In the bottom of the eighth, with the Reds behind 6-3, Amy walked up to the plate with two outs and the bases loaded. She barely glanced at Servace down the third baseline for the signs. The Astros pitcher got in front in the count with two quick strikes. Amy shook her head at the last call.

The pitcher threw another fastball in Amy's wheelhouse. She

strode forward and hit a sky-high pop-up to the second baseman to end the threat. On her way down to first base, Amy slammed her helmet onto the dirt and ripped off her batting gloves.

Lisa watched her while she paced around the bag and took her glove from Rawls on his way to his position. As Amy threw grounders to the infielders, Lisa wondered about her insistence to come back so soon from bereavement leave.

The Reds lost the game, 7-3.

Lisa followed Sarah into the clubhouse. While Sarah went to talk to one of the other players, Lisa walked up to Amy who was pulling her jersey out of her uniform pants.

"Hey, Aim. How are you?"

Amy kept her back to Lisa.

Lisa moved beside her and touched her shoulder.

Amy blinked a few times before meeting Lisa's eyes. "Don't you want to ask about me letting the team down in the eighth?"

"I think you know me better than that. I was asking how you're really doing, not about the game."

Amy began unbuttoning her jersey. "I'm all right."

Lisa waited for her to say more. Amy kept undressing in silence.

"You know you can talk to me anytime, don't you?"

Amy didn't respond.

"Aim?"

"Yeah, I know."

Lisa almost said more, but Stacy's words came back to her about Amy not talking. Lisa decided to let it go.

* * *

Cincinnati's home stand was not going well. They'd lost the series to the Astros the weekend before and to the Cubs during the week. Another loss followed Friday night against the Cardinals. If they lost this Saturday night game, they'd lose the series even if they pulled out a win tomorrow afternoon.

With each day, Amy became more and more withdrawn, answering reporters' questions but with little elaboration. She hadn't reached out to Lisa despite Lisa's best efforts to get her to talk.

Amy had grounded into a double play in the first and popped out in the third to end the inning with the bases loaded. She flung her bat after she popped out. Luckily, the netting in front of the dugout prevented the bat from doing any damage.

She came to bat in the bottom of the sixth with runners on second and third and one out. Amy strode to the plate and stared down at Servace who flashed the signs. She adjusted her helmet before stepping in.

The Cardinals pitcher fired a low fastball to the plate. Amy swung and missed. He toed the rubber, checked the runners, and tossed a slow curve that the umpire thought caught the inside corner of the plate. Amy jawed at the umpire for a few seconds while kicking her cleats in the dirt.

The pitcher tried another fastball that Amy stood and watched as the umpire called it for a third strike. Amy dropped her bat at the plate. The ump held up two fingers to indicate a fine. She was in his face in an instant, never bumping him, but screaming at him.

"That was a fucking ball! It was at least six inches off the plate!"

Servace sprinted down the third baseline to get between Amy and the umpire before he tossed her, but it was too late. The umpire pointed at her and with an exaggerated motion, threw his arm in the air, signifying she was gone from the game. Murphy hurried onto the field and pushed Amy toward the dugout. At the same time, he said a few words to the umpire.

Amy shouted one more "Fuck you!" before disappearing into the tunnel.

"There's something you don't see every game," Sarah said. "Isn't that her first toss?"

"I believe so." *Damn it, Amy.*

The game ended with the Cardinals on top, 3-2.

* * *

Lisa and Sarah entered the clubhouse at the same time. Amy had her back to the reporters as she zipped up her equipment bag. From her wet hair, it looked like she'd showered. She'd already changed into her street clothes.

"Amy, isn't that the first time you've been tossed from a game, including the minors?"

She didn't answer.

"What about the pitch you popped out on in the third?"

Still no response.

"Are you feeling added stress?"

Amy whipped around and scowled at the reporter asking the question. "From what?" she barked at him.

"Well, from… from…" His face reddened.

"*Don't* say it." She shoved a finger in his face and stared him down. "Don't you *dare* say it."

"Amy, we understand if you need some time to cool off," Lisa said.

"I don't need you to fucking speak for me, Lisa," Amy snarled.

Lisa stopped herself from taking a step backwards.

Nick Sanders walked up to his locker. "That's it, everybody. If you want to talk to someone, talk to me. I struck out in the bottom of the ninth with the tying run on third. Why don't you ask me about that?"

Lisa left to talk to Murphy.

Sarah passed her in the hall. "Damn, Lisa, you don't look so hot. Everything okay?"

"I'm fine." Lisa brushed past her to enter Murphy's office. "Murphy, a minute?"

"Lisa. Have a seat. Something happen?"

"Amy."

"And it's only her first week back."

"Is there any way to talk her into taking more time off?"

He laughed harshly. "Let me get this right. You want me to call her into my office and suggest she stay away from the game. How do you think she'll react? I tried telling her that on the phone when she called last week from Kansas. She about bit my head off. And I'm the goddamn manager. Why don't you try to talk to her?"

"She just dressed me down in front of the others. I don't think she wants to listen to me, either."

"What about her partner?"

"I don't know. I can give her a call." Lisa stood up. "I need to file my article."

"Don't take it personal, Lisa. She's hurting."

"I know, Murph."

Lisa went back to the lockers, but Amy was gone.

* * *

Amy entered the apartment.

Stacy was sitting in the recliner with her legs curled up under her. She set her cell phone down on the table.

"Hey." Amy dropped her equipment bag by the door. "I think I'll take another shower. I barely took one in the clubhouse." She stopped on her trip down the hallway when she saw Stacy's expression. "What's wrong?"

"Can you sit with me for a minute?"

Amy sat down on the end of the couch next to the chair.

Stacy uncurled her legs and knelt in front of her. She placed her hands on Amy's knees.

"Lisa called."

Amy stuck out her chin. "What'd she tell you?"

"That you lost your cool on the field and with the reporters."

"For one thing, it wasn't a fucking third strike I got called out on. And as for the other shit, I was pissed because of not coming through for the team."

"And taking it out on the reporters?"

"What the hell? Can't I have a bad night? Do I always have to be 'on'?"

"Amy." Stacy moved so she was in between Amy's knees. She studied her face. "Did you come back too soon? I think maybe—"

"You think maybe what?" Amy snapped.

"Maybe you should take off at least another week. And since you haven't talked about your mother's death with me, maybe it wouldn't be such a bad idea to see someone who could help you sort out your feelings."

"First of all, I'm not taking off another week, so drop it. Second, if you mean me seeing a shrink, you can forget it. I'm fine. I lost my mom. How am I supposed to react?"

Stacy caressed Amy's face. "That's just it. You have every right to react how you need to, but you should allow yourself to feel what you need to feel. I think you're suppressing your feelings and channeling them into anger."

Amy jerked away from her touch. "Hell, Stacy, with your expert analysis, I don't think I need to see a shrink. You've got it all figured out."

Stacy's eyes instantly filled with hurt. She slowly rose to her feet and left for the bedroom.

Amy dropped her head back on the cushion. "Damn it."

When Amy got to the bedroom, Stacy was taking her nightshirt out of the dresser drawer. She didn't look at Amy as she moved toward the bathroom.

"Wait." Amy grabbed Stacy's arm.

Stacy wrenched free from her grip and glared at her before brushing past.

"Stace…"

Stacy slammed the bathroom door.

Amy rubbed her hand over her face. She silently chastised herself for her insensitivity but was at a complete loss as to how to make things better.

Chapter 17

"I fucking beat that throw, and you fucking know it!" Amy charged the first base umpire. Jeffries jumped between her and her destination.

Amy's voice easily carried up to the Turner Field press box. Lisa watched the scene unfold with her chin resting on her fist. The Atlanta Braves pitcher paced around the mound while Amy's tirade continued.

"Goddammit, what do I got to do to get a break?"

Murphy ran from the dugout and stood between Amy and the umpire. He cocked his head and listened to the umpire as Jeffries pushed Amy toward the dugout.

"Fuck you, you mother fucking asshole!" Amy shouted.

The umpire promptly tossed her from the game.

Jeffries had to restrain Amy from charging the umpire again. He pushed her into the dugout. She stalked back and forth in front of the bench. She made a move toward the tunnel but did an about-face, grabbed a bat, and took it to the Gatorade cooler. Her teammates stared straight ahead. No one tried to stop her. But Donny, the hitting coach, put his arm around her shoulder. She shrugged him off. He placed his hand on her lower back and nudged her toward the tunnel.

"I guess when you've batted .200 the past three weeks and left as many men in scoring position as she has, it was bound to happen," Sarah said while shaking her head. "Jesus, Lisa, when will this end? Will Murphy bench her? They're falling out of the race, and she's making things worse."

"I don't know. But she can't keep going on like this."

The Reds were out of the running for the divisional title but still had a chance at the Wild Card. That chance dimmed with each lost series. They trailed the current game 8-2 in the top of the eighth. If they didn't rally, that would mean they'd dropped the first two games in the three-game series to the Braves. The Rockies had opened up some daylight between the two teams by jumping five games ahead in the Wild Card race entering the first weekend of September.

Lisa recalled her most recent conversation with Stacy. She'd told Lisa that she and Amy argued almost every day. Stacy had stayed away at the start of the road trip but came in for tonight's game. Lisa looked below and watched Stacy move along the aisle of her row above the Reds dugout and head up the stairs.

The Braves won the game 10-2. Sarah and Lisa stood with the others in the clubhouse as they interviewed Sanders. Amy was at her locker, her face red and her jaw tight. She undressed in jerking motions, leaving her uniform on the floor where she threw it. She pulled her T-shirt on and stepped into her jeans.

Lisa watched. *Okay. Not taking a shower here.*

Nick glanced at Amy and returned to the reporters gathered at his locker.

Lisa waited a few seconds to approach her. "Hey, everything okay?" she asked quietly.

Amy grabbed her bag and glared at Lisa. "Why don't you ask Murphy? He benched me."

Lisa kept her voice low. "Aim, you can't keep doing this."

Amy dropped her bag and shoved Lisa against the locker. "Guess what, Lisa? You're not my mother. She's fucking dead." Again, she slammed Lisa against the wood.

The sharp edges of the locker cut into Lisa's back. She bit her lip to keep from crying out.

Amy released her, picked up her bag, and stalked out of the clubhouse.

Nick and the group of reporters stared wide-eyed at Lisa. Embarrassed, she quickly left to see Murphy. She stretched her back on the way to his office. It felt like she'd have bruises.

She found Murphy pacing.

"Goddammit!" He kicked the trashcan and stomped around some more until he noticed her. "Didn't see you there."

"She didn't take the news too well."

"No shit. She's a competitor. I give that to her. But I have to do this. She needs to get her head on straight. If that means riding the pine for a few games, that's what we'll do." He stared at her. "I hate to ask this, but have you been able to talk to her?"

"I'm not sure I'm someone she wants to see right now. We had a little altercation a few minutes ago."

"What'd she do?"

"Took out her frustration on me." Lisa waved her hand. "But I'm fine. None of it's going into my article, either." She moved from where she'd been leaning against the doorframe and winced as pain rushed down her back. "Speaking of which, I need to grab a few quotes from the guys before polishing it off."

She turned to leave.

"Lisa?"

She waited.

He didn't say anything, but she understood his expression.

"I'll try talking to her, Murph. I'm not sure what good it'll do, but I'll try."

* * *

Amy tossed her bag on the hotel bed. She didn't acknowledge Stacy sitting in the chair by the window. Instead, she undressed.

"What are you doing?" Stacy asked.

"What does it look like I'm doing? I didn't get a shower at the park. I'm taking one now."

Amy waited for the water to get hot and washed away the dirt and grime of the game. She shampooed, scrubbing her hair in anger as she thought about Lisa's interference.

"Who does she think she is?" she said aloud as she rinsed out the suds.

After toweling off, she took fresh panties and a bra from her suitcase. She didn't look up at Stacy until she'd put them on and was pulling out a fresh T-shirt and pair of black jeans.

"I'm going out, if you're wondering," Amy said. "I need a night out to cut loose. You're welcome to come."

"I'm not sure that's a smart thing to do."

"Not you, too. I've already had Lisa treat me like I'm a child." Amy sat on the edge of the bed to put on her socks.

Stacy sat down beside her. "I'm only saying I don't know if this is a good idea. You had a rough game and—"

"And what? What, Stacy?" Amy ignored Stacy's shocked expression. "I had a rough game, and Murphy's benched me for I don't know how long. I need to relax and haven't been out in months. Is it a sin to go to a club and try to have some fun?"

"I'm just worried about you, Amy."

"Well, save it. You and Lisa and Murphy—all of you—can quit treating me like I'm in grade school." Amy jumped to her feet and stood in front of the mirror to check out her appearance. She stared at Stacy's reflection. "Are you coming or not?"

Stacy folded her arms across her chest. "No. Not if I have to sit there and watch while you get drunk. Is that what you intend to do?"

"Maybe I will. Maybe I won't. If you're not coming, I guess you won't know."

"Don't expect me to be here when you get back," Stacy said evenly.

"Fine."

Amy snatched her billfold and hotel keycard from the dresser and left. The door slammed behind her.

* * *

Amy entered the women's nightclub. The throbbing beat of the dance mix vibrated through her body. She pushed through the throng as she eyed her destination. A seat emptied at the bar, and she hurried to slide onto the stool. With wallet in hand, she waited for the bartender to make her way over.

Finally, the short blonde asked for her order. "What'll it be?"

"Foster's with a glass."

The bartender returned with the beer and glass. "Six dollars."

"Kind of high, isn't it?"

"You're in the hottest lesbian bar in town. What'd you expect?" She handed Amy her change from the ten dollar bill.

"Keep it," Amy said.

"For that, we need to be on a first name basis." The bartender held out her hand. "Madeline, but everyone calls me Maddie."

She took Maddie's hand. "Amy, but everyone calls me Amy."

Maddie laughed. "I like you." She furrowed her brow. "You look familiar. I know this is lame, but have we met before?"

"No, not unless you moonlight in Cincinnati." Amy poured her beer into the glass.

"Cincinnati… Cincinnati." Maddie snapped her fingers. "That's it. You're the Reds first baseman, Amy Perry. Christ, I can't believe I didn't recognize you right away."

"Helps keep my ego in check." Amy held up her glass. "I only ask that you keep these coming. I plan on staying awhile."

"As long as you didn't drive."

"Nope. Took a taxi."

"We're okay then. Rough game?"

"You could say that."

"You can run a tab if you want."

"Perfect. Thank you."

Another patron called out a drink order to Maddie. "I'll keep my eye on you," she said before walking away.

Amy drained her beer. True to her word, Maddie replaced it with another can of Foster's when Amy set down the empty glass. She sat there and observed the women around her, wishing she hadn't been such a shit to Stacy. Unsure how many Foster's she'd gone through, her lightheadedness told her it had to be more than five.

Maddie set a blue-colored drink in a tall glass in front of her.

"The lovely lady at the end of the bar there thought you might like to switch to something else." Maddie nodded at a smiling woman with long, dark hair. "Blue Hawaii, if you're wondering."

Amy was about to refuse the drink when the woman picked up her glass and slinked toward her.

Oh, crap.

The stool beside Amy emptied in time for the woman to sit down.

"You looked like you could stand a break from that Australian stuff you've been drinking." The brunette's voice was husky with a southern drawl, her eyes dark and inviting.

"Thanks for the drink, but I—"

"But you what?" The woman held up her hand as Maddie breezed by. "A gin and tonic when you have a chance."

"I don't drink these." Amy tapped the side of the glass. "They get me in trouble every time."

"What kind of trouble? I'm Cassandra, by the way. Cassie."

"I'm Amy—"

"Perry. I know who you are. At least half the women in this bar know who you are. Probably more like two-thirds."

Maddie set the gin and tonic in front of Cassandra and took her money.

"I don't know about that," Amy said.

"Have you looked around lately?"

Amy checked out the women in the bar. Cassandra was right. Most of them were either looking Amy's way or pretending not to be by casting furtive glances.

"Cassandra…"

"Cassie."

"Cassie. I appreciate the drink, but I don't want you to get the wrong idea."

"And what idea would that be, Amy?"

"Well… uh…"

"I'm simply buying you a drink. It seemed you needed something stronger. I'm assuming it's because of tonight's game?" Cassie sipped from her straw.

Amy stared at Cassie's full lips. "You were at the game?" she managed to say. Her mouth was suddenly dry, so she took a long drink.

"No. I wasn't at the game, but I caught the last three innings here." Cassie nodded at the plasma TVs above the bar. "They broadcast the Braves games. After all, it is Atlanta, and this is a lesbian bar."

"Things haven't been so hot for me lately."

"You've struggled the past few weeks. I've kept up on your play."

"You have?"

"Amy." Cassie covered Amy's bare arm with her hand. "You do realize you're the only woman playing on a professional men's baseball team, right? And that you're a heroine, not only to female athletes but to lesbians everywhere?"

Amy tried to ignore the warmth of Cassie's fingers. "I guess. I don't think about it all that much."

Cassie withdrew her hand. Amy hated herself for missing the touch.

"It might surprise you that I'm quite the baseball fan." Cassie leaned into Amy and managed to show more cleavage.

Amy took another drink before responding. "I have a partner."

Cassie's mouth twitched into a slow smile. "Kind of knew that, too." She made a point of searching the bar. "I don't see her here, though."

"She didn't want to come with me."

Cassie stared at her a long moment before speaking. "I'm with you." Her voice dropped to an even huskier level. "And we're just talking, right? There's no harm in that."

Her dark eyes reminded Amy so much of Stacy's. "No. I guess not."

"Good. Let's talk." Cassie raised her hand at Maddie again. "I think she needs a refill."

Amy was about to object that she hadn't drunk all of the Blue

Hawaii when she noticed the glass was empty. *When did that happen?*

"Let's talk baseball." Cassie raised her glass to Amy after Maddie brought over another Blue Hawaii.

Amy barely lifted the glass to acknowledge the toast.

"Relax, Amy. We're just talking, remember?"

Amy tried to think of a reason not to be there, tried to search for a reason it was all wrong, but maybe Cassie was right. They were only talking. It wasn't like she was going home with her.

Amy smiled. "Right."

Cassie hadn't been lying. An hour had passed, and they'd talked nothing but baseball. Cassie had moved her stool closer to Amy's and inched even further into her personal space. But Amy thought it was so Cassie could hear her better. The music seemed louder than before. It pounded her eardrums. Or maybe it was her head pounding…

* * *

"I must be getting old, Collins. This shit's way too loud."

"See an open table?" Lisa scanned the bar.

Sarah moved beside her and joined in looking. "You mean to tell me this is a tolerable level?" she yelled in Lisa's ear.

"Remember. I've had some practice with the Watering Hole, although this is pretty high-tech. Frankie read about it in *Out in Atlanta* on another trip here this summer. She wanted me to check it out to see if I could get any ideas for the bar." Lisa spotted a table emptying and grabbed Sarah's arm. "Come on. You have to be fast in these places."

They hurried to the table and got to it before two younger women arrived. The women scowled at Lisa and Sarah.

"Guess old ladies have to get their rest," one of them said with a smirk.

"Young enough to beat your sorry asses to the table, though, weren't we?" Sarah yelled over the music.

One of the women said something inaudible in response before searching for another table.

Lisa sat down. "You're too much."

"I don't ever remember being that rude when I was in puberty. They were in puberty, weren't they? I can't see how they got in."

Lisa waved over the floating server. "I'll take a Mich," she said. "Sarah?"

"Whatever's cheap on tap."

"Budweiser," the server said.

"That's good."

From where they sat, they had a good view of the huge room. It was bigger than any lesbian nightspot Lisa had seen before.

"The article said this is the newest hip scene for lesbians in Atlanta," Lisa said.

Sarah shook her head. "Maybe those girls were right, because I know I'm too old to dance to that shit."

Lisa watched the couples writhing to a techno beat.

"What's that goofy expression for?" Sarah asked after their server brought the beers to the table.

"Just thinking about how special it felt to dance with Frankie for the first time." Lisa brought the bottle to her lips.

They continued to watch the women dance until Lisa remembered something she'd wanted to discuss with Sarah. "Hey, I wanted to get your thoughts about writing columns to denounce these demonstrations against Amy, especially the one outside her mother's funeral."

"That sounds like an excellent idea."

They talked about what they'd say in their columns. After the waitress dropped off two more beers, Sarah changed the subject.

"Did you know Murphy benched Amy?"

"Yes."

"Was that why she was so upset?" Sarah asked. "How's your back by the way? She slammed you pretty hard into that locker."

"I'm all right," Lisa lied. She was still physically sore, but even more than that, she was hurt by Amy's actions. And now Murphy wanted Lisa to try to talk to her.

"Isn't that Amy over there?"

"Where?" Lisa whipped her head around.

"Sitting next to the dark-haired chick. Is that Stacy? It kind of looks like her from behind, but isn't Stacy's hair shorter than that?"

Lisa saw Amy slumped over the bar. "Shit."

The brunette had her hand draped over Amy's thigh and was running her fingers back and forth along the inseam of her jeans.

"No, that's not Stacy." *What are you doing, Amy?*

"Okay." Sarah drew out the word. "If that's not Stacy, is that her?" Sarah stared at Stacy standing at the entrance.

"Oh, fuck." *Please don't look at the bar. Please don't look at the bar.*

Lisa rose to her feet and pushed through the throng in her rush to get to the door. She was almost there when Stacy's gaze stopped on the middle of the bar, and she swayed slightly. Lisa hurried the remaining distance to reach her.

"Stacy."

Stacy's eyes were full of tears when she turned to Lisa.

"I went to a couple of bars before coming here. I was worried about her." Stacy's voice broke. "I wanted to make sure she was safe. She's been so messed up lately, and I…" She covered her mouth with her hand and bolted for the door.

Lisa ran outside after her. "Stacy. Stacy, wait."

Stacy slowed to a stop.

"She's hurting, and I'm pretty sure she's drunk," Lisa said. "I doubt she even knows what's going on."

"If Amy doesn't, the woman sitting with her knows exactly what she's doing." Stacy swiped at her wet cheeks.

"I'll go get Sarah to help me. Why don't you go back to the hotel room, and we'll bring her there."

"Oh, I'm going back to the hotel all right, but don't expect me to be there when you bring her back." Stacy walked quickly to the curb, raised her hand, and shouted for a taxi.

"She loves you, Stacy," Lisa said as she followed her.

A taxi braked with a slight squeal. Stacy opened the back door and slid into the backseat. She looked up at Lisa with tears streaming down her cheeks. "She has a funny way of showing it. I can't take watching this anymore, Lisa. I'm going home." She slammed the door shut, and the taxi drove away.

Lisa stared at the taillights until they were out of sight.

When she returned to the bar, Sarah was standing by the door.

"I think we need to pry Ms. Short, Dark, and Up-to-No-Good off of Amy," Sarah said.

As they drew nearer, Lisa overheard the brunette say, "Why don't we leave, Amy?"

Lisa moved between them. "What a great idea. Only she's not going with you."

The woman slowly lifted her hand from Amy's thigh.

Amy blinked a few times as if to focus in on Lisa's face. "Lisa? Hey." Her words slurred.

"Come on. We're taking you to the hotel." She put her hand on Amy's shoulder.

"No. I'm fine here with Cassie. We were just talking baseball.

Weren't we?" Amy cast a sloppy grin Cassie's way.

Cassie picked up her drink and attempted to move around Lisa and Sarah. "Excuse me."

Sarah glowered at her before stepping aside.

They got on either side of Amy and each hooked a hand under one of her arms.

"Come on, Aim." Lisa nodded to Sarah. They pulled Amy to her feet at the same time.

Amy looked around in confusion. "Where'd Cassie go?"

"She left," Lisa said. "Let's get you to the hotel."

The bartender picked up the glasses and wiped down the bar.

"Does she owe you anything?" Lisa asked her.

"No. Her friend there paid for everything after the Foster's."

"Did you ever think to stop serving her?"

"I did cut her off, but that chick must've gotten drinks from one of the other servers. I didn't see it, so I couldn't do anything."

Lisa let the matter drop as she and Sarah led Amy toward the door.

Amy suddenly stopped. "I wish Stacy were here. I made her mad, Lisa. I made Stacy mad. Why did I make her mad?" Her face twisted in pain as she slumped in their arms. "Oh, God, I feel sick."

"Let's keep going." Lisa urged her forward.

They picked up their pace in leading her to the exit. When they walked outside, Amy craned her neck to stare up at the sky. Then she paled. "I think I'm gonna puke."

They hurried her to an alley between the buildings. Amy bent over and vomited. After two more heaves, she rose and wiped her mouth with the back of her hand. They waited to see if the nausea had passed.

"Can you make it in a cab?" Lisa asked.

Amy didn't answer.

"Amy?" Lisa said a little louder.

"Yeah," Amy shouted in response and then held her head with a grimace. "Ow."

At the curb, Sarah waved down a taxi and got into the backseat first.

Lisa gently pushed Amy in between them. "The Omni," she told the driver.

Amy leaned her head against Lisa's shoulder and passed out on the way to the hotel.

After arriving at the Omni, Lisa paid the cab driver. They roused

Amy enough to pull her out of the taxi. They tried to appear casual as they led her through the automatic door.

"Do you have your keycard?" Lisa asked her. "And what's your room number?"

Amy fumbled with her back pocket and handed her wallet to Lisa. Lisa opened it and found the keycard in with Amy's credit cards.

"Amy? Your room number?"

"It's 1407, I think."

They struggled to the elevator, still holding Amy upright on the ascent to the fourteenth floor. At Amy's room, Lisa slid the card into the door slot and flipped on the light. They guided her to the bed and eased her onto the mattress.

"Where's Stacy?" Amy asked. Her eyes, which seemed more in focus, held only sadness now.

Lisa glanced over at the luggage and saw just the one bag. "Let's worry about getting you to bed, huh?" She knelt down and unlaced Amy's sneakers.

"I think I'll leave now, Lisa," Sarah said.

Lisa peered up at her. "Thanks for everything, Sarah."

"Give me a call later to let me know how she's doing."

Sarah left the room while Lisa eased off Amy's shoes.

"Lie back," Lisa said. Amy did as told. "I'm getting you out of your clothes." There was still no response, but she didn't expect one.

Lisa disrobed Amy of everything but her panties and bra and pulled the covers over her. Amy was already snoring when Lisa flipped off the bedside lamp.

Lisa walked over to the chair by the window. She saw an envelope propped against the lamp on the table. It was addressed to her. She opened it, pulled out a folded sheet, and read:

"Call me tomorrow and let me know how she's doing. Tell her I love her, but I need some time alone. Be her friend, Lisa. She needs someone now, and I don't think it's me. —Stacy"

Lisa switched off the other light and sat in the dark. She watched Amy sleep before drifting off herself.

Chapter 18

Amy awakened to a jackhammer drilling through her skull—at least that's what it felt like. She moaned and opened her eyes. Which was a mistake. Pain pierced every neuron in her brain.

"Fuck." She tried to sit up but immediately regretted the motion and lay back down. She heard someone beside the bed and attempted to focus on the face. "Stacy?"

"No. It's Lisa. I'm not even going to ask how you're feeling."

Amy eased up farther in the bed and held her head in her hands. Then the nausea hit. She flipped back the covers and shoved Lisa aside in her dash toward the bathroom. She made it to the commode just in time. Everything she threw up was liquid, but it didn't make her feel any better. She gagged some more and waited for the last wave to hit. Amy slowly straightened, went to the sink, and rinsed out her mouth.

After splashing water on her face, she looked in the mirror and saw Lisa standing in the doorway.

"Need me to get you some ibuprofen or aspirin?" Lisa asked.

"Stacy usually has that stuff. She must've gone downstairs for some breakfast." Lisa's expression changed. "What is it?"

"Why don't you sit down?"

Amy followed her and sat at the foot of the bed while Lisa sat in the chair.

"Where's Stacy?"

"What do you remember about last night, Amy?"

Amy thought back. She left the hotel room angry. It seemed that's all she was lately—angry. She went to the club and had some Foster's. Another woman's face floated into her mind. Then panic set in.

"Oh, God." She jumped to her feet and regretted the action as all of the blood rushed to her head. She swallowed down the nausea that threatened to make an encore appearance. "Oh, God," she repeated, while pacing.

She tried to remember other things. Blue Hawaii's. I never drink that crap, she thought. How many did I have? More came back to her. The woman had dark eyes that reminded her of Stacy's.

Amy looked up at Lisa. "Tell me I didn't do anything. Tell me you didn't find me doing something with that woman." Her stomach fell when she saw Lisa's expression. "God, Lisa, I didn't… didn't…" She felt faint and sank back down onto the mattress.

"You were drunk when Sarah and I found you. The woman was draped all over you and was rubbing her hand along the inside of your thigh, but I don't think anything else happened. When we came to get you, she was talking about taking you out of there."

Amy relaxed. "Thank God. Thank God you guys showed up. I can't remember that much, but I'd never forgive myself if I'd done something." Lisa's expression hadn't changed. "Why are you still looking at me like that?"

Lisa leaned forward and took Amy's hand. "Stacy saw you with the woman."

It felt like someone had sucked all the oxygen out of the room. "How did Stacy see me?" she whispered.

"She went searching for you because she was worried."

Amy noticed that only one suitcase remained by the closet.

"Please don't tell me she went home." She turned back to Lisa. "Please."

"She left me this note." Lisa handed it to her.

Amy read it and then read it again. "No," she sobbed. "What have I done?"

"Listen to me. You need help, Aim. You need to see someone. I can talk to you. I can tell you how I was after my mom died. I was about in the shape you are now. I was alone. I still don't know if my dad's alive or dead. He's never been a part of my life. My mom was an only child. I don't have any aunts or uncles, and my grandparents died several years ago. So, when my mom died, I knew I had no one else."

Lisa stared at her intently before continuing. "But when I drank myself to sleep for a full month after her death, a good friend sat me down and talked to me. Like I'm talking to you now. She suggested therapy. I resisted at first, but I knew I had to do something. I finally gave in and saw a grief counselor. You need to do this, Amy. For Stacy, yes, but more importantly, for you. If you keep running from your grief, you'll push everyone away until you're all alone."

Amy sobbed even more. "But it's too late for Stacy and me."

Lisa sat down beside her. "I don't believe that for a minute. You've pushed her away, but it doesn't mean she's not coming back. She loves you. She said so in that note. You have to take this step on your own. Then you have to focus on your relationship. If she sees you're getting help, it'll change things. Trust me."

Amy sniffed. "Think so?"

"You can bet on it. You two are meant for each other."

"We are, aren't we?"

"Absolutely. I suggest you see Murphy before the game this afternoon. Get to the ballpark early. Meet him in his office and ask him about the counselors the Reds use. While the team continues on this road trip to Miami, you go home."

"I'm sure it'd be a guy, considering all my teammates are men," Amy said. "This is going to be hard enough as it is. Do you think I could get a referral to a woman? I know I'd be more comfortable."

"Probably. You won't know until you ask."

"I hate that I can't be with the team. But I know you're right. I'm not much help to them in the shape I'm in." Amy struggled with her next words. "I'm sorry I shoved you last night in the clubhouse." She shut her eyes, trying to block out what she'd done. "There's no excuse. You're the best friend I have. There aren't too many friends who'd still be talking to me after what I did to you."

"You can't get rid of me, remember?" Lisa bumped shoulders with her. "I told you I'd stick with you through everything, and I meant it."

"Should I call Stacy?"

"Probably not. I'll call her today like she asked. I'll let her know what's going on. Give her some time. I have a feeling you're about to take another leave of absence from the team. Take as long as you need. Then you talk to her." Lisa stood up. "I need to get to my room and take a shower." She checked her watch. "I'm supposed to be at the ballpark in a couple of hours. I'm sure you want to get washed up, too."

Amy rose to her feet and hugged Lisa. "I don't know where I'd be without you."

"We don't have to worry about that now, do we?"

* * *

Amy tapped her sneaker in cadence with the ticking of the wall clock in the waiting area. It was almost time for the therapist to call her back into her office.

The door swung open. A short woman with close-cropped dark hair graying at the temples greeted her with a smile. Dressed in jeans and a green polo, she reminded Amy of a middle-aged leprechaun. Her appearance screamed "family."

"Amy?"

"Yes, ma'am."

"Hi, I'm Kelly O'Brien." She extended her hand to Amy as she entered the room. Amy felt like a giant towering over her. The woman couldn't be more than five-foot tall. And after hearing her name, Amy had to suppress a grin. *Maybe she is a leprechaun.*

The room wasn't anything like what Amy expected of a therapist's office. Two windows offered a stunning view of the Ohio River. Early morning sunlight streamed into the room through the lightly tinted glass. A long, comfortable-looking maroon couch lined the wall to Amy's right and faced the two windows. Two dark green chairs angled toward the couch, one at either end. A wooden coffee table sat between the chairs and couch. The carpet was thick and springy under Amy's sneakers. A coffeemaker bubbled in the corner of the room.

"Take a seat," Kelly told her. "Wherever you feel comfortable. Would you like some coffee?"

"No, thank you." Amy debated about where to sit, wondering whether it was some sort of test.

"Water?"

"Yes, please, if you have it."

"I do. Bottled." Kelly went to a small refrigerator, took out a bottle, and brought it to Amy.

"Thank you." Amy still hesitated about the seating arrangements. She watched as Kelly poured a cup of coffee with her back to Amy.

"It isn't a test as to where you sit, Amy," Kelly said over her shoulder.

Amy laughed nervously and sat down on the couch.

Kelly carried her coffee to the chair facing Amy, settled into it, and held the mug in her hand while observing Amy. "Why do you think you need to be here?"

Nothing like getting right down to it, Amy thought.

"I've been pretty messed up since my mom died a little over a month ago. I haven't handled it well. I thought I could do this on my own, but I guess I was wrong." She thought about Stacy. Amy hadn't talked to her since she'd gotten into town on Sunday. She'd arrived at the apartment to find Stacy gone, and apparently for a while, since she'd taken some clothes with her. Amy remembered the overwhelming relief she felt upon discovering that Stacy hadn't taken all of her belongings.

"Tell me about how you've been feeling."

"Helpless, angry. And I feel alone, especially now."

"Why is that?"

"I did something stupid and drove my partner away." Amy stared at her hands. She waited for Kelly to ask her what it was she'd done to make Stacy leave, but no question came. She raised her head. Kelly still observed her as she took a sip of coffee. "I went to a bar, got drunk, and let this woman buy more drinks for me. She was hitting on me, I guess." Amy stopped. "Ah, hell, there's no guessing about it. She was hitting on me, and I told myself nothing was happening. 'We're just talking,' she kept saying. But I knew better."

Kelly rotated the mug in her hand. It was then Amy noticed the writing, "World's #1 Therapist," on the side.

"Where do people find those?" She gestured to the mug.

"My partner found it online." Kelly set the mug down on the table between them and picked up a legal pad and pen. She waited for Amy to continue.

Amy shifted on the couch. "I was already drunk when the woman sat down next to me. I was attracted to her. She reminded me of Stacy, and I missed Stacy not being there. I was in a horrible mood after finding out Murphy was benching me. When Stacy didn't come with me to the bar, I was even angrier. This woman was easy to talk to. It was the most relaxed I'd felt in so long. But it was wrong. Deep down, I knew it was wrong. Then I proceeded to get even more plastered. God, I'm such a shit." Amy pounded the arm of the couch with her fist.

Kelly stopped scribbling notes and looked up. "You said something interesting there. Do you know what it is?"

Amy wanted to say, "Isn't that your job to tell me?" Instead, she said, "No."

"You said this woman was easy to talk to. Why was that?"

"Well, for one thing, I think she was good at what she did. She wanted to pick me up or for me to pick her up."

"Why else?"

Amy tried to think of any other reason. "I'm not sure."

"Did she know you, Amy? I mean other than the fact you're the starting first baseman for the Cincinnati Reds."

"No. In fact, we talked baseball mostly. It's like she knew that was the safe topic to get me to relax."

"And how has it been talking with Stacy?"

Amy heard her heart throbbing in her eardrums. "It's been hard. I've lashed out at her when all she's been trying to do is help."

"Have you been able to show her your grief?"

Amy choked up. "I can't. I'm a strong person. Strong." She repeated the word with a little more conviction. "I've always been that way. And I've had to be even stronger struggling with making it in the majors." She thought back to a time several years ago. "Even when my dad died, I didn't break down that much. I wanted to be there for my mom, to let her know she could count on me."

"Amy, it's okay to cry. It doesn't mean you're weak. It means you're human."

"I did cry. Stacy held me at the hospital and then later."

"But have you been able to talk to her about your feelings and your fears?"

"I don't think I have any fears."

Kelly tapped the legal pad with her pen and stared at her, as if waiting for her to say more.

"I don't," Amy said defensively.

"We'll let that go."

The unspoken "for now" lingered in the air.

"Why don't we talk about your mom and what she meant to you?"

Amy struggled to fight the tears but lost the battle.

"Take your time," Kelly said gently.

* * *

Lisa unlocked the front door of the house. Frankie's truck wasn't in the driveway, so she knew she'd find the house empty. Frankie had been in Indianapolis for a few days, checking on inventory and going over payroll—things she couldn't do from Cincinnati. With the Reds having an off-day on Thursday after the first leg of their road trip, Lisa had flown into Indianapolis for the day and night. She'd made her own arrangements to fly to Chicago tomorrow for the last four games of the ten-game road trip that would end Monday afternoon.

Lisa took her bag to the bedroom and left for the bar.

She entered the Watering Hole and saw Stacy behind the bar. Lisa wanted to talk to her but wasn't sure this was the time or place.

"Hey, Lisa. How are you?" Stacy asked with a sad smile.

"I'm good." Lisa looked around. "You alone this afternoon?"

"For the next thirty minutes or so until Billie gets in."

"I need to let Frankie know I'm here. But after that, do you maybe want to go somewhere to talk?"

"I'd like that."

"I'll be out in a few minutes."

Stacy's somber expression stayed with Lisa as she tapped on Frankie's door. She poked her head inside.

"Feel like a break?"

Frankie checked her watch. "Wow. You made good time. You weren't doing eighty on I-74 again, were you?"

Lisa splayed her hand across her chest. "Moi?"

"Right. I forgot. You never speed."

"Have I ever gotten a ticket, unlike someone else I know?" Lisa planted a quick kiss on Frankie's lips before sitting down in front of the desk.

"I think you're tempting the speeding Fates with that comment, which isn't a smart thing to do. They're very unforgiving." Frankie shuffled through some paperwork and glanced up again. "Why the sad face?"

Lisa tilted her head toward the door.

Frankie sat back in her chair. "According to Billie, she's been very quiet since she came back. She's been staying at Billie's house all along. Been quiet with me as well."

"I asked if she wanted to go somewhere to talk. She said Billie would be in to work soon, and then we could go."

"What are you going to tell her?"

"I'm not sure. I want her to know she's my friend. That hasn't changed."

"She didn't say much when you called her from Atlanta?"

"No. She asked how Amy was and to tell her to give her some time before Amy tries to contact her."

"Speaking of Amy, has she made an appointment yet with a therapist?"

"She had her first appointment earlier this week, I believe. I thought she might call me, but maybe she's trying to process stuff."

"You told me how drained you were the first few

times you saw the grief counselor."

"I felt like someone had thrown me into a heavy-duty dryer and put it on high heat."

"It got better for you, and I'm sure Amy will get there soon enough. Any idea how long she'll be out?"

"I'm thinking at least a week, probably more. The Reds need her, but this is more important."

"Which is why they referred her to this therapist."

"I only wish I could help her more than I have."

"Lisa, you've helped her more than you realize. She never would've taken this step if it weren't for you. I think she would've gone in the opposite direction and buried her feelings even more if you hadn't talked to her in Atlanta."

"I guess." Lisa still felt like she should do something. Anything to take away Amy's and Stacy's pain and to see them back together. She stared down at her feet and didn't see the object flying toward her until it struck her forehead.

"What was that for?" She bent down and grabbed the wadded up piece of paper from the floor.

"For taking on stuff you have no control over," Frankie said. "You're a good friend. That's all you can be right now. Let this therapist try to get through to Amy. She'll talk when she's ready. Just be prepared that it might not be as quickly as what you'd like."

"You're right." Lisa thought of something else. "Can I ask your opinion on something?"

"Always."

"One thing I thought I could do to help Amy relieve a little of the pressure is to get her hitting straightened out. I think she could use some advice from Marge Tompkins, but I don't want to upset Amy by calling her old coach."

"That shouldn't upset her, Leese. It shows you care. Do you know how to get in touch with Marge?"

Lisa patted her cell phone on her hip. "I have her number stored from that mess last year with the steroids allegations."

"Then my opinion is to call her."

"Okay, thanks. That's what I'll do. I'll give Max a heads-up, too. He can set up a time at Great American for the workout. But only when Amy's ready."

Frankie motioned to the stack of papers on her desk. "I'm sorry, but..."

"Don't apologize. I'll see if Billie's made it in yet. Do you need anything while I'm out? Or should I just plan to see you later at home?"

Frankie checked her watch. "I'll be home by six. We can go out for dinner if you like."

"Give your eyes a rest every now and then."

"I'll try. Good luck with Stacy."

* * *

"Is this okay?" Lisa asked as they approached a picnic table in the park. She'd suggested going out for a sandwich, but Stacy said she wanted some fresh air. The trees surrounding the grassy area exhibited the onset of the inevitable march of autumn colors.

"This is fine."

Lisa sat on a bench facing Stacy. She watched as Stacy gazed up at the sunlight that filtered through the branches, cutting bright, splotchy patterns onto the picnic table.

"I never thought I'd be in this situation. Never in a million years," Stacy said. "Our relationship was perfect. We never raised our voices. We made a pact early when it was plain it was getting serious between us that we'd always communicate with each other and never try to shut the other one out. And that's what we did until her mom died. Then it was like she was alone, like I wasn't there." She wiped away a tear. "Like I was invisible," she finished saying in a whisper.

Lisa put her hand on top of Stacy's.

"She was lost there for a while, Stacy, but I think she's making the effort to come back. I talked to her about my mother's death and how I dealt with it." Lisa told Stacy about her conversation with Amy about her own isolation. "Seeing the therapist was a godsend for me. The fact that Amy's seeing a grief counselor is a positive step. She needs to work through her issues, and then she needs to talk to you."

"Finding her with the woman at the bar…" Stacy stopped.

Lisa held Stacy's hand a little tighter.

"It was like she'd ripped my heart from my chest. It hurt. It really, really hurt." Stacy began crying harder.

Lisa walked around the table and sat beside her. She placed her arm around Stacy's shoulders. "She was so lost that next morning when she realized what she'd done. It tore her up, Stacy. She knows how wrong she was. She's giving you the time you need right now, just like she needs this time to get her head on straight."

"But what about her heart?"

Lisa fought back tears hearing the anguish in Stacy's plea.

"Her heart's with you."

"Is it? Is it really?"

"I'll tell you what I told her when she was afraid she'd lost you. You two are meant to be together."

"Can you tell her I'm thinking about her? That I haven't stopped thinking about her? And now I'm ready to talk whenever she's ready?"

"I'll tell her."

* * *

Amy perused the *This Is Cincinnati* magazine for a second time while waiting for Kelly to call her to her office. She couldn't believe this was the second week of sessions. Each visit had left her feeling drained.

The door opened. "Amy?" Kelly motioned toward her.

Amy took her customary seat while Kelly went through the same routine as the other visits. She brought over her mug of coffee and, without asking, handed Amy a bottle of water.

Kelly sat back in her chair. "Why don't we pick up where we left off from our last session? I believe I asked you again about your fears."

Amy stiffened. "And I believe my response was I didn't have any."

"This is where we disagree."

Amy squeezed the plastic bottle a little tighter. "I think I'm a better judge of this than you."

"You've said some things in our sessions that I'm not sure registered with you. You may not have come out and said everything I suspect you're feeling, but you've said enough to make me think you have one big fear you haven't faced."

Amy was about to object again, but her curiosity got the best of her. "Then tell me. What is it?"

"You're afraid of being alone. Of everyone leaving you."

"Oh, come on, Kelly. The stupid crap I've pulled has shown the opposite of that. Why did I push Stacy away if I was afraid of being alone?"

"It's called self-fulfilling prophecy. Because you fear it, you unconsciously make it happen."

"That's bullshit."

Kelly didn't seem to mind the outburst. "Who has left you in your life?"

Stunned, Amy sank back into the cushion of the couch. *What the hell?*

"Think about it."

Amy did just that as she remembered her former lover, Carly, who'd left her because Amy was so closeted. Amy had maintained her distance until Carly couldn't take it anymore. Her father, who had taught her the love of the game and how to hit and field—he was gone. Her brief romantic relationship with Lisa. That had hurt. And now her mom.

"I guess you might be right."

"You've told me about these people in our sessions. I'm not sure you were aware you were revealing as much as you did." Kelly smiled slightly. "Which means I'm doing my job."

"So I was pushing Stacy away?"

"Yes, I believe you were. You weren't consciously doing it, but you cut her off from your feelings. Like I told you before, it's natural to grieve and to cry. And it's natural and healthy to do these things with the woman you love and trust the most. She won't leave you if you show yourself to her. She won't think of you as weak."

"I hurt her, though."

"You're getting the help you need by coming to therapy. From what you've told me about Stacy, she loves you very much, and she'll be ready when you want to talk. You have some mending to do, yes. But you'll do it."

They talked more about how Amy was feeling and whether she was ready to return to baseball.

"I think you're ready," Kelly said. "But you have to agree. How would you feel about keeping a weekly appointment with me? Not indefinitely, but until we both feel you've worked through everything."

Amy hesitated.

"Amy, you've gotten to the core of your issues in these sessions, but you still have a lot of work to do."

Amy never thought she'd agree to see a therapist on a regular basis, but she said, "Okay."

"Good. I'll report to the Reds management that you're ready to return, but I'm going to ask you to trust me on this next one. Why don't you give yourself the weekend and come back Monday on Cincinnati's road trip to Milwaukee?"

Waiting disappointed her. The Reds had been playing well in her absence, and she was itching to get back into action. But she realized Kelly would never ask her to do anything that wasn't in Amy's best interest. "Monday's good."

"Let's schedule your next appointment." Kelly stepped over to her desk and opened her laptop. "How about next Thursday? Same time in the morning? You'll be back in town next week after your series with the Brewers."

"Next Thursday's fine."

Kelly handed her the appointment card and led her to the door.

"Thank you for everything, Kelly."

"No need to thank me." Kelly reached up and clasped Amy's shoulder, surprising Amy with her strength. "Why don't you give Stacy a call this weekend?"

Amy's stomach fluttered at the possibility. Even though Lisa had told her Stacy was ready to talk when Amy was ready, the thought of making that phone call scared the hell out of her. "I will."

"Now get back to what you love to do."

Chapter 19

The shrill ringing of the phone jarred Amy from her sleep. She tried to focus on the numbers of the digital bedside clock: 6:38. In the morning. On a Saturday. She fumbled for the portable.

"Hello?" She didn't try to hide her irritation.

"Is this Amy?" The gravely voice sounded familiar.

"Who is this, and why are you calling so early?"

"It's Marge Tompkins, sweetheart. And good morning to you, too."

Amy threw the covers back, swung her legs to the side of the bed, and sat up. Her old Bandits manager tended to have that effect on her.

"I'm sorry, Coach Tompkins, I didn't realize—"

"Hell, Amy, don't apologize. I'm calling to ask you a favor. I'm in town this morning on my way to Marietta, Ohio, to scout someone for our team. I'd like to see you, if I could."

"Sure. Can you give me a few minutes to take a shower? Where'd you like to meet?"

"I'm sitting in my car in front of Great American. Why don't you drive down?"

"Okay." Amy wondered what was up but didn't question Marge any further.

"You're not far from the stadium, right?" Marge asked.

"No. I can be there within the hour."

"I'm parked by the main gate."

"Be careful, Coach. They tow cars from there."

"Don't worry. I have an arrangement."

Amy was even more intrigued. "I'll see you in a little while."

* * *

Amy parked her Mazda next to the curb behind the lone car in front of the stadium. She missed the SUV, but she missed the woman driving the SUV even more.

She approached the dark sedan and tapped on the driver's window, startling Marge who was reading the *Cincinnati Enquirer* sports page.

Marge got out of the car. "Give your old coach a hug."

Surprised, Amy bent down and returned the embrace. The only other time she'd received this kind of physical affection before from Marge was at her mother's funeral.

"Wondering why I'm here, aren't you?"

"Kind of, but it's good to see you."

"You might not think that in a few minutes." Marge, dressed in a maroon Kansas City Bandits sweat suit, started for the gated entrance to the ballpark.

"Uh, I don't think we'll be able to enter the park yet." Amy hurried to keep up with her. "The earliest they've allowed me in for batting practice is ten."

"We'll see."

They walked to the gate. Shirley, the security guard who'd winked at her that first game back and quite a few other times, stood nearby.

"Shirley," Amy said. "What are you—"

"No time for questions," Marge said. "We need to get going. I only have an hour before I have to hit the road again."

Shirley once again winked at Amy before unlocking the gate. "Good to see you again, Amy."

"Good to be here." *I think.*

Marge continued toward the back entrance of the clubhouse as if she'd been there a million times before. Another guard finished talking on his two-way radio before opening the door.

"You must be Coach Tompkins."

"That's right. You know who this is, of course." Marge jabbed her thumb at Amy.

"Sure do."

Amy had a lot of questions but was afraid to ask.

"If you're wondering what's going on, Lisa Collins called me," Marge said over her shoulder as they headed down the long hallway. "She explained you'd taken another leave." They stopped outside the clubhouse entrance. "I was thinking that was a good thing." Her tone had softened. "You needed time away from the game, time you didn't allow yourself before."

"I know."

They entered the clubhouse, and Marge motioned toward the lockers. "You're already in sweats, but why don't you change into your cleats."

Amy gathered the courage to ask what they were doing. "Are we heading out on the field?"

"That's generally what you need cleats for." Marge looked at her in bemusement.

Amy changed from her sneakers.

"Grab a pair of batting gloves and a couple of your favorite bats there. Lisa also told me she thought you needed some work on your hitting. Which is exactly what we're going to do."

They walked out from under the covering of the dugout. Amy stared at the sight before her. The batting cage had been set up, and Wally stood out on the mound behind the protective fencing. He tossed a baseball a few times in the air and nodded her way. Max Murphy stood beside the cage.

"Come on, Amy. I told you I don't have all day."

"Right. Sorry."

"Good to see you again," Max said as Amy stopped in front of him.

"Hey, skip."

"How you doing?"

"Better, thanks."

Marge leaned against the cage next to Murphy. "Why don't you stretch out a little while Max and I chat?"

Amy dropped her bats and gloves beside her and went through her usual stretches. She heard the low burr of the conversation between Marge and Murphy but didn't try to make out the words. She stood up, went over to the pine tar rag, and rubbed it along the handle of the bat.

"Get those gloves on, and let's see what we've got," Marge said.

Amy picked up the batting helmet someone had left for her and scrunched it into place. After tugging her batting gloves on, she walked up to the plate.

"I'm gonna feed you nice fat fastballs for as long as you need them," Wally shouted at her. He threw the first pitch.

Amy lunged forward and hit a high infield pop-up. She waited for the next pitch and again popped the ball up.

"Hang on, hang on." Marge waved Wally off. "You're dropping your back shoulder like you used to on the Bandits when you tried to do too much." Marge grabbed Amy and positioned her in the batter's box. She tapped on Amy's right shoulder. "Keep this shoulder up." She got out of the way and motioned to Wally on the mound.

He lobbed in another fastball. Amy popped it along the first baseline.

"You're not listening to me, Amy. Not only are you dropping your right shoulder, you're striding into the ball way too early. But let's go at this one problem at a time. Let's fix this shoulder thing first." Marge tapped her right shoulder again. "Remember Joe Morgan? How he used to flap his back arm? It was a reminder for him to keep that shoulder in place. If you need to try it, try it. You don't have to do it forever, but at least until you get your timing back. What is it I always stressed while you were with the Bandits?"

"Timing is everything."

"That's right. Now, try again."

As Amy waited for the pitch, she tried to flap the arm slightly. It wasn't as pronounced as Morgan's action, but it was still something she'd never attempted before. She hit the next pitch on a line between second and first.

"Good. Keep that up for a few."

Wally pitched her fastballs, and Amy lined them to all parts of the field, depending on where the ball crossed over the plate.

"Stop," Marge barked.

Amy wiped the sweat from her eyes and waited for Marge's next instruction.

"Let's get that footwork going. Remember, this is where your power comes from. It's your balance." Marge grabbed the bat and marked a line in the dirt at the front of the batter's box. "Try getting that left foot here but no farther." She handed the bat to Amy and moved behind her.

Amy hit the next five pitches into deep left field.

"Keep it going, Amy. Try to shut out all the noise in your head and concentrate on the ball. Watch for the stitches. Make it all that you see."

Amy settled into a rhythm, spraying the ball to different parts of the park. She'd hit about twenty more pitches before she realized she wasn't even flapping her back arm anymore. She wasn't thinking about where her left foot landed. She was enjoying the simple thrill of hitting a baseball.

Amy squinted through the sweat stinging her eyes and hit the next pitch into the left field seats. And the next one. The one after that bounced against the fence.

"Take a breather, Perry," Murphy said from behind her.

She took off her helmet and wiped the sweat away with her forearm.

Wally yelled at her from the mound. "There's a towel beside the cage, you goofy rookie."

Amy snatched it up and wiped down her face. She glanced over to see Marge grinning at her.

"Feeling better?" Marge asked.

"A lot. I'm more relaxed. It feels natural again, like I'm not even thinking about it."

"That's the Amy Perry I remember coaching. Well, I need to get on the road."

Amy held out her hand. "Thanks for everything, Coach."

"Anytime. I'll be watching your games, so don't let up."

"I won't."

"And I'll see that she doesn't," Murphy said. He shook Marge's hand. "I'm glad Lisa suggested this and that you were able to make it."

"Anything to help one of my former players."

If Amy didn't know any better, she'd swear Marge had tears in her eyes.

Marge cleared her throat. "Time to go. Take care and keep in touch, Amy." She turned, descended the dugout steps, and disappeared into the tunnel.

"Why don't we go to my office?" Murphy asked.

Amy took off her gloves and wiped her face again as she followed Murphy toward the dugout. Once they entered the clubhouse, she grabbed an iced bottle of water from a nearby cooler before taking a seat in front of his desk.

"This is where I ask you to be honest with me and tell me how you're feeling, because if you're not honest, I can't help you." He gave her a pointed look.

"I'm better, like I told you out on the field. My therapist has helped so much."

"She called Dan Taylor with the go-ahead for you to return to play, but I don't want to see you until Monday morning when we take the bus to the airport." He picked up a baseball lying on his desk and rubbed it in his hands. "I'm sure you're aware of where we are in the Wild Card standings. We still have a shot at this thing. There are two weeks left in the season, and after this last road trip of the season, the schedule's finally in our favor. We made up a couple of games this last week and have moved to within two-and-a-half of the Rockies. But we need your bat and defense. Hell, we need *you*."

"You got me, skip." Amy waited for the words she wanted to hear.

"Yes, you'll be starting again, so wipe that worried look off your face."

She grinned. "I won't let you down, and I won't let the team down."

"Do your job. It's all we ask. Get some rest, and we'll see you Monday."

Chapter 20

Amy stared at the portable phone as if it were a snake that would strike if she tried picking it up. She wiped her sweaty palms on her jeans.

She'd returned to the apartment after her early morning batting work-out and a long run in the park. On her run, she'd gone over in her head what she wanted to say to Stacy. Even though Lisa had told her Stacy was ready to talk, it didn't make it any easier or less nerve-wracking.

Amy grabbed the phone from the charger and paced the living room. *What do I say to her? I know I'll apologize, but what else? I'm more nervous now than I was on our first date.*

She stopped pacing and opened the sliding glass door to the balcony. The late afternoon sun shone on the river below but failed to warm the cold fear inside her chest. Without another thought, she punched in the number. Amy held her breath as the call went to four rings.

"Hello?"

Stacy's voice was tentative and shaky. Amy longed to reach through the phone and take her in her arms.

"Stace. Hi."

"Hi, Amy."

There was a long pause. Amy said a quick prayer before continuing.

"I'm sorry. God, I'm so, so sorry." She sat down in the lounge chair, afraid of what she'd hear next.

There was silence.

Amy was about to say more when Stacy spoke.

"It hurt, Amy," Stacy said and sniffed.

She's crying. It was as if someone had stabbed Amy with a knife and twisted it into her side, knowing she was the cause for Stacy's pain.

"I wish I could go back and do things over," Amy said. "I wish I could've told you how I was feeling, but I didn't. Instead, I treated you like crap and then went out that night. Even though nothing happened between me and that woman at the bar, it was still wrong."

"I couldn't believe it when I saw you sitting there. It was like it wasn't real."

"I haven't shown you my love these last few weeks, but can you give me another chance? I've been working hard with my therapist. I have some insight into why I've been acting the way I've been acting. It's me, Stace. Not you."

"I'm not ready to come back yet. I still need a little more time. Can you understand?"

Amy's heart sank. "I understand," she whispered. She suddenly thought of something and hoped Stacy would at least give her this. "Can I ask you a favor? Can I come there this week? We have an off-day Thursday when we get back from our road trip. I can drive up to Indianapolis. Can I take you out to dinner? It'd be like a date. Maybe it sounds silly, but—"

"I have to work until four, but I can see you in the evening. So, yes."

"I mean, I understand if you wouldn't want to—"

"Amy, I said yes."

Amy thought she heard a smile behind Stacy's words, and it made her heart beat a little faster. "I'll call you when I'm on the road. How about I pick you up around six-thirty?"

"I'll be waiting to hear from you."

Amy didn't want to hang up. She needed this connection, even though it was tenuous.

"Take care, Stace. I love you." She tensed as she waited for Stacy's response.

"I love you, too," Stacy said softly.

"Bye."

"Goodbye."

Amy clicked off the phone. Thursday seemed light years away.

* * *

Soft kisses traveled from Lisa's neck down to her breast. "I thought you'd be wiped out after last night," Lisa said.

"I can't help it. You do this to me every time."

In one quick move, Lisa flipped Frankie onto her back.

"Frisky, are we?" Frankie asked with a chuckle.

Lisa nipped at her neck and kissed her. "The feeling's mutual."

"What time do you need to get to the park to make the bus?"

"Nine." Lisa glanced at the clock. "Which is in two hours."

"Have you talked to Amy anymore this weekend?"

"She called yesterday morning to thank me for calling Marge. She and Stacy talked. Amy's driving up to Indianapolis Thursday on the off-day, and they're having a date."

"That's not such a bad idea."

"I didn't think so, either."

Frankie rubbed her thumb against Lisa's nipple.

Lisa groaned. "As much as I'd love to pick up where we left off last night, I need to shower and get going."

Frankie kissed her again. "I know. Off with you, then."

Lisa reluctantly climbed out of bed. She padded across the carpet toward the dresser and pulled a drawer open.

"Hey, Leese?"

She turned.

"The view's mighty fine from here." Frankie grinned.

Lisa's gaze traveled the length of Frankie's body and back up again to meet Frankie's eyes. "I could say the same."

"Get your shower before I come over there and pull you back into bed."

*   *   *

Lisa approached the batting cage at Miller Park. Amy was hitting line drive after line drive to every part of the outfield. She entwined her fingers into the netting of the cage and didn't say anything until Amy took a breather.

"How's it feel coming back?"

"Hey, Lisa. Feels good."

"You seem to have found your timing."

"I think I'm where I need to be again." She pointed her bat out to Wally. "A couple more. How about right here?" She leveled her bat to the middle of the plate.

Amy hit the next fastball into the left center gap.

"Let's try the knuckleball again, princess." Wally lobbed a floater to the plate.

Lisa could tell Amy was concentrating on holding her swing as long as possible. She stepped into the pitch and launched it to the left field foul pole where it bounced off the netting.

"Show off!" Wally shouted.

Amy laughed. "That's it, Wally, I'm done." She unsnapped her batting gloves, shoved them in her back pockets, and took off her helmet before gathering her bats.

Lisa grabbed the towel hanging on the cage and tossed it to her.

Amy wiped down her face. "Why don't you come into the clubhouse, and we'll chat before I catch a shower."

Lisa followed her down the dugout steps and through the tunnel.

Amy threw the towel in the laundry basket and took a seat in front of her locker. Lisa carried a chair over.

She glanced down at Amy's bouncing knee. "You seem a little nervous. You're not worried about the game tonight, are you?"

"No. A few butterflies, but nothing major. Baseball, I can handle."

"Is it Stacy?"

Amy's knee stopped bouncing. "I'm worried about Thursday. It's like our first date all over again."

"But the difference is she's your partner now."

Worry clouded Amy's face. "A partner I've hurt deeply."

"Who still loves you." Lisa tried to lighten the mood. "Where are you taking her?"

"Huh?"

"You know. For dinner? You've thought about it, right? Please don't say you're taking her to McDonald's."

"Very funny. I thought Bynum's Steakhouse on the south side. We've gone there a couple of times for special dates. We went there for Valentine's Day, now that I think of it."

"Better make reservations. Tell them to put you in a booth, too. Much more intimate."

"Let me guess. You've taken Frankie there before."

"Maybe."

"I'll call them Wednesday when we get home from our afternoon game to make the reservations." Amy held her eyes with a long look.

"What is it?" Lisa asked.

"I was thinking how glad I am you and I worked through everything and remain friends. That's all."

Lisa felt her face redden. "You're a good person, Amy. Always have been."

"Right back at ya."

"What is this? A mutual admiration society meeting?" a voice boomed behind them.

Lisa looked up at Nick Sanders standing over her.

"Hey, Nick."

"Lisa." He turned toward Amy. "Good to see you again, rook."

"You, too."

"I'd better let you take your shower and have some downtime." Lisa stood up from the chair. "I'll see you both after the game."

Amy watched Lisa walk away and enter the tunnel leading to the field. She smiled, thinking back to the first day she'd met Lisa on the practice field in Indianapolis. Life had a funny way of working itself out.

"She was more than a friend once, wasn't she?" Nick asked while taking off his shirt.

Amy looked at him in surprise. "How'd you know?"

"You can tell. Was she the one you were dating when Stacy met you?"

"Yes," she said quietly. "Stacy was attracted to me from the beginning, but she was such a friend to Lisa she'd never think of doing anything behind her back. I was attracted to Stacy, too, but didn't realize how much until Lisa and I broke up. Stacy asked about dating me last summer."

"And the rest, as they say, is history." Nick pulled on his long-sleeved undershirt.

"A history I don't know the ending to yet."

"What's wrong?"

"I did something stupid down in Atlanta."

He sat down while she told him what had happened. She even told him about the counseling sessions.

"We're going on a date Thursday night, and I'm as nervous as I was the first time."

"Maybe that's not such a bad thing. It's like a do-over from when you were kids. Remember those?"

"You think?"

He finished dressing. "She loves you, Amy, and I can't see her giving up so easily. You were hurting. It was stupid, like you said, but you still get to have a do-over. Just don't screw it up. Ryan would be very disappointed. He still talks about your visit in July and wants to see you both again. Both, not just you."

"Let's work this out first, and we'll see."

"Why don't you concentrate on baseball tonight?" he said while lacing up his cleats. "We need you."

She grabbed her towel. "I'll take a shower and see you on the field in twenty minutes, tops. Then we'll see how much your swing has suffered since I've been gone."

He laughed. "Go on before I drag you into the showers with your clothes on."

*   *   *

Amy took the pick-off throw from the pitcher and slapped the tag on Dillon, the diving Brewers runner. The umpire signaled safe, and Dillon asked for time. He shook the dirt from his belt buckle and stayed on the bag when the Reds pitcher waved the catcher out to the mound with his glove.

"Sorry about your mom," Dillon said. "I know it's rough. I lost my dad two years ago."

Amy tried to swallow the lump in her throat before responding. "Thank you."

The next batter lined a one-hopper to the shortstop for a tailor-made double play.

The Reds trailed 3-2 in the top of the eighth, and Amy came to the plate with runners on second and third and two outs. She had lined out in her three previous at-bats but tamped down her frustration. She briefly acknowledged Servace for the signs, knowing the only thing she needed to do was get a hit.

Sharper, the Brewers's talented set-up man, fired a ninety-nine-mile-an-hour fastball toward the plate. Amy swung late, just getting a piece of it. The next pitch was a slider down and in. She held back on it for a ball.

Fastball. It has to be a fastball. Amy was guessing but hoped it was a good guess. *Stitches. Watch for the stitches. They may be a blur, but they're still there.* She heard Marge Tompkins's voice as though she were standing right behind her.

Sharper fired a fastball over the heart of the plate. Amy connected and drove the ball to right center field. She kept her head up as she took off out of the box. The Brewers center fielder made a sliding stab at the ball, but it skipped under his glove and rolled to the fence.

Jeffries yelled at her to keep going. She pivoted around first base, never breaking stride as she approached second and looked up for direction from Servace. He held up his arms to keep her there. She skidded to an abrupt halt past the bag and hustled back before the throw came in from the center fielder.

Both runners had scored.

Amy clapped her hands. This was more like it.

*   *   *

"Amy! How does it feel your first week back?"

"I'm feeling pretty good, especially with the win tonight. I think my swing is coming around to what it was before."

"You have a big series starting Friday when the Rockies come to Cincinnati. How do you see yourself doing against their pitching?" Lisa asked.

"I've had a little bit of luck against them, but they're locked in as of late. What's their team ERA dropped down to now? Isn't it under 4.00?"

"I think they're at 3.89."

"The Rockies are a tough team. They're showing it by staying in front of us for the Wild Card, but we've been playing better lately and have picked up a couple of games. We can only take care of what we can control, which is to keep pushing and try to win as many games as possible between now and the end of the season. Let's get through this series first, though."

*   *   *

Amy stepped down from the bus and started walking toward the players' lot. The afternoon loss against the Brewers, coupled with the loss Tuesday night, weighed on her mind. After picking up a half game on Monday on the idle Rockies, the Reds had fallen back to four games behind Colorado when the Rockies won two more.

She heard Nick's voice behind her when she reached her car.

"Good God, Perry, please tell me that's not your car."

"It runs," she said as she tossed her bag into the backseat.

Nick strolled up and kicked at the rust behind the back tire of her eleven-year-old Mazda. Large flakes fell off.

"Stop! This old baby's delicate."

"No. This old baby's a piece of shit."

"Stacy has the SUV for now."

"Why don't I help you get your mind off tomorrow night's date and take you car shopping? Even though you're a rookie, you make enough on the minimum salary to get yourself a new set of wheels."

Amy thought about it. "Might not be such a bad idea. Where do you want to meet?"

"You remember how to get to our place, right?"

"Give me the directions again."

She took out a pen and paper from her glove compartment and jotted down his instructions.

"I have a therapy appointment in the morning at eight, but I can get to your place around nine-thirty," Amy said.

"Nine-thirty's good." Nick tapped the rust again with his shoe. Another large flake fell off.

"Will you stop?" Amy jumped between him and the car to prevent further damage.

He stepped backwards toward his Lexus. "Drive it if you can make it to the house, and I guarantee you'll drive home in something much easier on the eyes."

"You're hurting her feelings."

"Just bring the car," Nick yelled before climbing into the driver's seat of the Lexus.

* * *

"You have to admit, this is one smooth ride." Nick stroked the dashboard with his fingertips.

"It should be for the frigging price." Amy merged onto I-75 for her test drive. She maneuvered the Audi R8 Spyder into traffic. "I am so not buying this car."

"I figured you weren't, but I wanted you to see how one drove for your future purchase."

"I'd be just as happy with a Chevy Malibu." Amy made a quick exit onto the next ramp.

"What are you doing?"

"Driving the damn thing back before I get into an accident and have to pay for it."

He laughed as they took city streets to return to the dealer.

Amy said her "thank you, but no thank you" to the young, pushy salesman and drove on to the Chevrolet dealership a few blocks away.

"You've got to be kidding me," Nick said as Amy looked at the sticker price on a new, midnight blue Malibu. "You were serious?"

"It's practical, and it's a good car." Amy opened the door and got into the driver's seat. "Besides, Stacy wanted one of these, and I talked her into the Equinox," she mumbled.

"What was that?" Nick bent his ear toward her with his index finger as though he were hard of hearing. "Did you say Stacy wanted one?"

"I had my heart set on an Equinox, but I liked these, too."

"I was about to call you kitty-cat whipped."

"Kitty-cat whipped? What the hell is… hey, that's not funny."

He grinned. "I'm teasing. It's a solid car. Let's get the salesman and see about taking it out."

An hour later, they waited in the tiny office of the financial manager for Amy's paperwork.

"You don't think Stacy will take this as me buying her a gift because of my screwup, do you?"

"Let me ask you a question. If she was here and I'd talked you both into car shopping, would you have ended up at this dealership buying this particular car?"

Amy didn't hesitate. "Yes."

"There's your answer. Get the car."

On their way to Nick's house, they discussed the importance of the Rockies series. Nick and Ryan tried to persuade her to stay for lunch, but she was anxious to get home and take a shower again before she left for Indianapolis.

She dried off after her shower and stared into her closet a good fifteen minutes before choosing a pair of black dress slacks and a long-sleeved green cotton shirt. The shirt was one of Stacy's favorites. She'd said it brought out the color of Amy's eyes.

Amy got into the new car and sat there as she envisioned the evening ahead. Then she turned the ignition.

It was time.

Chapter 21

Amy parked in front of the old double house Billie rented in the eastside community of Irvington. She checked her watch. It was six-thirty. Their reservation was for seven at Bynum's. She ascended the porch steps of the brick home and was about to knock when the door flew open, and she came face-to-face with Billie.

"Hey, Amy."

"Hi, Billie."

"I need to get to the Watering Hole. Sorry I can't chat, but you're not here to see me. She's almost ready." Billie opened the door farther. "You know how femmes are. Takes them awhile. Why don't you sit down in the living room? Good luck tonight, and try not to look so worried, man." Billie slapped her on the back. Then she was gone.

Amy felt like a mini-tornado had swept over her, but Billie often left her feeling that way.

She sat down on the couch and crossed her legs. Then she uncrossed them, sat up straighter, and ran her fingers through her thick brown curls. She shut her eyes to center herself but snapped them open when she heard the stairs creak.

Stacy stood on the landing. Like Amy, she wore a pair of black dress slacks. But Stacy's slacks clung to her hips like a second skin. The sleeveless light peach blouse showed off her dark tan. She'd swept her hair back in an elegant French braid and was wearing a hint of makeup.

Amy realized she was staring. She jumped to her feet and knocked over the book that sat on the edge of the coffee table. She bent over to pick it up. When she looked up again, she caught her breath at the sight of Stacy standing right in front of her.

"Hi," Stacy said in a shy voice.

"You look beautiful, Stacy."

Stacy blushed. "Thank you. You wore my favorite shirt."

Amy fingered the material. "I remembered how much you like it."

They stood there shifting in place like two teenagers before their senior prom.

"I guess we'd better go," Stacy said. "We have reservations for seven?"

"We should make it just in time." Amy opened the door for her and waited while Stacy locked up.

"Did you rent a car?" Stacy asked when she saw the Malibu.

"No. I bought it this morning. Nick talked me into going car shopping."

Stacy stuttered to a halt. "You bought it?"

"I hope you don't mind. You liked them so much, and the Equinox was my idea. I thought maybe—"

"It's okay, Amy. I'm not upset. I'm just surprised."

Amy hurried to open the passenger door. "I thought you could drive this when you came back."

Stacy got into the car and began checking out the stereo and the knobs on the dashboard.

She didn't say she wasn't coming back, Amy thought with relief while getting into the driver's seat.

"I love the color," Stacy said. "And this has everything I wanted."

"I only want you to be happy with it. But I didn't get it as a makeup gift," Amy added in a rush. "I needed to get rid of the Mazda, and this seemed like the logical choice. It's yours, though."

Stacy touched Amy's cheek.

"It's very thoughtful. And, no, I don't think of it as a makeup gift, so don't worry."

Amy relaxed. She was about to take Stacy's hand, but Stacy pulled it away. "The reservations are for Bynum's. Hope that's okay," Amy said.

"It's perfect."

They spoke in quiet pleasantries on the way to the restaurant. Amy pulled to a stop and hopped out to open Stacy's door. She linked her arm in Stacy's as they walked to the entrance.

"Reservations for Perry," Amy told the hostess.

The hostess picked up two menus and led them to a booth in the corner. She poured ice water into their glasses before returning to her station. Muted overhead lighting and lit candles adorning each table added to the romantic ambience. The server appeared at their table and introduced himself as Dale. He asked if they'd like to try the house wine as he held out the bottle for their inspection.

"Stacy?" Amy asked.

"Yes, please."

Dale poured her a glass. "Ma'am?" He held the bottle toward Amy.

"Yes, thank you."

"I'll let you have a few minutes to look over our menu."

Amy's hand was shaking as she picked up the glass of wine. She took a small sip, hoping Stacy hadn't noticed.

Stacy reached across the table and took her hand. "There's no need to be nervous," she said softly.

Tears burned Amy's eyes, and she tried to hold them back. She made a silent plea. Please, God, not in the restaurant.

"We're going to be okay, Amy. Seeing you again, feeling what I do for you, it hasn't changed. It's the same as the first time I saw you." The candlelight danced across Stacy's face.

"I need to tell you things," Amy said. "Things I've discovered about myself and how I handle loss." She fidgeted with her fork. "Which hasn't been very well up to now."

"We'll talk, but let's figure out what we want to order first, okay?" Stacy squeezed Amy's hand.

Amy decided on the New York Strip while Stacy chose a filet served with lobster tail. They handed Dale their menus, and he left for the kitchen. Amy took Stacy's hand in hers again, not caring if any of the other diners noticed.

"I've been seeing a therapist who's been so helpful. You were right about me needing to work through everything, and I've been doing that these past couple of weeks."

Amy didn't go into all the detail, but she knew what she wanted to say.

"I've been afraid of being alone but, in the process, pushed you away. It might not make sense."

Stacy stroked the top of Amy's hand with her thumb. "No, it does. Go on."

"What I did in Atlanta is inexcusable. In my state of mind, I never should have left the hotel room. I was only asking for trouble. But I want to tell you again, that woman meant nothing to me, Stacy. Nothing."

"I won't lie. You did hurt me." Stacy paused before continuing. "But the important thing is for us to keep communicating and not shut each other out. Even if it means we have to go to a counselor together when we're having trouble, you have to promise me that's what we'll do."

"I promise. But more than that, I promise to make the effort to let you in on what's going on with me, no matter how lost I feel. I learned I don't have to be strong all the time. That by letting you see my vulnerability, I'm showing you my strength."

Stacy smiled. "You've been working overtime with this therapist."

"I have. For you and for us."

"And for you, Amy."

Amy didn't realize Dale had returned to their table until he cleared his throat.

"Honey mustard?"

"Mine," Stacy said, holding up her index finger.

He handed her the salad. "That would make yours the house dressing." He placed Amy's plate in front of her. "Enjoy. Your dinners should be out in a few minutes."

While they ate their salads, Amy filled Stacy in on all the extras she'd gotten on the Malibu.

"I can't believe you remembered everything I liked on the one we test drove," Stacy said.

"I remember everything you tell me, honey."

They'd just finished their salads when Dale showed up again. "We have lobster tail and filet." He set the food in front of Stacy. "And New York Strip. Anyone need A1 sauce?"

"Yes," Stacy answered.

"Ketchup please." Amy hated the incredulous expressions she received whenever she asked for ketchup with her steak. Dale was no different.

He quickly recovered. "I'll be right back."

Stacy giggled. "I love it when you do that. It never gets old."

"I figure I'm paying for the damn thing. Why should they care?"

"Here you go, ma'am." Dale handed her a small container of ketchup.

"Thank you."

Over dinner, Stacy talked to Amy about her hitting. "I caught a couple of your games on TV against the Brewers. You have your stroke back," she said as she dipped a bite of lobster into her melted butter.

Amy watched, mesmerized, while Stacy brought it to her mouth, closed her eyes, and pulled the piece off the fork, slowly running her tongue along her lips.

"Delicious as always." Stacy tore away another piece of lobster and paused mid-bite. "What's wrong?"

"N-nothing." Amy's face warmed. She concentrated on cutting into her steak.

"You're sure everything's okay?"

"The steak's fantastic," Amy said around a bite.

"Anything else wrong?" Stacy dipped another bite of lobster into the melted butter and brought it to her lips, once again letting the fork linger in her mouth.

"You know exactly what you're doing to me, don't you?"

"Maybe." Stacy grinned and waggled her eyebrows.

* * *

Amy walked Stacy up the stairs to the porch, unsure of the next move.

Stacy, her hair suffused in the soft glow of the porch light, turned to Amy. "Why don't you come in?" She unlocked the door and waited for Amy to enter before shutting it behind her. "Do you want a Pepsi or something?"

"No thanks." Amy sank into the soft couch.

Stacy jiggled her house keys. She looked anywhere but at Amy.

"I won't bite." Amy patted the cushion.

Stacy maneuvered around the coffee table to sit beside her. "Are you as nervous as I am? I mean, isn't this a little silly?"

"I was so nervous on the drive over here I almost had to pull over. And no, it's not silly, just like you saying this date wasn't silly." Amy brushed some loose strands of hair away from Stacy's face. "I've missed you so much."

Stacy stared at Amy's mouth. "If you don't kiss me right this instant, I think I might lose it."

Amy pressed her lips to Stacy's, gently at first, before dipping her tongue inside. Stacy met her stroke for stroke as she tugged her closer. Amy got lost in the feel of Stacy's lips against hers.

They broke free from their embrace, both breathing heavily.

Amy pressed her forehead against Stacy's. "I want to make love to you," she whispered. "But maybe we should wait. I don't want to rush you."

Stacy kissed her again. It was soft and yielding, the passion simmering under the surface like a placid sea before an unexpected storm. "And I want to make love to you," she said as she ran her finger along Amy's lips. "But in our home and in our own bed."

Amy captured Stacy's finger with her teeth, nibbled it, and sucked it into her mouth.

Stacy gasped. "You're not making this easy."

Amy released her finger and planted a kiss on Stacy's palm. "I love you enough to wait until the time and place are perfect for both of us. When are you coming home?"

"Soon. I'll surprise you."

"Don't wait long."

"I won't. I promise."

"It's late. I should probably get on the road." Amy stood up.

"You're welcome to stay tonight and drive back tomorrow." Stacy rose to her feet.

"No. If I sleep here tonight, I couldn't stay away from you."

"That's good to know, because I feel the same."

She followed Amy to the door.

Amy kissed her one last time. "Come home where you belong."

"I'll be there before you know it."

Chapter 22

Lisa grappled with her nerves as she sat in the press box. The Reds had the tying and winning runs at third and second with two outs in the bottom of the ninth. If they rallied against the Rockies, they'd take a game off the Rockies lead in the Wild Card race. They needed to sweep to have any kind of hope.

Nick Sanders strode to the plate. He'd had a bad night thus far, striking out twice and popping up with the bases loaded in the seventh.

Amy took her lead off second. She possessed above-average speed and could score on a single. Lisa checked positioning of the outfielders. Medium depth, playing Sanders to pull. There was a big gap in right center.

Sanders gave a cursory glance to Servace, the third base coach. He stepped into the batter's box and tugged the bill of his batting helmet.

The first pitch from Reynolds, the Rockies closer, was a slider on the inside part of the plate. Sanders swung through it. The next pitch was a slow curve that dipped into the dirt, but not before Sanders swung wildly at it. He backed away from the plate, regrouped, and repositioned himself in the box. He closed his stance by moving his front toe toward right field.

The next pitch was a fastball on the outer half of the plate, the last place Reynolds should have thrown it based on the defensive placement of his outfielders. Sanders's bat sliced through the air and sent the ball like a laser over the second baseman's head. The right fielder hustled over and cut it off before it made it to the wall.

The runner on third easily scored. Servace waved Amy home. The right fielder fired the ball home. Amy hooked her slide to the back of the plate and swiped at it as she went by. The catcher grabbed the one-hopper and slapped her hand with his mitt in a bang-bang play.

Amy looked back and up at the umpire. He ruled her safe, and she jumped up to meet the players who flew out of the dugout and pounded her on the back and helmet. They then ran to Sanders as he trotted in from first base. He disappeared into a scrum that went on until he lost his helmet. He emerged, grinning, with his jersey untucked. Amy was the last to greet him. She held him in a neck lock and ruffled his hair.

Lisa entered a jubilant locker room. She interviewed several players, including Sanders and Amy, then wandered into Max Murphy's office. The *Cincinnati Enquirer* reporter was wrapping up with his last question. He passed by Lisa on his way out.

Lisa sat down and took out her notebook. Max's red hair was in disarray, and exhaustion lined his face. But he also looked the happiest she had seen him in a long time.

"Feeling good, Max?"

"I am. I'm excited for the team, especially the young players. I'm glad to see Amy back to her old self. She went through a rough period after her mom's death, but she's focused on the game. I couldn't ask for a better team player. And the camaraderie between her and Nick has spilled over to the others."

"I noticed that, too. How's his hamstring holding up?"

"He's not complained. As long as he can walk, he'll play."

"The young guys are gelling."

"Yep. I think they can smell the playoffs. It's an exciting feeling. Hell, I'm excited. I know what winning's like in the minors, and some of these players do, too. You know that—you covered them in Indianapolis. But this is a very different ballgame, so to speak. They're playing against some of their idols. I'm glad they're not awestruck."

"How about the rest of this series?"

"This is between you and me. I don't want to give the Rockies any more ammunition to use against us these next two games. I think we can sweep. We've got the rotation lined up like the playoffs. We had our ace tonight and have the number two and three going Saturday and Sunday. But we have to play within ourselves. If the guys"—he paused with a smile—"and gal stay within the game and the game situations, I think we'll be within one of Colorado by Monday."

Lisa stored the last comments in her memory bank, not jotting them down.

She stood up. "I'll let you take your shower and get out of here."

"See you tomorrow afternoon for warm-ups."

She flipped through her notebook and went over her quotes as she walked through the clubhouse on her way to the press box.

Amy still sat at her locker with a half smile on her face. The other players were in the shower.

"Nice game, Aim," Lisa said as she walked past. She stopped when she saw Amy's distant expression. "You seem far away."

"Thinking about how lucky I am. I have the game I love back, and Stacy should be home soon."

"Any word on when?"

"No. She said soon, but each hour that passes means it's not soon enough."

* * *

"Lucy, I'm home!" Lisa called out when she entered the apartment. She didn't get an answer, but she saw Frankie sitting on the balcony. She opened the sliding glass door.

Frankie glanced back at her. "Hey, Leese."

Lisa kissed her and sat down in the other lounge chair.

"Tired?"

"Beat," Lisa said around a yawn. "I'm not a member of the team, but sometimes I feel like I've played nine innings, too."

Frankie reached over and took Lisa's hand. "I saw where Nick came through for them tonight. I love watching them act like kids when they win."

Lisa swung their hands back and forth between them. "It'll be even funner if they sweep the Rockies this weekend."

"Funner? Did my wife, the esteemed sportswriter, just say 'funner'?"

Lisa laughed. "I think I'm entitled, don't you?"

"I think you're entitled to a lot of things."

Lisa sat up and gazed out at the river. "I don't think I'll ever get tired of this view at night. There's something about lights on the water."

"Can I get you something to drink? I'm sure you've already had your dinner of a hotdog and Coke. Tell me I'm wrong."

"Nope, which is why I'm not arguing. I'm good. I don't need anything to drink."

After several minutes passed, Frankie spoke. "When I was at the bar this morning going over inventory, I noticed Stacy had more of a bounce in her step. I wouldn't be surprised if she showed up this weekend."

"Kind of like when I haven't seen you for a long time."

"Right." Frankie caressed Lisa's hand.

"How've you been since you relinquished management of the bar? I worry about you giving up something you love so much."

Frankie continued with the soft stroking. She dipped into the sensitive area between Lisa's thumb and index finger.

"It wasn't a sacrifice, Leese. I still go there when I want, like today. Billie keeps me posted on any problems. I'm able to spend my nights with you where I belong." She brought Lisa's hand to her mouth, softly kissing each knuckle.

A steady pulsing settled between Lisa's legs. "Was there a reason you were sitting out here, or can we go to bed?"

"It's time I be taking ya to our bedchamber." Frankie stood and pulled Lisa to her feet.

"Let me guess. You've been reading more of that pirate novel."

"Aye, and I be planning on having my way with ya, wench."

* * *

"What'll Murph do here?" Nick asked Amy.

She popped a handful of sunflower seeds into her mouth and eyed Murphy as he relayed the signs to Servace.

"I'd say a double steal."

The Rockies pitcher went into his windup and threw to home plate. As he released the pitch, the runners at first and second took off and stole their bases with ease.

"Nice, Perry. You must be able to read Murph's mind. Or is it that you checked out his relay?"

She grinned. "Dunno, Sandy. You don't think I'm smart enough to figure out what he'd do in this situation?"

"I didn't say that. Wait. I guess I just did."

She slugged him on the arm.

"How come you can get away with hitting me, and I can't hit you?" he asked as he rubbed his arm.

"Rookie privilege."

They were in good spirits, as were the rest of their teammates. The Reds led Colorado 5-4 in the bottom of the seventh on Sunday afternoon. If they took this game, they'd be one game behind the Rockies for the Wild Card with a week remaining in the season.

The next batter flied out to the center field warning track to end the inning. Amy grabbed her glove and tossed Nick's glove to him. They trotted out to their positions, and Amy threw grounders to the other infielders for warm-up.

The Rockies got two runners on with no outs. Murphy trekked to the mound and replaced the reliever with McKinley. McKinley struck out the next batter. The Rockies third-place hitter popped out to Nick. Their cleanup hitter, Alexander, came to the plate. He'd already knocked in three of the Rockies runs.

McKinley checked the runners, went into his windup, and fired a ninety-two-mile-an-hour heater on the inner half of the plate, right in Alexander's power zone. He smacked it into the left center gap. Both runners scored, giving the Rockies the lead. Alexander stopped at second with a stand-up double.

Murphy made another trip to the mound and put in Danny Lopez, their closer. He made a double switch by bringing in Thomas to replace their right fielder. Thomas would lead off in the bottom of the inning in what had been the pitcher's spot. Lopez struck out the next batter.

Amy trotted into the dugout, already thinking ahead to her next possible at-bat. She'd be the fourth batter up if it came down to her.

Thomas hit a single into right. The next hitter lined the ball to the second baseman, who fired it over to first base in an attempt to double off Thomas. He safely slid back to the bag headfirst.

Reynolds, the Rockies closer, walked Rawls. The pitching coach strolled out to the mound for a conference with the catcher and the infielders.

Amy rubbed the pine tar on the handle of her bat. While she took a few practice swings, she glanced around at the fans. That's when she spotted a familiar face with dark, shoulder length hair, three rows above the Reds dugout.

Stacy blew her a kiss.

Amy's heart started beating double-time as the conference on the mound ended. She attempted to settle her sudden onset of jitters before she got into the box.

Reynolds threw a slider down and away. She held back. The next pitch was a slow curve on the inner half of the plate. Amy timed it and hit it fair down the left field line. The two runners scored. She ended up on second, sliding in before the shortstop's tag.

She stood up and dusted herself off. The roar of the crowd was deafening. She looked in Stacy's direction. Stacy pumped both fists in the air.

Nick flied out, and Roberts, the fifth-place hitter, grounded out to second to end the inning.

Lopez shut the Rockies down in order in the top of the ninth.

Amy joined the line of her teammates as they slapped hands in celebration after the last out. She trotted over to the railing where Stacy was waiting.

Stacy gave her one of her full-dimpled grins. "I said I'd be here soon."

"I'm glad, Stace. See you outside the clubhouse?"

"Yes."

Amy jogged down the dugout steps into the tunnel. Nick joined her and clapped his arm around her shoulder. "Hell of a game."

"You made some outstanding defensive plays, Nick, or the score would've gotten out of hand."

"You've got more important things to worry about. I saw Stacy in the stands."

Amy couldn't stop grinning as they entered the clubhouse.

"I'll tell the guys to be fast because your woman's back in town."

She grabbed a towel and threw it in his face.

* * *

Amy didn't think there was ever a time she was so glad to see the reporters leave the clubhouse. She waited impatiently for the last teammate to finish dressing so she could take her shower.

After what felt like an eternity, she emerged from the clubhouse back entrance with wet hair. She worried about her attire of faded jeans and a long-sleeved polo. She should have brought something else to change into.

"Hey." Stacy's voice cut into her silent recrimination. She sported a smile as she leaned against the side of the building. She pushed away from the wall and walked slowly toward Amy. Touching Amy's cheek, she searched her face. "You look exhausted."

Amy grabbed Stacy and hugged her tight. *An anchor,* Amy thought. *That's what she is to me. While she was gone, I might as well have been one of those barges out on the Ohio, floating around aimlessly, waiting for someone to come to my aid.* She started crying.

"Hey, shh," Stacy whispered while rubbing her back in soothing motions. "I'm here now." She pulled back and met Amy's eyes. "I'm not going anywhere. I'm yours, if you'll have me."

"God, yes." Amy didn't care where they were. She bent down and kissed Stacy.

"I'll drive you to the players' lot," Stacy said. She dropped Amy off and waited at the exit for Amy to follow.

Amy pulled in behind Stacy at the apartment. She motioned at Stacy to take their allotted spot while she parked in one of the visitor's spaces. She grabbed her bag from the backseat, hustled to where Stacy was stepping out of the SUV, and reached in to get her suitcase.

They took the elevator up to their floor. Amy opened the door and moved aside for Stacy to enter first. Stacy studied the living room.

"You didn't think I'd keep it up?"

"I didn't say anything." Stacy's face reddened. "I mean, I wasn't sure—"

Amy set the bags by the door. "I was joking, sweetie." She took Stacy in her arms. "I can see where you and I need to get reacquainted. Even more than our date in Indianapolis."

"You're right." Stacy started to pull away. "Do you want me to make you a sandwich or something? You have to be hungry."

Amy wouldn't let her go. "I'm hungry." She brought her lips to Stacy's and kissed her until Stacy moaned. "But not for food," she said against her mouth. "I've missed you." She nibbled Stacy's earlobe. "I've missed us."

Stacy stepped back and stared at Amy as she unbuttoned her own shirt.

Amy reached out to help, but Stacy swatted away her hand.

"I'll do this." A flush covered Stacy's throat while she removed the shirt. She took Amy's hand and brought it to her breast.

Amy rubbed her thumb against the thin fabric of her bra until Stacy's nipple hardened. She reached behind her and unclasped the bra. "Just how I remembered you but so much better." She took the nipple into her mouth.

Stacy arched her back. "Bed," Stacy whispered. "Please."

Amy lifted Stacy into her arms and carried her effortlessly down the hall to their bedroom. Sunlight peeked through the cracks in the blinds. She laid Stacy gently down on the bed and made quick work of Stacy's jeans and panties.

Stacy reached for Amy's polo shirt, but Amy didn't give her the chance. She undressed and lay beside her.

"Tell me what you need," she whispered into Stacy's ear.

"You. I've only needed and wanted you."

Amy answered the silent plea hidden in those words. She brought her mouth to Stacy's breasts, taking one nipple in her mouth while rubbing the other with her thumb. Then, she moved to the other nipple and gave it the same attention until Stacy squirmed beneath her.

Amy lowered her hand past Stacy's abdomen as Stacy raised her hips and parted her legs.

"Inside," Stacy said hoarsely.

Amy pressed two fingers inside and settled into the rhythm she remembered Stacy craved. She thrust one last time until Stacy tensed and cried out her name.

Amy flipped onto her back and tried to catch her breath, but before she could, Stacy was on top of her. She captured Amy's mouth and plunged her tongue inside. She didn't stop there as she kissed her way to Amy's full breasts. She pushed Amy's legs apart to kiss along her thighs. Then she dipped into Amy's wet folds and ran her tongue up until she captured her clit between her lips. Stacy took her higher with each movement of her mouth. Amy felt the passion building and savored the feeling until her orgasm thrummed through her body.

Stacy kissed her way back up Amy's stomach and chest. Amy held her while she stroked Stacy's thick hair.

"I pictured us taking this slow the first time, didn't you?" Stacy asked.

"Is there a problem?"

She felt Stacy smile against her breast.

"Do you hear me complaining?"

* * *

They made love until darkness filled the room and sleep overtook them, only to awaken and make love again in the early morning hours.

"You asleep?" Stacy asked Amy.

"Yes. This is Amy's subconscious speaking. You can ask her anything."

Stacy poked her in the side where Amy was the most ticklish.

Amy squeaked. "No fair."

"I have something serious to talk to you about." Stacy placed her hand above Amy's left breast. "Hey, I didn't mean to scare you. Your heart's pounding like crazy." She sat up more, so that their eyes met. "Everything's okay, but this is, um, pretty serious. And if it's too soon to talk about it, or if you're against it, then I want you to be honest. It's that while we were apart, and I knew we'd be getting back together and that we were on solid ground again, well..."

Amy touched her finger to Stacy's lips. "Tell me what it is, sweetie."

"Remember, if you say no, you won't hurt my feelings. Promise me you'll keep that in mind before I ask you."

Amy crossed her heart. "I promise."

Stacy took a deep breath and let it out, the air cooling Amy's bare breasts. "Would you ever want to have a baby?"

Amy sat up so fast that she smacked her head against the headboard.

"Not now, Amy, but maybe a couple of years from now?" Stacy said in a rush. "The main thing is I want you to be okay. And, like you said, you and I need to get reacquainted." She smiled. "In more ways than making love. We need some time for just us first."

Amy rubbed the back of her head. A baby. She wants to know if we can have a baby. That means we're a family. Amy knew Stacy was her partner, of course, but she hadn't thought of them in the family sense of the word. Until now.

A baby. In her imagination, Amy pictured a little girl with dark hair and dark brown eyes. She'd even have Stacy's dimples. Amy tensed. *Wait. She doesn't think I'll have the baby, does she?*

"Tell me what you're thinking, Amy. Please."

Amy remained mute.

Stacy lowered her head. "Well, it was only a thought."

Amy tried to find her voice. "I think..." She stopped, overwhelmed with emotion. "I think it's a wonderful idea," she choked out.

Stacy's eyes filled with tears. "You're not just saying that?"

Amy shook her head. "No. But I have one question."

"I'd be having the baby, hon. I mean, I love you and everything, but I'm not so sure about you giving birth."

Relief hit Amy, along with a slight sense of indignation. "You don't think I could handle it?"

Stacy tried to hide her smile.

Amy started laughing and couldn't stop. Stacy joined her until they collapsed back onto the bed and fell into each other's arms.

Their laughter eventually died down.

Amy pulled Stacy close. "I could see us having a baby together, Stace, but you're right. We need some time for just the two of us. Then, somewhere down the line, we can talk about it again." She gave Stacy a gentle kiss. "There's one thing I'm asking of you before we have a baby, though."

"And what would that be?"

"Will you marry me?" Amy searched her face for an answer and became more nervous with each passing second. "Well?"

Stacy launched herself on top of Amy and showered her with kisses.

"Is that a yes?" Amy asked, laughing.

"Oh, it's most definitely a yes."

Chapter 23

The phone jangled in Amy's ear. She untangled her arms from Stacy's embrace and reached over to pick up the receiver.

"Hello?"

"Damn, Perry, aren't you out of bed yet? Oh, wait. Stacy's there with you, huh?" Nick asked.

"Nick, it's six-freaking-thirty in the morning. You do know this, don't you? And I just woke up from the best dream ever. To top it off, you made me leave the warmth of Stacy's arms."

Stacy shifted in her sleep.

"What's so important at six-thirty that you couldn't tell me at the park later?" Amy whispered.

"I wouldn't be calling at this time if it wasn't important," Nick said. "But I wasn't sure when we could talk in private in the next few days, and I knew it had to be early because you're usually at the park by ten."

"Oh, tell her the truth." Amy heard Ryan's voice in the background. "Your husband pestered you until you picked up the phone."

"Shut up, Ryan. Sorry about that, Amy. We were wondering if you two maybe wanted to have breakfast here. He makes killer omelets. You can't pass this up."

"Is that Nick?" Stacy asked, her voice raspy.

"Yeah."

Stacy wiggled her fingers. "Hand me the phone." She took the receiver from Amy. "This better be good, Sanders." She grew quiet while she listened. "We can't pass up Ryan's omelets, and you have some news you want to share with us?" Stacy quirked an eyebrow at Amy.

Amy shrugged.

"I believe we also have some news to share with you and Ryan. What time?" Stacy giggled. "Yes, we can be showered and presentable by eight, you shit. We'll see you then."

Amy took the receiver from Stacy and replaced it on the cradle.

"What do you think it is?" Stacy asked. She leaned on one elbow, and the sheet dipped below her bare breasts.

Amy's gaze lowered to Stacy's nipples. She licked her lips. "Right now, I don't care. He said eight, right? Don't we have some time before we take our showers?"

* * *

"Hello, darlings," Ryan gushed when he opened the door. "It's good to see you again."

They entered the foyer and took turns embracing him.

"I'm so glad you two worked it out," he whispered in Amy's ear as he hugged her.

Buster bounded into the living room and skidded to a halt on the tiled floor of the entryway. He jumped up on Stacy.

Nick hustled behind him and tugged on his collar. "I'm sorry, Stacy. He doesn't have the best of manners."

Stacy knelt down and rubbed behind Buster's ears. "Don't apologize. Buster and I are good buddies, aren't we boy?"

In answer, Buster licked the side of her face.

"That's enough loving, big guy. Outside for now." Nick clamped on his leash and led him toward the deck in the back.

Amy and Stacy followed Ryan into the dining room.

"You two have a seat. What would you like to drink? We have some fresh coffee brewing or orange juice."

"Juice okay, Stace?" Amy asked.

"Yup."

"Glad to see you two together again." Nick entered the dining room and joined them at the table. "She's not the same without you, Stacy." He pointed his finger at Amy.

Stacy placed her hand on top of Amy's. "I'm not the same without her, either."

"I'll get the juice." Ryan continued to the kitchen.

Nick propped his feet up on another chair. "So what's your big news?"

"And talk loud so I can hear you," Ryan shouted.

Amy questioned Stacy with her eyes.

"Go ahead."

"I've asked Stacy to marry me, and she's accepted."

"Oh!" Ryan came around the corner from the kitchen and rushed over, clapping his hands. "I knew you two were destined to stay together. Didn't I tell you that?" he asked Nick.

"Yes, dear."

Nick's sarcastic tone earned him a ruffling of his blond hair.

"Congratulations." Ryan kissed them both on the cheek.

"Yes, congratulations, but enough of this schmaltzy marriage stuff," Nick said. "It's time for my news."

Amy turned to Ryan. "Do you know what this is about?"

"Yes, I do. My lips are sealed. Let it come from the mouth of the babe." Ryan went back into the kitchen for a minute and returned with a tray of glasses of orange juice. "I've got everything ready to make the omelets, so get to it," he said as he sat down next to Nick.

"Tomorrow I'm meeting with Murph and Dan Taylor to tell them next year's my last."

"You can't be serious," Amy said. "You're still in your prime."

"Amy, I'm thirty-five. I could play a couple more years, but my body's not what it used to be. I've had this bad hammy all year. My left knee swells after every game. I'm tired. I love the game, but I'd like to go out while I still have some dignity."

Nick took Ryan's hand in his. He looked at him as he spoke. "But more than anything, I want to live my life openly as a gay man with a wonderful partner. I'm tired of lying." He turned to Amy. "To watch you and how you've handled yourself with poise and dignity throughout this season, living out of the closet, it's made me realize even more what kind of life I'm missing. I'm not coming out while I'm still playing. Not like you. But I'm telling them this next season is the last. That way they can bring up Jody Harrelson from Indianapolis, and I can mentor him during the year. He's a damn good third baseman for the Indians, and he will be for the Reds, too."

Amy still hadn't recovered enough to comment.

"Do you remember Smokey the Bear?" Nick asked her.

"The forest fire bear?" Amy wondered about the change in topic.

"When I was a kid, about four or five, I went to the National Zoo in D.C. with my family. They had these two adjacent pens running several feet deep. One held the original Smokey the Bear. The other caged his replacement, this young bear cub. My older brothers and sisters rushed over to take pictures of the young cub, but I didn't. I felt sorry for the old Smokey." He smiled. "You're sitting there questioning why I'm telling you this."

"Kind of," Amy said.

"I'm the old Smokey, but I want to leave the game before anyone feels sorry for me."

"I don't know what to say, Nick. I'm happy for you and Ryan, but I'll miss you."

"I'm not going anywhere," he said, the fondness evident in his voice. "We'll still see each other."

"You know what I mean. On the field. In the clubhouse."

"You'll be fine. You've earned the respect of the team."

"You had a lot to do with it."

"You did all of it on your own. I never said anything to anybody."

"But they took your lead."

"And now they'll take yours. You're an outstanding player, Amy. If you'd played enough games this season, you'd be right there for Rookie of the Year." He reached across the table and patted her arm. "You'll be okay."

"You will, you know," Stacy said.

Amy met Stacy's eyes, and her insecurities melted away.

Ryan went to the kitchen to fix the omelets. Nick helped him bring the food out, and they dug in.

Talk turned to baseball and the last week of the season.

"Tell me your thoughts on the Dodgers series and the rotation," Nick said.

"I think it'll be tough. They're coming in here on a roll."

She and Nick got into the nuances of the pitching staff while Ryan and Stacy chatted about recipes. The time passed quickly.

Nick and Ryan walked them to the door.

"Thanks for having us over, guys." Amy pulled Stacy close. "We enjoyed ourselves. And your omelets were most excellent, Ryan."

"I'm glad you shared your news with us," Ryan said. "We couldn't be happier for you."

"See you at the park, rook. Bring your A-game," Nick shouted as Amy and Stacy got into the car.

* * *

Friday night was unseasonably warm for late September and the first game of the season-ending series against the San Francisco Giants. Lisa wiped the sweat from her forehead while interviewing the Giants pitching coach before the game. Sarah, talking to Murphy, looked as miserable as Lisa felt in the sweltering heat.

They entered the press box at the same time and set up their laptops.

"Jesus H. Christ. Who turned on the fucking furnace?" Sarah said.

"I don't know, but I sure wish they'd find the off switch."

"Thank God for air conditioning."

"And thank God they shut the windows for the night." Lisa powered up her computer. "Not that I'm a baby or anything."

"Oh, no. Me neither." Sarah flipped open her laptop. "It's a shame with the four-game sweep of the Dodgers, they weren't able to pick up a game on the Rockies."

"Yeah. Well the Rockies went on their own streak. That's baseball for you."

The Reds took the field and made short work of the Giants in the top of the first. The Reds went out in order in the bottom of the inning. Amy hit a gapper, but the speedy Giants left fielder ran it down for a shoestring catch.

They were into the fifth inning with no score when the Giants plated two runs. It remained 2-0 with the top of the order coming to the plate in the bottom of the eighth. The leadoff hitter lined out. The pitcher walked the next hitter and walked Amy as well.

Nick stepped up to the plate. He worked the count to 2-1.

"Fastball or slider?" Sarah asked.

"Slider, outside corner."

The pitcher fired in a slider that hit the outside corner of the plate for a strike.

Nick backed out of the box and stared down at Servace.

"Now a fastball," Lisa said with confidence. "The only question is if he makes a mistake pitch."

The answer came quickly. A ninety-four-mile-an-hour fastball up and across the middle of the plate. Nick launched it over the left field wall. The capacity crowd rose to its feet and cheered as Nick ran his patented fast trot around the bases. Amy greeted him at home plate with a slap on top of the batting helmet.

The Reds held on to win the game 3-2 with Lopez striking out the side in the top of ninth.

Before Lisa followed Sarah and the others down to the clubhouse, she checked online for the latest Rockies score. They trailed the Cardinals 5-3 in the top of the seventh.

* * *

"He'd struck me out on a high heater earlier in the game. I thought he'd try it again," Nick was saying as Lisa moved in behind the reporters in the clubhouse.

"How's your hamstring holding up?" Lisa asked. "I noticed you limping a little on a groundout in the third inning."

"It's as good as it'll get. I'll hang in there and hope we can make the playoffs. Anyone catch the Rockies score?"

"I checked before coming down," Lisa said. "They're behind 5-3 in the top of the seventh."

Lisa walked to Danny Lopez's locker and jotted down some quotes from him about his outstanding pitching in the past couple of weeks. She then shifted over to Amy's locker. Amy's uniform was dirt-stained from the top of her jersey to the hem of her pants from a headfirst slide into third on the front end of a double steal in the sixth inning.

"How does it feel still being in the hunt for a playoff spot?" Lisa asked as Amy sat down to pull off her cleats.

"Awesome."

"Care to elaborate?"

"You don't miss my one-word answers from our first meeting in Indianapolis?"

Lisa laughed. She'd felt like she was extracting top-secret information from a government operative in their first interview on the University of Indianapolis practice field.

"No, I don't miss your one-word answers," Lisa said. "I have a feeling you're messing with me right now."

"A little." Amy's face lit up with a grin. "How do I feel? I'm loving every minute of it. Of course, I'd love it even more if the Rockies lost a game. We're running out of time."

"You've handled the pressure very well this year, and I'm not just talking about the game. You had to deal with those protesters and some hate mail you shared with me."

"I've always thrived off game-time pressure. I love all of the nuances and intricacies in each situation on the field. It's fun. It's my job, but I still keep in mind that this is a game. As for the other stuff..." Amy's expression darkened. "It wasn't easy walking past people shouting hateful words at me. It was especially difficult dealing with those people at my mother's funeral. But I remembered what she told me right before she died. To play the game. To not let their bigotry get to me. I've tried to follow her advice and remain focused on my play and how I can help this team win."

Lisa finished scribbling down the last of Amy's words. "Your mom would be proud."

Tears came to Amy's eyes. "Thanks, Lisa." She lowered her head and began rolling down her socks.

Lisa patted her knee. She headed down the hallway to get a couple of quotes from Murphy. Sarah was leaving his office as Lisa made it to his door.

Lisa was about to step into Murphy's office when Sarah stopped her. "Top of the ninth with one out and one on for the Rockies. Still 5-3 Cardinals. Thought you'd want to know."

Murphy had his back to her when she entered while he watched the Rockies-Cardinals game on the MLB network.

The Rockies were now down to their last out. Marty Alexander, their cleanup hitter came to the plate. He jumped on the first pitch and hit a deep fly ball to dead center field.

"Goddammit!" Murphy shouted. "What the hell kind of fucking pitch is that to a guy with forty home runs?"

The Cardinals center fielder leaped with his glove outstretched over the wall. He landed back on his feet. Lisa tensed as she waited to see if he held onto the ball. He waved his glove to the umpire who'd sprinted in from behind second base. The umpire threw a fist up in the air for the final out.

"Yes!" Murphy jumped up and down and did what Lisa could only describe as an Irish jig. She heard shouts from the clubhouse and assumed someone switched on the game in there.

"You're tied now."

Murphy whipped around at the sound of Lisa's voice. His face reddened.

"If you tell anyone what you just saw, you'll never get another quote from me."

"My lips are sealed." She joined Murphy in taking a seat. "As your rotation stands now, you have Patterson, your number five starter, pitching Sunday's game. Any thought in bringing your number one back on short rest?"

"No. Not at all. Patterson's been pitching strong for us down the stretch. He's young. Hell, most of our roster's young. But I have confidence in him. I'm not trying to look ahead, but if we have to play a tiebreaker game, I'll need Rick Fowler on the mound."

"How about the health of the team, Murph?"

"We've got a couple of players banged up, but we're in pretty good shape."

"What about Perry's performance since she returned to action?"

"What can I say other than she's a big reason we're sitting where we are. It's either her or Sandy each night. They seem to feed off each other. It's a shame…" He stopped.

"Yes?" Lisa glanced up from her notebook.

"This is off the record. Management won't make the announcement until after the season."

Lisa closed her notebook.

"Nick's retiring at the end of next season. Dan and I tried to talk him out of it, but he wouldn't budge. He's only thirty-five for Christ's sake, but it was like he was holding back on giving us the full reason for his decision. We'll miss his bat and defense. Even more than that, we'll miss his leadership in the clubhouse."

Lisa tried to think of any reason he'd walk away from the game. "That's surprising."

"It makes any chance we have at getting to the playoffs this season even more pressing."

"Well, I'll let you go, Murph. Thanks for the quotes."

She left to file her article and had to smile at the exuberance of the players when she passed by on her way to the press box.

Chapter 24

Amy woke up around one in the morning after a nightmare. In the dream, she was running from room to room at her mom's house. She'd call to her mother. Her mother would answer, but her voice was faint. When Amy would run to where she heard her voice, it shifted to come from another direction. At last, Amy gave up and sat on the landing of the stairs, exhausted and in tears.

She had awakened crying. Not wanting to disturb Stacy, she went to the living room.

And there she was, two hours later, quietly crying in the darkness.

The bedroom door creaked open, and Stacy's footsteps advanced down the hall.

"Amy? Is everything okay?" she asked.

Amy almost said yes. Almost sent Stacy back to the bedroom. Instead, she choked out, "No. I'm not okay."

In an instant, Stacy was at her side, pulling her close. "Let it out, sweetheart. Let it out."

That's all it took for the dam to break. Amy buried her head in Stacy's chest and sobbed, her whole body shaking with emotion.

"Why?" she cried. "Why did God take her from me?"

"I don't know. I don't think we're meant to know." Stacy rocked her gently. "One thing I am certain of is how much I love you."

Amy cried until her throat was raw. Stacy held her until Amy pulled out of her arms.

Stacy grabbed some tissues from a box on the end table. "Here."

Amy blew her nose. "Thank you."

"For what?" Stacy asked.

"For being with me. Holding me. Telling me you love me."

Stacy leaned forward and kissed her. "No. Thank you for opening up to me."

Amy managed a smile. "I guess I did, huh?"

Stacy used her thumb to wipe another tear away. "Yeah, you did."

"And it's good?"

Stacy returned the smile. "It's very good." She stood up and held out her hand. "Why don't we go back to bed, and you try to get some sleep. You've got a big game tomorrow night." She glanced at the digital clock on the cable box. "Well, considering what time it is, I should say tonight."

Amy rose to her feet and took Stacy's hand. They walked to the bedroom. Stacy got into bed first and opened her arms.

Amy slid under the covers and into Stacy's embrace. She heard Stacy whisper, "I love you," just before she slipped into a deep slumber.

*   *   *

"Watch for his move and Servace's sign. Don't be surprised if Max doesn't send you," the first base coach, Jeffries, whispered into Amy's ear.

Standing on the first base bag, she nodded. She was well aware of the importance of the situation. Bottom of the ninth, and she represented the winning run. A quick observation of the left field scoreboard emphasized how vital it was for her to score. The Reds and the Rockies had won their respective games the night before. This afternoon, the Rockies were pounding the Cardinals, 11-0 in the sixth inning.

Amy checked the sign. A steal on the first pitch to Nick. Got to love Murph's aggressiveness, she thought as she took her lead.

Rodgers, the Giants reliever, stepped off the mound and fired over to first.

She dove back into the bag, waited for the first baseman to deliver the ball to the pitcher, and kept her foot on the bag while she brushed off her uniform. She took a couple of steps to inch a little farther away. Rodgers stepped off and looked her back to the bag. She moved another step farther this time. Rodgers looked her way one last time before firing a fastball to the outside part of the plate.

Crap, Amy thought as she took off for second. A freaking outside fastball. They might as well have called for a pitchout. She prepared to launch into her slide. The ball hadn't reached the second baseman yet. She dove headfirst and reached for the outer half of the bag as the second baseman pushed his glove into her face. Her hand hit the bag an instant before his glove knocked her helmet off.

"Safe!"

Amy called for time, and the umpire granted it. She stood up and wiggled her belt to shake away the dirt. Some of it dribbled down the inside of her uniform. But she was safe, and their best hitter could knock her in.

Nick took a strike. The next pitch looked inside, but the home plate umpire called it a strike. Nick said something to the umpire, then leveled his bat a few times and waited for the pitch. Amy made sure the shortstop wasn't sneaking in behind her to the bag and took a bigger lead. Rodgers threw a slow curve that would have been a ball, but Nick dipped his bat down and lined it over the second baseman's head into right field.

Servace was motioning for Amy to keep going. She hit the third base bag with her toe and sprinted toward home. The Giants catcher, Reed, stood at the plate, decoying like there was no chance a throw was coming. But Roberts, the on-deck hitter, knelt on the ground and slapped the palms of his hands in the dirt for her to slide.

Reed moved to block the plate. The only way Amy could score would be if she knocked him out of the way. He was about Amy's height but probably outweighed her by twenty pounds. She braced for the impact before launching herself into Reed. The ball arrived at the plate at the same time. It was a jarring hit. Pain fired through every muscle in her left shoulder as she bowled him over. She managed to touch the plate with her hand before lying sprawled on her back. She didn't see what happened to the ball. The umpire's intense face hovered over her. Amy watched his lips move, but the ringing in her ears prevented her from hearing anything. He threw his arms out to the side.

Safe. I'm safe.

The next thing she knew, strong arms lifted her from the dirt. Her teammates surrounded her, everyone hopping up and down. They hustled over to first base to greet Nick. She limped along behind them and rubbed her left shoulder with each step. *God I hope this is just a bruise.* Amy joined in pounding Nick by using her right hand.

Nick enveloped her in a bear hug. "What a collision," he shouted over the crowd's cheers.

Amy winced.

He immediately released her. "Are you hurt?"

"I might have dinged my left shoulder."

"Let's get it checked out in the clubhouse."

*   *   *

Alerted about her possible injury, Tom, the trainer, had already greeted her on the field. She followed him to the trainer's table. He helped her unbutton her jersey and take it off, and he gingerly pulled off her undershirt.

He probed her shoulder.

"Jesus," Amy hissed.

"It's not dislocated. This is going to hurt."

Amy braced herself. Anytime a member of the medical profession told her something was going to hurt, it meant it would hurt like a sonofabitch. She was surprised this time when the pain was minimal.

"Seems to be only a bruise. Try rotating it."

Amy complied. The more she moved it, the looser and better it felt.

"It's a little swollen," Tom said. "I'll have the doc confirm it's not anything worse."

He left and returned with Dr. Krivitch, the Reds team physician. The doctor went through the same routine.

"I think it's badly bruised, but as a precaution, we'll take you to get an MRI."

Murphy entered the training room. "Well, Doc?"

"I think she needs an MRI. From examining it, I don't feel anything out of place, and she's not reacted to palpable probing. Unless she's hiding the pain."

They scrutinized her.

"It's sore," Amy said, "but it doesn't hurt as much as it did when I hit Reed."

"Can you do the MRI this afternoon?" Murphy asked Krivitch. "If it's nothing serious, we need her bat tomorrow for the Wild Card game."

If the Rockies won, the league had scheduled the tiebreaker game for 1:05 at Great American Ballpark. The Reds had earned the right to host the game based on having the better head-to-head record between the two teams.

"Sure, Max, we can do it today," Dr. Krivitch said. "Get showered, Amy. We'll take you over to the hospital and run the MRI."

* * *

Stacy joined Amy after she showered, and they drove to the hospital together. They listened to the Reds radio network on the drive and heard that the Rockies had won their game. Amy's shoulder hurt, but it didn't feel like a serious injury. At least she hoped it wasn't serious. Maybe she was kidding herself.

Amy had endured other MRIs, so she knew the routine. When it was done, she dressed and sat with Stacy to await the results in the doctor's office.

The door opened, and Dr. Krivitch entered.

"You've got some inflammation that's indicative of a deep bruise. Nothing that won't heal, but I'm not sure you'll be able to play tomorrow."

"I can play," Amy said through gritted teeth.

"Amy…"

"I said I can play." Her voice rose.

Stacy squeezed her knee. "Honey, he's just doing his job."

"Will I do any damage by playing?" Amy asked.

"No. But I'm not sure by tomorrow morning you'll be able to lace your cleats let alone swing a bat."

"What about a cortisone shot?"

His mouth set in a thin line. "We can give you a shot, but we'd need to do it now. It takes a few hours to recover from it."

"Fine. Let's do it."

"I need to call management for approval."

Amy was about to protest, but he shot her down. "No argument on this one, Amy." He left the room.

"Are you sure?" Stacy asked.

"It's the biggest game of my life, Stace. I can't miss it."

A few minutes later, Dr. Krivitch reentered the room followed by a nurse pushing a cart. On the cart was a tray. And a very large needle.

Holy shit.

* * *

The next morning, Amy tried out the shoulder. It was a little sore but nothing like the pain she'd experienced right after the shot. She'd iced the shoulder down overnight as the doctor suggested. The pain lessened with each passing hour. By game time, she hoped to be pain free or at least in little enough pain that she could keep her mind off it for the game.

She and Stacy left for the ballpark together, with Stacy driving.

Nick greeted Amy when she entered the clubhouse.

"How's the shoulder?" he asked while putting on his undershirt.

"As good as it's going to get."

Murphy stopped by their lockers a few minutes later.

"Your shoulder?" he asked Amy.

"As good as new, skip."

He grunted and continued toward his office.

She and Nick dressed in silence. Nausea hit her in waves. She'd never felt this nervous before a game.

"It'll pass." Nick took his glove out of his locker.

"What'll pass?"

"The sick feeling in your stomach."

"How'd you know?" she asked as they walked down the tunnel to the dugout.

"Your face is as white as a sheet."

They took their usual batting practice. Nick was right. She was more at ease with each step back into her routine. While she followed through on a line drive, she saw Lisa out of the corner of her eye.

"How's your shoulder?" Lisa asked.

Amy left the batting cage and motioned for Nick to take over.

"How'd you find out?"

"See, I have this job as a sportswriter. And part of it is to, well, find out shit."

Amy burst out laughing. Lisa grinned at her.

Amy stripped off her gloves. She glanced toward the stands, spotted Frankie sitting next to Stacy, and waved at them. "The shoulder's okay. Like I told Nick, it's as good as it's going to get."

Lisa looked back and waved. "The wives are here." She turned and followed the path of a ball Nick hit into the left field stands. "How you feeling about the game?"

"Until ten minutes ago, I felt like I was going to puke. But I'm better now."

They chatted for a while. Amy went out to right field for wind sprints, and Lisa left to interview the Rockies manager.

* * *

"Hey, Lisa." Sarah had set up her laptop before Lisa entered the press box.

"How you doing?"

"Tired. Not as tired as them, I'm sure." Sarah gestured to the players below. "Amy's shoulder holding up?"

"She says it is, but she's a jock. It's what I'd expect her to say."

"Frankie made it, I see."

"Said there's no way she's missing this game."

"How do you think Fowler will pitch today?" Sarah asked. "It was a little rough on his last outing when he gave up those five runs."

"I think he'll recover."

The Reds took the field. Amy tossed the ball around the infield while Fowler went through his warm-up pitches. It was a beautiful day for a game—low humidity, with the sky clear and temperatures in the sixties.

Fowler threw the first pitch over for a strike. He retired the Rockies in order and in rapid fashion. The first two batters flied out in the bottom half. Amy walked to the plate and watched two pitches out of the strike zone.

The Rockies starter, Rollinson, was a left-hander with a sneaky fastball and a wicked curve. Other times when Lisa had seen him pitch, he'd throw his curve ball, regardless of the count.

He tossed a slow curve to the outer half of the plate.

Amy waited and unleashed her swing, hitting the ball on a line over the right field fence. She trotted around the bases and took congratulations from Servace as she passed third. Sanders slapped her on the helmet in the on-deck circle. Her teammates waited for her in the dugout. Murphy smacked her on the butt as she went down the steps. Everyone else gave her high fives.

Sanders flied out to deep left to end the inning.

The game remained 1-0 until the fourth when the Rockies scored two runs on a homer by Alexander.

* * *

"I can't believe I watched that called third strike from him in the fourth," Amy told Nick in the bottom of the seventh. The score remained 2-1. She popped more sunflower seeds into her mouth. "He dropped that frigging curve in. I didn't think he'd try it again."

"Hang in there. You'll get another chance in the ninth if we don't go ahead before then."

The Reds sixth-place hitter grounded out. They grabbed their gloves and trotted to their positions. Fowler got into trouble in a hurry. The first two hitters reached base with singles.

The pitching coach made a trip to the mound and talked with Fowler until the home plate umpire broke it up. A lefty and a righty were warming up in the bullpen. Whatever the pitching coach said must have done the trick. Fowler struck out the next batter.

Alexander lumbered toward the plate.

He has that look about him, Amy thought. Like he could hit every ball out of the park. She glanced into the dugout in anticipation of Murphy making the move to put in their short reliever. But Fowler remained on the mound.

Fowler got in front 1-2. The next pitch was a mistake pitch over the inner half of the plate. Alexander knocked it down the third baseline. Sanders dove and picked it off on two hops. He jumped to his feet. It was too late for the runner on third. He fired it to Rawls at second. Rawls leapt in the air over the sliding Rockies' runner. His throw to Amy was high and wide. Amy jumped to get the ball, then swooped her glove down on Alexander's back before his foot hit the bag. She felt a twinge in her shoulder, but she ignored it on her way back to the dugout.

Nick hustled over to smack gloves with her. Rawls came up to her in the dugout. "Thanks for bailing me out."

"No problem."

Nick and Amy remained standing with their arms hanging over the padded railing with the rest of their teammates. They watched as the bottom of the order went down quietly with the pinch hitter making a loud out to deep left field. It brought the fans to their feet, but it fell a foot in front of the wall.

Danny Lopez retired the side in order in the top half of the ninth.

The Rockies closer, Reynolds, came in to pitch the bottom of the ninth. The Reds leadoff hitter popped out. Amy rubbed pine tar on her bat handle as she watched Rawls work the count to his favor. She hadn't used the weighted bat at all in the game and wouldn't start now. Rawls lined a single into left.

She walked toward the plate. The Rockies pitching coach hopped up the steps and went to the mound. He motioned the infielders in for a conference. Amy ignored it and concentrated on what she'd need to do against Reynolds.

Fastball in the upper nineties. Slider. But he also throws a screwball for strikes.

The umpire broke up the huddle on the mound.

Amy snapped and unsnapped her gloves before taking some more practice swings and stepping into the box. A ninety-seven-miles-an-hour fastball zipped across the inner part of the plate, painting the black for a called strike. She anticipated another one and hit a long fly ball to left, bringing the crowd to their feet, but the ball landed well foul.

Too eager.

She was down in the count 0-2 and knew she couldn't chance letting anything close to a strike go past her. She settled back in the batter's box. It was guessing time. He had some pitches to waste. Amy guessed screwball.

She guessed right.

Her bat connected with the ball and sent it on a low line toward the gap between third and short. Just as her mind screamed, "double," Alexander dove for the ball. Amy had taken only two steps out of the box when Alexander made a miraculous catch. Everything seemed to move in slow motion. From his knees, he fired across the diamond to double-up Rawls who was already halfway to second.

It was over.

Amy felt like she'd been kicked in the gut. The other Rockies players scrambled out of the dugout and mobbed Alexander. She joined Nick in the on-deck circle to watch the winners' celebration on the field.

"Remember this," Nick said, "and bring it to spring training next year." He turned to Amy. Sunlight bathed his face as his eyes met hers in steely determination. "We'll be back. Only next time, we won't need a fucking tiebreaker game."

* * *

They entered a subdued clubhouse. Murphy gathered them around for a pep talk, but even Amy could tell his heart wasn't in it. It was too soon.

She sat in front of her locker with her cleats off and stared down at her dirty socks. But she made no move to undress. She listened as Nick answered the questions thrown his way, knowing she'd be next.

Lisa asked her what she was thinking as she watched the game-ending double play. Amy heard the apology in Lisa's voice. She was doing her job, and it was Amy's turn to do hers.

"Like someone kicked me in the gut," Amy said.

"How do you see the team doing next season?"

"Right now, I can't even think about it. But in a few days, I'll reflect on the year and realize we went above and beyond what anyone expected us to do." Amy softened her expression. "Except for you."

Lisa smiled sadly.

It hit Amy then that Lisa had to be just as disappointed in the outcome. "I'm proud of this team and the season we've had. We'll be back."

*   *   *

Amy finished showering and dressed slowly. She paused every now and then as a play from the game flashed through her mind.

She slung her equipment bag onto her right shoulder and kept her head lowered as she walked down the hallway to the back entrance of the clubhouse. She rotated her left shoulder. It had bruised to an ugly black and blue, despite the icing overnight.

Amy opened the door. The security guards were there, along with a few fans.

"Amy! Can I have your autograph?" a teenage boy shouted.

She didn't say anything, but she took the baseball and Sharpie from him and scribbled her name. She signed three more, the last a special program for the day's game. She and Nick were featured on the cover in split photos.

"Don't be sad, Amy. You'll win next year."

Amy looked down into the hopeful blue eyes of a little blonde-haired girl who searched Amy's face for reassurance. Amy studied the woman standing behind the girl with her hand on the girl's shoulder. She had dark hair, cropped close. Another woman with shoulder-length blonde hair stood beside her and held the woman's hand.

The dark-haired woman spoke first. "Our daughter's right. You'll be back better than ever."

Amy tried to speak around the lump in her throat. "Thanks."

"You're such a role model for us, you know," the blonde said as she stroked her daughter's hair.

Amy swallowed. "No, you've got it wrong. You're the role models."

The couple shook her hand and walked away.

She watched as they exited the ballpark.

"I'm sorry about the game," a familiar voice said behind her.

Amy turned to Stacy as she approached. Here was everything in her life that really mattered. Yes, baseball was important, but it wasn't something Amy could wrap her arms around at night and keep close to her heart.

Stacy held out her hand, "Come on, babe. Let's go home."

Author Chris Paynter

About the Author

Chris Paynter is the author of six novels, including the *Playing for First* baseball series. Her *Survived by Her Longtime Companion* was a 2013 Lambda Literary Award Finalist and winner of the 2013 Ann Bannon Popular Choice Award. Her short stories have appeared in two anthologies: Regal Crest's *Women in Uniform: Medics and Soldiers and Cops, Oh My!* (2010) and Cleis Press's *Love Burns Bright: A Lifetime of Lesbian Romance* (2013). After earning a Bachelor's degree in journalism, Chris worked as a general assignment reporter and sportswriter until accepting her current position as the editorial specialist to a law journal. A sports junkie, you can find her screaming at the TV during a Colts game or living vicariously through her Cincinnati Reds. She resides in Indianapolis with her wife, Phyllis, and their beagle, Buddy the Wonder Dog, also fondly known as "He who must be obeyed." When not writing or editing books, Chris loves to get lost in a good romance.

Visit her website: www.ckpaynter.com

Email her at: ckpaynter@ckpaynter.com

Visit her Author Page on Facebook:

www.facebook.com/ChrisPaynterAuthor

Find her on Twitter: @ckpaynter

If you enjoyed this book, be sure to look out for Chris Paynter's next book in the *Playing for First* series,

FROM THIRD TO HOME

Available Spring 2015, only from

COMPANION PUBLICATIONS

www.ckpaynter.com

"Ohmygodohmygodohmygod! I can't believe I'm standing here getting Amy Perry's autograph again. It's like it's not real, you know? Me and my best friend decided at the last minute to make a trip to Arizona for spring training because we just love you."

Amy waited for the petite blonde with the butch haircut to take a breath, but she wasn't finished yet.

"We, like, traveled to Phoenix two years ago to watch you play in the Arizona Fall League when the Reds signed you with the Mesa Solar Sox. Does that help your memory? We had you autograph the back of our T-shirts."

"No, I'm sor—"

"You're sure you don't remember us?" The woman, probably in her early twenties, motioned to her dark-haired companion. "What about when you were in Double-A Chattanooga? We drove down to a couple of your games. But we're not, like, stalkers or anything. Right, Cheryl?"

"Naw. We just like watching you play."

"Then last year, when you came up in May from Triple-A Indianapolis and were with the Reds for the season, how many games did we go to?" the blonde asked her friend.

"Wow. I dunno. Twenty?"

"That's a lot of games—" Amy started to say.

The blonde cut Amy off again. "We wanted to go to a lot more, but we have to work. Sorry about that loss at the end of the season. I bet that double play you hit into at the end of the tiebreaker game against the Rockies still haunts you, huh?"

By now, Amy wanted to smack the woman over the head. She'd had nightmares in the off-season over the play that had ended the Reds year and any chance to make the playoffs.

"Amy! Amy! Can I have your autograph?" a little boy yelled, hopping up and down beside the blonde.

Thank God, Amy thought. A reprieve. "I need to sign some more," she told the two women. "Thanks for your support." She managed to give them a tight smile before signing the boy's baseball and two more that kids thrust in her face. She took the program someone offered to her, not looking up.

"Could you make that out to 'the love of my life'?"

Amy's mouth pulled into a grin before gazing into the dark eyes of her partner, Stacy.

"I don't think so, ma'am. I'm taken," Amy said.

Stacy's face lit up and her dimples became more pronounced. She leaned over the railing and kissed Amy on the cheek. "Right answer, babe. Frankie asked if we wanted to go out to dinner tonight with her and Lisa. Is that okay?"

Amy spotted the reporters who hung out on the field at the Reds Goodyear, Arizona, spring training camp. Lisa Collins was talking with another sportswriter, Sarah Swift. Amy caught Lisa's eye and waved. Lisa waved back.

"Sure. The guys told me about a great Mexican restaurant. Would that be okay?" she asked Stacy.

"Sounds good."

"Come on, Perry, quit talking to your wife. We've got work to do."

Amy turned at the sound of her friend, third baseman Nick Sanders's voice.

"Keep your uni on, Sandy. I'm almost done."

"The next voice you hear won't be mine, you know," he said as he trotted off into the outfield to begin loosening up.

Max Murphy, her manager, stared at her from the infield grass with his hands on his hips. He jabbed a thumb toward the outfield.

"Guess I'd better let you go, huh?" Stacy said with a teasing lilt. "Don't want to get your boss upset on your first day in camp."

Amy squeezed her hand and jogged out to right field to join Nick in loosening up.

9 781942 204053